ALL THY CONQUESTS

ALL THY CONQUESTS

BY ALFRED HAYES

HOWELL, SOSKIN, PUBLISHERS

Are all thy conquests, glories, triumphs, spoils
Shrunk to this small measure?

—Julius Caesar, Act 3

Chorus

So MANY PEOPLE and the sun so bright. One would not have thought there would be so many people. So many of them, from all the quarters of the city, and the sun on the stone angels of the bridge, the sun on the avenging Michael above the Castel Sant' Angelo, and on the leaves of the horse-chestnut trees, on the decks of the river bath-houses around whose rotting keels the Tiber swirled.

Ah, Antonio, do you remember the bridge? Of course. How could one forget the bridge? The sentry I knifed stood there, and from there I pushed him into the Tiber below.

That was six months ago, when the city was occupied.

Ah, Gina, Gina of the peculiar mouth and the difficulties with the husband, do you recall, amore mio, the patrols in their deadly fives? Che bestie! They were very correct, but they did not patrol the streets in less than fives. And they arrested so many, and Maspaccio says (you know his store off the Via Nazionale? He rents evening clothes) they bought, very legitimately, his entire stock of tuxedos, but of course their occupation money was worthless.

Nine months we lived under them.

Do you know what it was like the night of the liberation?

I went out into the street, not daring to believe that our misery had come to an end, and there, in front of Rompoldi's, I saw, sitting on the curb outside the cafe, two soldati Americani.

Two young ones, very tired, with guns.

I would have, if I were not so shy, kissed them. But I was polite and I inquired if there was something I could do to help them.

Yes, said the older of the two: when does this joint open?

It was three o'clock in the morning.

At nine, I replied.

Okay, said the older of the two: we'll wait.

That was four months ago.

But there are so many people now here on the Lungotevere around the Palace of Justice, and the sun is so bright. One would not suppose this to be a day of judgment with the sun so bright. There should be thunder, should there not, on a day of judgment? Thunder, darkness, and divine lightning. Instead, the air is so clear, the sky so flawless, there is such quietness in the heavens.

They are convening now in the courtroom. The light comes filtered into the marble halls. Someone coughs, a paper rustles. Always at trials someone coughs or a paper is rustled. It will begin soon. It is a day of judgment.

Who knows, perhaps they will acquit?

How can they acquit? How can they dare acquit?

He has too much money, says Paolo Benedetto, who will begin driving a bus again for his old company as soon as the directors can find some tires. Besides, says Benedetto, they are all former fascists themselves. Which one of them, says Benedetto, has really clean hands?

Benedetto knows. He is a man with experience in politics. Was he not arrested at the time of the arrival of Hitler in Rome and compelled to lie ten days in a cell in the Regina Coeli? He is a man with experience.

Impossible, says Lavognini, a garage mechanic. Lavognini will again, as he did before the war, fix the tires on Benedetto's bus when, of course, the directors find tires. Impossible, says Lavognini. How can they acquit him?

Lavognini means it will be difficult because the dead have been disinterred from the sandpit on the Street of the Seven Churches out beyond the catacombs of San Callisto only a short time ago. Lavognini means the smell of the dead is still there in the caves. The bones coming out of the earth and put into the coffins still have the mouldy ends of clothing on them, and in the city the widows are still lamenting. He means it is too recent. He means it is so recent the guards at the entrance to the cave have not yet become tired of saying: Here they shot them, on the twenty-fourth of March, and show the pilgrims where they placed the machine guns.

That is why Lavognini thinks it will be impossible for them to acquit him.

But tell me, Carlo, what do you think?

Me? You know my opinion. They're all bastards. They all ought to be taken to the Regina Coeli and shot.

There you are, there is an opinion, an opinion of the people.

There are Latin inscriptions on the Palace and there are many famous statues of many famous lawgivers in the courtyard. If we had a priest here he could read the inscriptions. The inscriptions probably say many wise things about justice. But what do the inscriptions say about corrupt judges and false courts? If we had a priest here we could ask the priest if the inscriptions say anything about corrupt judges and false courts.

Anyway, the court is convening.

I'm thirsty, caro. Buy me a lemonade.

Drink water.

No, buy me a lemonade. Look how pretty the lemons look in their wire cups, there in the chiosco. And the woman sitting among her lemons.

They want twenty lire for a lemonade. You drink water. So many people, and the sun so bright.

The Trial

HE DID NOT LOOK, to those who did not know him, as they had expected him to look. He was short, he was not very powerfully built except perhaps for the suggestion of strength in the thick sloping shoulders. He was dark, his dark hair was a little gray at the temples, he had a full mouth, the eyes were black and set at an average space either side of the nose, he wore a white shirt, open at the throat, a dark pinstriped suit obviously slept in, he did not look menacing, he did not look like a tiger, he did look like a man who had been born in Maddaloni and had become rich in Rome, but he did not look too rich, the broken arm was better but he still carried it in a sling. He did not look like a man about to die, but he did look like a man with a strong possibility of being condemned. He did look like a man who had come to the end of something.

The court was crowded. The great oak doors at the end of the crowded room were guarded by carabinieri. There were carabinieri all about the walls. He saw the benches reserved for the newspaper reporters, and he saw the lawyers in their robes, with their professionally intent faces, and he saw, behind them, occupying the bulk of the room, the people who had come upon invitation, for tickets were required for this trial.

He had told himself calmness was the important thing. He had prepared himself in the cell during the long nights in the Regina Coeli when he lay with the small black Bible unread on his chest, to make the sort of entrance he would have made were he about to attend a party meeting at which his position would have been threatened. It was only a question of being careful, as though something had gone wrong and he had incurred the displeasure of the party leaders. In the political atmosphere in which he had lived for twenty years that was the important thing to beware of, this displeasure of those with power.

But when he entered the court he sensed immediately that perhaps this time his situation was really dangerous. He was bothered by the fact that he had no tie, by the fact that he had not been permitted to shave. Then the sling, in which his arm hung, gave him a physical sense of defeat.

He could feel, too, how every eye in court was centered upon him. Although he was not a particularly clever man (he had, as a matter of fact, always despised the clever ones in the party to whom things came quickly and easily—those who were good at languages, for he could speak only his own, or who were witty, for he had no appetite for humor, or who were successful with many kinds of women, for he was not) or a particularly sensitive one, he nevertheless could feel a real physical sensation of all those anonymous eyes in the courtroom crawling over him.

He walked slowly, accompanied by his guards, across the room toward the defense table where Spezzano sat. What did they expect? he thought angrily. Should I have horns, and a tail? Why should they expect me to look different?

He knew that to them his entrance into the court was like the introduction of a fabulous monster. It was because of this man, they were thinking to themselves, that in a sandpit, during a March afternoon, three hundred and fifty innocent men had been machine-gunned to death, and their corpses dynamited and buried in the raw earth, and the crime was of such incredible proportions, the dead of so huge a number, they felt he must share some of the un-human characteristics of the deed. He knew, therefore, that because his eyes were narrow, and the lids made a slightly hooded effect, a family peculiarity, they would read some extraordinary cunning into his face. And that because his lips were full, and a trifle thick, as they were, this would assume the dimensions of a physical deformity; when, as a matter of fact, one could take a dozen obscure citizens out of the Piazza di San Silvestro at any hour of the day and find eyes as hooded, lips as thick.

It was bad luck. Sitting beside Spezzano, he blamed it all on his luck. The family luck, the old haunting fear that he had thought he had at last outwitted when he was finally successful and of consequence in the party. That tree, and the burning car on the Bracciano road. If it hadn't been for the tree he would have gotten away to the north and the safety of the black republic when the city had fallen, and he would have been safe now. Keppler had gotten away, the whole S.S. staff with him, Pucci had escaped, all of them had escaped, but it was his luck to have been in the car that crashed into that tree on the Bracciano road. He had planned it badly, or was it because he was really in-capable of planning that it had happened? Was it because that for years the planning had all been done for him by others, and in the crisis when he was compelled to make his own plans he had failed? If only he had not waited for the phone call from the Albergo Babuino! Eleanora had told him not to wait, but she had known, as she knew practically all his secrets, that because of the incredible fetish of obedience and discipline by which he had succeeded in the party, and by which he lived, he would wait patiently until the phone rang and the S.S. gave him at last permission to leave.

The whole day had been a joke. A gruesome, a disastrous joke perhaps, but a joke. The reassuring statements had kept coming all day from the press and the radio, statements about the impregnability of the city and the powerful defenses, when there was actually no defense, and the broad asphalt road from Velletri to Rome lay open. All one had to do to convince oneself of the idiocy of the statements was to go to the dusty windows of his office in the Questura and listen to the allied guns in the hills. Closer and closer. That was the third of June. Another date, one remembered the exact historic dates, it was a peculiarity of the time. And the newspapers in the end had become fantastic. It was impossible, of course, to report on the true situation, and the Messenger had appeared that morning with three columns devoted to the legend of Orpheus! Orpheus! It was insane, the whole thing had become insane. The bombers burned in their black protective earthworks on the air-strips outside the city, and the columns of armored traffic moving northward over the Ponte Milvio increased each hour, there was confusion, gathering disaster, the hints of panic, and the seething of the people, but on the front page of the Messenger—Orpheus!

Fogliani came into his office that afternoon. It was near evening. They could hear the guns somewhere in the Alban

Hills, still distant but unmistakably closer than the day before. No one, not even Fogliani, dared ask what the exact German strength was. There was a panzer division supposed to be guarding the approaches to the city.

He had said, stubbornly: "They'll never get out of the hills," although he had not really believed it, had not wanted to believe it, and Fogliani had said, standing by the window, "What are we going to stop them with? The blondes in the telephone exchange?" He had filled the glasses. And then: "What does Keppler say?"

"The usual."

"Rely upon the German to take care of his own skin."

"It is not hopeless," he had insisted. "Besides, whatever happens, they won't desert us."

"Oh," Fogliani said, "they'll drag us along for a little while longer. Why not? Somebody has to give the occupation the appearance of legality."

They drank, and then they had begun to sing, Fogliani sitting on the edge of the desk, and the sound of the guns coming across the great distance from the hills, an old song of the squadristi, of the triumphal days, a song he had not sung for years, not since the days of his youth in Naples after the war. Sitting there in the gloomy room, which held the political fate of so many men in this city, the very room in which he had spread the dossiers out on his desk and taken from them the fatal names he had given the S.S. the day of the reprisals, they had sung of the early and almost forgotten victories.

Even now he could remember the song.

He had felt fine after the song. But it had not lasted. At the Plaza, later, there was Lucia, worrying him with her questions, and his secretary Dario. He waited. What was there to do but wait? It was all going, the years of power, but there was nothing to do but wait. At midnight Keppler had still not called. Was Fogliani right? Were they going to leave him, here, knowing what this city would be once it escaped their control? Once the allies were in these streets?

Then, not being able to sleep, not being able any longer to prowl in the bedroom, or to watch the phone that did not ring, he had gone to see Eleanora. There, in the studio on the Via del Plebiscito, with Eleanora, he felt better, as he always did. At least here, the only place he knew, there was no pretense, no front to be kept up, no mask to be worn.

She had watched him, given him coffee, moved her paintings, those strange submarine landscapes of hers.

Was he afraid?

To her he'd admit it. He was afraid. Of what? The cells in the Regina Coeli at last opening. The men who had survived the terrible rooms in the Via Tasso. Those who had been exiled, those who bore old unavenged humiliations, those who had waited, waited twenty years for this moment.

Rome deadly quiet now among her hills. The assassins who still wore, because of the danger, the meek face and the innocuous bearing. But who were waiting. As he waited. In these last moments as they all waited.

If Keppler would call!

But why should he wait? Eleanora had said. If she were he, she would go to the Babuino, now, while there was still time, and see Keppler. There was no point going slowly out of his mind like this, waiting. Why should he be such a fool always, following with such blind devotion every order they gave him? After all, this was a question of—

His life.

And that night, for perhaps the first time in twenty years, he had disobeyed his instructions. Outside the Babuino, at three o'clock in the morning, he had seen the big cars, parked at the hotel entrance: Ottavio's, Motta's, Pucci's. It was obvious they had made their preparations; and now, with the evidence of the cars, a feverish anxiety took hold of him. So they intended to leave him—waiting like a fool for a phone call that would not come. He cursed, went into the lobby, past the S.S. sentry. The lobby was deserted. The faded man at the desk who had once been the manager of the Babuino in the days when the hotel had been a famous tourist place bowed and cracked his face into the smile he almost perpetually wore these nine months: a placating grimace which he detested. No; the colonel was not here. No, Excellency; he did not know where the colonel was. Did the signor perhaps know what the true reports from the front were? The guns had kept him awake, and this morning his wife had had the most terrible headache. Could the signor suggest what preparations he, or the hotel, those indivisible twins, should make?

He stormed back into the street. Even that fool in the lobby knew it was all over, even while he was still trembling with fear and scrubbing one dry palm against the other. Even he was waiting to be liberated.

The sentry stomped as he went by.

Outside, it seemed to him the volume of armored cars, bicycles, mules, troops going north had increased. But there was nothing orderly about the withdrawal. Soldiers were carrying fantastic loot; he saw one with a huge clock, another with a pair of hens. Near the Aurelian Gate a truck burned. What vehicles stalled they were setting fire to. Toward the river there was a faint crackle of shots.

He found Keppler at last on the Via Tasso. And in time,

too. The stocky, bald and bushy-eyebrowed man was descending the stairs of the headquarters, talking with an aide. At the curb there was a huge staff car.

What? Keppler said. Oh, you. Yes, what is it?

I've been waiting, Colonel, he said.

Waiting? Waiting? What for? Looking at him under the excessive eyebrows, to Keppler it seemed incredible that somebody in this city was still waiting.

Your orders, he said. I was to wait for a telephone call from your office.

Oh? And you waited?

Yes, Colonel. Since yesterday afternoon.

Incredible, Keppler said. He turned to the aide. He's been waiting for me to call him, since yesterday.

Do we abandon the city, Colonel?

Abandon? To the aide: He waits for a telephone call and now he wants to know if we abandon the city. Then to him: Yes, we abandon it.

And I?

Get out, you fool, Keppler said violently. Get out! And he climbed into the staff car.

Two diamonds, two gold women's purses, five gold watches, three diamond pins, a pearl ring, about four hundred and fifty thousand lire, drafts on the Bank of England, drafts on the National Bank of Labor, three hundred and fifty francs and a set, his wife's, of pearl ear-rings.

He sat in the rear of the big car.

As they took the road that goes to Lake Bracciano (it is deep, cold, blue, among the mountains) the planes had come. He would remember that. The plane diving, the bomb, the armored car in front of him, in that panicked procession, hit, and burning, and then Sziggetti, at the wheel, shouting violently, pulling on the wheel, then the sickening lurch, all quick, all telescoped, then the tree.

The morning of June fifth. On that morning.

Now he was here, in the courtroom, helpless at last among his enemies.

The Liberated City: I

AT ONE O'CLOCK, on the street which goes from the Corso to the Tiber, and which passes the tomb of the Emperor Augustus, that circular and ponderous ruin landscaped with cypress trees, a soldier who had read Gibbon a long, long time ago said to the brunette he was walking down the street with: "There's the tomb of the Emperor Augustus."

The brunette was very good looking, wore no stockings, danced in a night club on the Via San Steffano del Cacco, had a five-year-old son, had been deserted by her husband, lived with her aunt, a former seamstress in a provincial acting company, liked soldiers, and the brunette said: "Where?" and then, "Who?"

The soldier, who had read Gibbon, said: "Skip it," or its equivalent in the peculiar Italian he spoke, and that night slept with the brunette in an apartment borrowed from his first sergeant who was on a ten-day leave in Capri, and thought it did not matter about Augustus anyway, he was dead such a long time.

While on the street corners, where the trams stopped

and one could pick up from the pushcarts an old Dante in a battered edition for about thirty lire, if anybody was still picking up old Dantes, there were stanchions, and on the stanchions placards which said:

"We have driven the Germans out of Rome. Soon we will drive them out of all Italy. Long Live Democracy. Long Live the Constitution. Long Live the Allies."

The city was liberated.

Giorgio

As the american officer approached, under the shadow of
the arches, his shoulder burdened with a heavy musette
bag and the camera in his hand, the rosary man, holding
open the tray in which the mother-of-pearl scapulars and
the mosaic bracelets lay bedded in white cotton, got to him
first and asked, whiningly, "Nice rosaries, Lieutenant? To
be blessed by the Pope," but the lieutenant said no, he did
not want any rosaries to be blessed by the Pope, and by
that time the woman with the ricordi da Roma and the
town maps had gotten to him, and the officer said no, he
did not wish any ricordi da Roma or any pianti da Roma
either, and then he was compelled to chase off the kids who
eyed the musette bag with perhaps more than curiosity
and who quoted him the current market price on cigarettes
and chocolate, and the lieutenant said beat it, scram, va
via, and finally, as he was emerging from the shadows of
the archways, Giorgio got to him and said politely, to distinguish himself from the others, "Good morning, sir. You
wish a guide?"

"No," the lieutenant with the camera said.

"Very good guide, sir."

"No," the lieutenant said. He shifted the musette bag. "Say, Mac," the lieutenant said to Giorgio, "this is the Colosseum, isn't it?'"

"Yes," said Giorgio. "This is the Colosseum."

The lieutenant had been born in York, Pennsylvania, and had gone to school there, and had in time become the assistant manager of one of the two motion picture theaters in York, Pennsylvania. When he looked at the Colosseum which even he realized was considerable older than York, Pennsylvania, he thought it appeared, cupping the sunlight, with the blue shadows falling on its ruined tiers, surprisingly bigger than he had ever supposed when he had seen pictures of it in his history book at school. It occurred to him vaguely that the Romans must have been pretty good engineers to have hoisted into position a monument the size of this one, and he wondered equally vaguely how they had accomplished it without derricks, bulldozers and cranes. He felt, too, in a way he would not have been able to explain, rather uncomfortable about the idea of the length of time associated with all this stone, and the nice thing about York, Pennsylvania, he realized, was that you never thought of history at all there, even when you found an old Indian grave, and you never felt uncomfortable about time. Anyway, the family would sure get a kick out of it when he sent home a snapshot of the Colosseum, and he had been there.

Giorgio watched the officer clamber up what remained of the stone barrier which had once surrounded the sanded arena in which the gladiators had fought, and watched him, too, as he slipped the bulging musette bag from his shoulder and dropped it to the ground beside him. Doesn't he know better? thought Giorgio. Besides, the fool obviously needed a guide but was too miserly to hire one, and in addition Giorgio's head was killing him with pain.

He went back under the arch to where the group of men stood. The American was shifting about with his little camera. Giorgio sat down on a block of stone fallen from the tiers and put his head, with all its pains, into his hands. At the moment, two of the lesser disasters of his life were causing him anguish. He had lost, yesterday, at the Villa Glori, a thousand lire on a horse. And he had promised this evening to take Maddalena, his wife, to the cinema. He knew that he was not going to take Maddalena to the cinema tonight because he had already lost a thousand lire in the Villa Glori yesterday. In a little while, however, the other deeper disasters of his life flooded up and swept away the thought of Maddalena and even of the Villa Glori.

He heard a voice say, from among the group of men, "Io voglio lavorare," repeating the simple sentence over and over. "Io voglio lavorare."

Who didn't want to work?

"Cheer up, amico," said one, who was whittling a walking stick full of delicate scrolls. "What's work? Look at Baldini: all his life he has worked. Haven't you, Baldini?"

"All my life," Baldini said.

"Now he is fifty-eight and he has two sons, a pair of bulls, and they sit home and eat, and the old man goes out every day to work. Those are the rewards of labor."

"Io voglio lavorare," the voice said.

"It is better to play the black market."

"Of course."

"Like butter. Who has butter if they are honest and simply work?" the rosary man said. "But in the Tor di Nona yesterday I saw all the butter you want."

"All you need is the money."

"Exactly. The money."

"Io voglio lavorare," the voice said stubbornly.

"Be quiet, fool," the one with the knife and the walking stick said. "Work is for horses."

One sits, Giorgio thought, feeling the pain come and go inside his skull, here in the Colosseum, listening to people of no consequence talk, one comes to this eventually, begging ignorant foreigners to be hired, one descends and descends toward the bottom of a pit which has no bottom, losing everything on the way down, one's profession, one's happiness, one's sanity. One sits, with his head in his hands, like this, enduring agonies which baffle the doctors, every day more hopeless. How long was it, how many centuries ago, in what lost world had he existed as a man with self-respect and secure of his place in an ordered and normal and comprehensible universe?

"They will send us trucks. I heard it yesterday in the Piazza Colonna. Trucks from America."

"With tires?"

"Of course with tires. The Americans have tires. They have everything. Do you think the entire world is bankrupt because in Italy there are no tires?"

"In Italia c'è niente."

"The Americans have them."

"The Americans," said the one with the knife. "Look at them: peasants with mechanical educations. They have too much of everything, including the divorce."

"With you a woman wouldn't want a divorce, eh?"

"I'd thaw them out. They are all frozen from the neck down, the American women. A good Italian would thaw them."

"Come té."

"Come mé."

It was all lost, Poggio and his youth, and the days when his father had led the village band, the days of the devoutness of his mother. He could remember his youth only with difficulty now, it was as painful as the memory of his marriage, a mistake, or the children, two mistakes, and it had vanished into that pit, into that bottomless yesterday in which he had once been a barman at the Cafe Tivoli in the days when the Tivoli had been one of the fashionable bars on the Via Veneto and in the evenings the gagàs used to stroll down the street, under the chestnut trees, and Rome had blazed with light. They had all come to the Tivoli in those days: Farinacci, now blustering in the north, Edda Ciano, the young Umberto, all the officials and their women, the cream of the party, glittering, powerful.

And so sure of themselves.

And he had been there, Giorgio, this desolated and obscure imitation of a guide sitting on a dusty slab in the shadow of an arch in the Colosseum, part of it, a man with a future in an orderly world.

Had not Farinacci himself, he was a monster of course, one of the cruelest, the most ferocious, but had not Farinacci himself once, leaning on the bar, said to him: "That is what I should have been, Giorgio. A barman. Dropping a maraschino into a cocktail. Politics is too complicated."

Had not Edda Ciano, it was common gossip about the kind of life she led, her father's energy but all directed toward the bedroom, had not Edda Ciano sent back once a glass of orange juice three times because there were, she claimed, still orange pips in the glass?

And had not he, Giorgio, furious of course (he despised these people, in his heart of hearts he was an unregenerate democrat but what was one to do when one could not work

or send one's children to school without the party button)
strained the orange juice three times before the imperial
lady was satisfied?

Now they were gone, blown away by the violent winds
of change, blown down into the nothingness of yesterday,
the ferocious Farinaccis, the sexual Eddas, the cocktail
hours at the Tivoli, and Rome was in darkness.

"Emilio, quando finisce la guerra?"

"Mai."

"Never?"

"I say never."

"But it has to end."

"In your opinion yes. But this one never. Now the tedeschi. Then the Russ. Then the Inglese. Then the tedeschi will be strong again. This one doesn't end."

"The Inglese. That's one war I fight."

"Emilio the cynico."

"I say what I think."

"You know what they say: a man's worst enemy is his
own opinion."

"They say, they say. What are you, a book of proverbs?"

"That's what they say."

Somehow all his troubles went back to the Tivoli. They
were shooting fascists now, weren't they? Arresting them.
Well, he could show them one, a real spotted and striped
one if they wanted a fascist, right in there in the Cafe
Tivoli under their noses.

That animal, La Pina, what was he if not a fascist?

Look what had happened: there he had been, a barman,
making good money, with a reputation, for everyone used
to say Giorgio was the best of them, a martini by Giorgio
was incomparable, and then, in '42, when the news was
bad and the African business looked so gloomy, he had

ventured to say once to the busboy, Giovanni, that in his opinion it was very foolish for Italy to have gotten into the war.

As God was his witness, that was all he'd said. A phrase, an opinion uttered to a busboy, he had, so to speak, merely opened his mouth and exercised his tongue a little, but would you believe it that La Pina, that profiteer, that bastard, that incontestable fascist, who stuck his own daughter-in-law behind the cash register in order to save himself a cashier's salary, suddenly he, La Pina, was the big patriot, and had made such a stink about it threatening him with the Militia, the Ovra, God knows what, that he, Giorgio, had thrown his apron into his face and marched out. And what had he said? Nothing! It was perhaps stupid to get into the war! Who didn't think that in his heart? But La Pina, oh he was the patriot, he was all for the glory and the triumph of Italian arms, and what kind of a patriot was he now? An allied patriot. Now, with the Tivoli packed with soldiers and the officers of the Alleati and the black marketeers, he was the biggest and loudest democrat of them all!

A fury consumed Giorgio.

Dio, if he were only on the committee di epurazione! If they would put into his hands the purging of the city, and allow him to do the shooting and the hanging, he, Giorgio, this nonentity, would empty the villas fast enough! They wouldn't be sitting long with such complacency at their tables in the Cafe Tivoli sipping their iced vermouths or their cocktail Americanos, or dancing at their supper parties to which they so cleverly invited the colonels and brigadiers of the Alleati. No, out in the bright sunlight, tied backward in a chair, that's where they would be, saying their ultimate paternosters to a deaf Virgin.

That's what he would do, Giorgio, with his own bare hands if they gave him the authority just once, not sitting here dying from these terrible mysterious headaches, sickened and ill and crazy from his own existence.

Ah, how he had wanted the Alleati to come!

With what passion, with what hope, he had heard the guns speaking from the Alban Hills, with what secret joy he had crouched under his blanket in the living room listening to the radio while Maddalena had cautioned the neighbors to be quiet.

There had been the time, for example, when during the war he had been employed in the War Department building as a clerk, and the planes had come, the first of the days when the Alleati had bombed the stazione, and the air-raid sirens, late as usual, had sounded throughout the city. They had poured out of the offices then, racing for the cellars, all of them, but he, Giorgio, had gone up to the roof looking up into the sky for the neat silver squadrons in the afternoon haze, and had seen them wheeling and wheeling, and they had gone over once and wheeled and come back, and when they had come back Giorgio had not been able any longer to endure it, and so great a lust for annihilation and revenge had overtaken him that he had danced on the roof in a kind of gleeful rage, waving at the sky his white pocket handkerchief, screaming to the drumming squadrons:

"Here! here! Drop one here! This is the War Department! Imbeciles, drop one here!"

An insane act, insane, an act full of comedy and tragedy, because then the planes had gone on over, ignoring the War Department and his frantic pocket handkerchief, dropping their eggs, and what had they hit? In all this great city, full of so many splendid targets, full of such excellent material for destruction and death, of things worthy of a long delayed punishment, what had they hit? Yes, on the Via Ostia, beyond the gate of St. Paul, in the vicinity of the railroad, they had hit an apartment house which contained the apartment belonging to the wife of Giorgio's brother, and which held some expensive furniture he had loaned to them. On this the last bomb had fallen, effectively destroying all of it, and only by some incredible charity of fate not taking his brother's family with it.

It was crazy, absurd.

He was being made a buffoon of by history, by he knew not what, God, fate, chance, a comedian full of disasters, the clown whose head is laughingly broken. No wonder he had these headaches. Logic and reason, in revolt, were trying to batter their way out of his skull.

"Tell me, Baldini. Do you pray?"

"Me? I pray."

"For what?"

"That worse shouldn't happen."

"Listen to him," said the rosary man. "He asks about praying. Tell me, lazzarone, how long is it since you went to mass?"

"The signor grande can take care of himself without my prayers."

"Ah, but he likes the sinner's prayers best."

"He gets enough of that kind from the priests."

"What are you, Emilio? An atheist?"

"I am me. An Emilioist."

"We need to pray," Baldini said. "Not for the rewards. I do not so much believe in the rewards. But just for the necessity of it."

"What necessity, old man?"

"A man feels bad without at least religion."

"Then pray," Emilio said, gesturing with the knife.

"Pray to the buon Dio. No shoes on their feet, and they sprinkle their horsemeat with salt extracted from the sea, but still they pray. I have different ideas of salvation."

"What ideas?"

"Different."

"He prays to the east now, Emilio. Non è vero, Emilio? Like the Arabs, he prays to the east."

"Ah, with a red handkerchief he'll look handsome."

"Be quiet, you fools," Emilio said. "If you were wise men would you be so poor?"

"Speaking of fools," said the rosary man, "there is a real one. Up there with the camera."

"Who? The American?"

"Yes."

"Look at him. He is walking away from his property to take the photograph."

"In a little while there will be no property."

"Should we warn him?"

"Why?"

"Well, I was an honest man once."

"Look at him. What world does he think he is in, leaving property behind him like that? What do you think is in the military bag?"

"Cigarettes. They carry in their bags very often cartoni di sigaretti."

"He walks away from sigaretti like that nowadays?"

"The uniform I would like. With such a pair of trousers I could live through the winter."

"Sometimes they have blankets in their packs."

"Blankets?"

"The woolen kind. I have a cousin made a wonderful coat of just such a blanket."

"In that color?"

"Of course not. He dyed it."

"Ah, cigarettes, blankets. And the fool walks away leaving such treasures to take photographs."

"Look, look."

"We are watching the education of a fool."

"In a little while I think you will see the wrath of a fool."

"Is it gone yet?"

"Going."

"Who is it?"

"The hunchbacked boy. Whose father was killed in Caiazzo. The wild one."

"Now?"

"Si, now. Vanished is our fool's treasures. All one has to do is to leave such a thing alone, like a lamb in a jungle."

"Look, look. He has finished taking the photograph."

"How old is he?"

"A young one."

"All the ufficiale Americani are young ones. It is an army made up of young ones. Have you watched them salute?"

"Si."

"In our army you would go on bread and water a week for a salute like theirs."

"But they win all the wars."

"And we lose them. With our magnificent salutes."

"Is he looking for it yet?"

"I think it has begun to penetrate that he does not have what he once had."

"He can afford the loss."

"Too bad a remnant of honesty still clings to me. Or is it a remnant of cowardice? I could be enjoying the sigaretti now."

"And his blanket."

"And his blanket."

"He is beginning to shout at the woman with the maps."

"He shouts loud, doesn't he?"

"Very."

"La voce degli conquistadori."

"He is indignant. His faith in humanity has been violated. I think, compagni, it is time we made a little walk in the direction of the Corso. His indignation is loud enough to be heard by the carabinieri."

"Andiamo."

"Si. Come along, Giorgio. He has begun to shout loudly and to pursue the children. Listen to what the children are shouting back at him."

"It is an obscenity they learned from the soldiers."

"Nevertheless it is not a nice thing to say about anybody's mother."

"Well, let us hope the photograph at least turns out well."

"Speriamo."

"Come along, Giorgio."

They walked leisurely from under the old stone arches, shabby, cynical, kicking the white sand, indifferent to history. Incomprehensible ecstacies had once sustained men in this arena. What ecstacies, what men? Limp mortals who stiffened the palsies of their souls with hosannahs. What souls, what hosannahs? And the lions roared. What lions? Sacred, the bishops had made it sacred, the bishops and the lions. Scusi, amico, you wish a martyr? Here is one, in the pants that don't match the coat, his feet out of his shoes. You wish lions? Here, look where they have left the marks of their teeth.

Our Father who art. Well, he's still there. Sacred, the bishops had made it sacred and profitable, the bishops and the lions.

Ciao, Emilio.

Ciao, Baldini.

Ciao, Giorgio.

The Via del Impero was warmed by the sun.

One walked, as Giorgio walked, thinking how in the Via Francesco Crespi not two nights ago a certain professor of political economy had assassinated his entire family with an army pistol. Of course. A rational act, why should one think it was not a rational act? A point comes when a pistol must be used even against oneself, the suffering makes one one's most terrible enemy. He understood completely the soul of that certain professor of political economy in the Via Francesco Crespi. Look how it shines, the sun, there in the valley of the Forum, making the grass greener, the white broken columns whiter, and how neat the wreckage is, how carefully arranged this debris of an empire, like one's grandmother on her deathbed, while the family, assembled, marvel at her great antiquity. From what one heard it was excellent, the Forum, at night for the whores. Among the old stones, the temples, in the grass of the basilicas, why not, it was as good a place as any, but damp probably. For the negri it did not matter; once, do you remember, almost in broad daylight, against a tree in the Villa Borghese you saw one, un negre, and she, the woman, with her skirt up against the tree. Soldati and women, it was all soldati and women, thieves and whores, that was a war. First they had said the headaches were sinus, so one paid for the injection against sinus, then it turns out not to be sinus. So a cardiograph is advised, and the heart is perfect, miraculously despite everything the heart is perfect, there is nothing whatsoever wrong with the heart, meanwhile one pays also for the cardiograph. When the dottore had suspected an old case of the disease one wor-

ried: after all, it was possible, how careful had one been
in Milan in one's youth? That crazy time when one went
four times to the brothels the same day, including the one
with the queer contraption in the ceiling, and woke up in
bed with three of them. A disease of that kind he was ready
to believe, reappearing even after so many years and sup-
posedly cured, but the test had been negative. Nothing:
headaches! They were headaches of a mysterious origin, the
doctors agreed, nerves, it was all to be traced to his nerves.
Meanwhile a thousand lire each visit.

From the balcony, in the Piazza Venezia, hung a crimson
square of velvet. An art exhibition where once the Grand
Council had assembled. So? That was dead, too; it had happened, and that was the end of it, his sitting under the
barred windows eating grapes, the barking from the balcony, the vivas, the long imperial speeches, ended, wiped
out, an art exhibition deposes Caesar, a parking lot dis-
graces the center of the piazza where the squadristi had
sung, the black legions flashed their daggers. It was not important any more; it was more important that the Alleati
have a parking lot to park their jeeps and lorries, it was
more important that he win once in a while at the races
in the Villa Glori. History: history had become a pair of
shoes. Look at his, the ones he was wearing, the sport ones,
shoes he bought in 1939, the brown all scuffed and the
white cracked open, the seams gaping, these were the shoes
one wore. Maddalena, she took the polish every morning
but go polish holes. Do? Piss in one's tears, that's what to
do. Blow out one's brains and let a little peace in.

Around him, as he crossed the piazza, the afternoon
throbbed. A traffic Rome had never known flooded the
streets. Squat topheavy British lorries tented with dirty
tarpaulins, driven by pokerfaced Englishmen in cocked

blue berets. Olivegreen jeeps with cigar-smoking Americans, naked little vicious engines of destruction. Stuttering Italian taxis (O patria mia) and backfiring camionettas banging along on some kind of incredible fuel with only the vaguest chemical kinship to gasoline. (O quanti feriti, che sangue, che lividor!) And in the open carriages a drunken and grinning soldiery while the old capped vetturini flicked their whips at their starved mares.

The narrow ledgelike sidewalk of the Corso. Step off into the gutter and one ended in the Policlinico, in a plaster cast. Scusi, signor. Of the British, what would one say? They have magnificent officers; all the officers have magnificent mustaches; it was quite possible they smiled during the Boer War, not since. Look, with the riding crop. For what? They have horses? Scusi, signor. How the sun shines. On all this pile of merde how the sun shines. Guarda: that one is being amusing, the blonde one, he hits the other with his military cap, the other hits him back, a pair of jovial drunkards. Gli Americani. What stables were they educated in? Such faces, look, all shapes, as a people they have no racial beauty, a kind of rude health, a youngness, and rich, unquestionably rich. Why give them everything, us nothing? Ask the buon Dio. He knows all—and keeps it a secret. Scusi, signor.

One walked, walked. In this shop window, ecco: shoes. One said shoes, but meant diamonds. Diamonds were priced like this, not shoes. Ten thousand lire for that thick-soled pair, there, with the tasseled laces, and the leather probably only pressed paper, perhaps wood, Jesu knew what they manufactured shoes of now with the cattle driven off by the Germans, and no trade, and the factories blown to bits. Ten thousand lire! Why did not all the Corso come crowding here at this window to laugh? A wild hysterical murderous laughter such as he felt looking at shoes which cost ten thousand lire? A suit bankrupted a family, a shirt starved the children, an overcoat cost more than a funeral. He walked, outwardly a reasonable being, except perhaps for the twitching of his eyelids, shoes priced like pearls floating through his mind. O Madre di Dio! And she heard? Who heard, who cared? The tears fell on a world of iron, fire consumed the bewildered heart.

Even as he turned the key, later, exhausted by the long walk, and entered his house, he could feel the repugnance and irrationality, the self-hatred, overwhelming him. Maddalena was in the kitchen, a woman full-breasted, in her late thirties, with a round patient face and a double chin, whose every movement for months now had inspired nothing but thoughts of violence in him. He firmly believed at times that if he had not married this daughter of a shopkeeper from Pistoia thinking she would come into possession of money, which she had not, the whole course of his life would have been different. It was true that during the occupation she had acted with great energy and even a certain amount of courage for a woman, when he himself had been terrified at the idea of being taken by the Germans in one of their labor dragnets and shipped off to some factory on the border, and had as a result not dared for weeks and weeks to venture out of the house, but cowered here in the dining room, listening to Radio Roma and doing the crossword puzzles in the weekly papers. But this did not alter the fact that Maddalena's great crime was that she existed at all, because her only existence was as his wife, and as his wife she now inspired nothing but thoughts of violence in him. There were a hundred accusations he could bring against her: she was stupid, she was a log in bed, she had a double chin, the understanding of a cow, the appetite of a horse, the ambitions of a fishwife. Above all, she existed. And she imposed such problems and such obligations on him as taking her to a cinema when he had already lost a thousand lire at the Villa Glori and had spat on himself all night as a will-less fool for doing so.

In the dining room, on the wall, were the portraits of his parents, the leader of the village band, the dark devout mother. There was a bowl of waxed fruit on the dining table.

Maddalena had prepared eggs, in the pan, and mozzarella, the white cheese fried between little squares of bread. He decided he did not like the eggs. Didn't she know he needed fish, he was dying for a piece of fish?

Fish! Where was one to get fish now?

And if there was fish in the market, how would *she* know? Did she ever go and look what they had in the markets? It was too much trouble for her to go look at what they might possibly be selling in the markets!

"What are you screaming about?" Maddalena said. "Mother in heaven, what are you screaming about?"

Didn't they perhaps scream in Pistoia? He supposed in that stable in Pistoia in which she was brought up her family was of such magnificent manners they did not scream. They were all aristocrats, her family. With snot in his mustache, that's the kind of an artistocrat her father was.

"Mother in heaven," Maddalena said, "help me, help me. What have I done to him, tell me!"

He shouted what she had done.

The portrait of his father, the leader of the village band, stared out into the dining room from its oval frame.

He shouted about the bad luck he had marrying her.

Then about her habits in bed.

"Mother in heaven!" Maddalena screamed. "Mother in heaven!"

He shouted that she was driving him out of his mind and why didn't she pack up and go back to her father that animal in Pistoia and that when he was young and in Milan and free he should have broken both his legs before he met her because that would have effectively prevented him from cutting his own throat with a marriage license. He shouted that at night he might as well go to bed with a bag of potatoes as her and then he shouted the advantages of going to bed with a bag of potatoes and when she began to cry and scream hysterically which was what he had intended her to do from the beginning he got up and slammed the door into the bedroom hearing her calling upon the Madonna to witness the insanity of the cannibal she had united her fortunes with, and then knowing with a sick sense of shame that it was all to prevent her from asking him about his promise to take her to the cinema he flung himself down on the big bed in which they slept and suffered and in terrible meaningless moments coupled together, burying his hot face in the pillow in rage and anguish and humiliation and so finally escaped into what was the only escape the world gave all the Giorgios, sleep, and even then he dreamed.

Harry

HE WENT INTO the bar, recognizing it, the bead curtain, the cane chairs, the same tiled floor. He was very tired. It was cool inside the bar, and the proprietor, glancing up from behind the cash register where he sat on a high stool reading Il Tempo, saw only another hot, tired soldier in the clumsy buckled boots, wearing, as they all did, a khaki handkerchief wound about his throat, and the back of his heavy woolen shirt all stained with his own sweat.

A big nickeled caffe espresso urn glittered on the counter.

The bartender said: "Buon giorno."

There was nothing to distinguish this soldier, coming into the Bar Americano now, from any other soldier, and there were so many of them. Jesu alone know how many. All over Italy. Too many, and of such different uniforms. All sweaty, on a hot September day, and all asking, when they should know it was forbidden, for cognac. This one, of course, would ask for cognac.

"Cognac," the soldier said.

The proprietor sighed. Il Tempo was less predictable.

"It is not the hour," said the bartender. He indicated on the wall the military notice which prohibited the sale of intoxicating liquors to the soldiers between the hours of one and five.

"How about vermouth?" said the soldier. "Is it the hour for vermouth?"

"It is the hour only for aranciata."

"It is the prohibition against the drinking of the military," the proprietor explained. How many times did that make it he had explained the notice today? Always the cognac, and then the order for vermouth, since the Americans did not somehow class vermouth as an intoxicant, and then the explanation.

"No liquor at all?" said the soldier.

"Aranciata."

"I can't drink that damned soda pop," the soldier said. "How about a cherry brandy?"

"Proibito," said the bartender.

"For chrissake," said the soldier. "Isn't there nothing you can get a drink of?"

"Aranciata."

"All right," the soldier said. "Aranciata."

The bartender uncapped the bottle of orange pop.

"Things sure have changed," the soldier said to the bartender. "In four months they sure changed things in this town, didn't they? I even saw barbed wire up. That's when you can tell they've got it all changed."

But they always changed, all the towns. When you came into them at first, maybe while they were still burning a little, and nobody was sure about boobytraps, they were good. But when you came back to them, later, they were changed. A town was great until the first redcross opened up, and the first station hospital moved in, and the first vietato signs appeared, and the barbed wire came up to keep the kids off who hung around the mess lines, and then the first MP's in white helmet liners and white gloves, the first bars closing at seven o'clock and the first off-limits signs marking the wooden doors of the little trattorias. Up to then the towns were fine. Then they changed.

But he hadn't thought Rome would change the way the towns in the south had changed. Rome had been different from all the other towns for him. But evidently they had changed it.

"Don't you remember me?" the soldier asked.

That, too, was one of the inevitable questions, thought the proprietor of the Bar Americano. Always they expected to be remembered. But he had difficulty even remembering the noisy ones who broke the glasses, let alone the quiet ones.

"I hit this bar on the fifth of June," the soldier said. "I thought you might remember because of the day."

"Ah," said the proprietor, "the fifth of June."

"I thought you might remember," said the soldier.

"It was a wonderful day. Do you remember, Vincenzo? It was a day when the people went crazy."

"Really a day," said the bartender.

"You were here on the fifth of June?" the proprietor asked the soldier.

"I was here."

"In the night it was all Germans," the bartender said. "Then in the morning it was all Alleati."

"There was shooting. Do you remember the shooting, Vincenzo?"

"Of course I remember the shooting. I contributed to it."

"With a beretta."

"Could I have hidden a cannon in the house?" said the

bartender. "It was a beretta of my brother. I fired it, mostly into the darkness, from my window. In the general direction of the sounds."

"Some hero," said the proprietor.

"What has being a hero got to do with it?" said the bartender. "I had a beretta and I fired."

"From the window."

"Your wife didn't even permit you to open the window."

"My wife," said the proprietor. "You know my wife. She is always seeing me killed."

"At least I opened the window," said the bartender.

"So you're a hero," said the proprietor. It was evidently an old argument. "You fired from the window. You would have closed it fast enough if the tedeschi had fired back."

"What a day," the bartender sighed.

"Yes," said the proprietor. "It was the kind of a day a person does not see twice."

"That's right," the soldier said. "That was a day to remember."

All the way up from Velletri they had pushed hard and because the rumors said the city would not be defended they had hand-carried the machine guns and the mortars, and the guys with the baseplates and the tripods really had it rough. There wasn't much left of the little towns going up to the city and in the fields the telephone poles lay broken trailing their wires and the airforce had caught the bombers sitting on their strips because they were still burning behind a kind of earthwork the Germans had built to protect them from strafing. The aqueducts bulking out there under the perfectly blue sky gave a guy a funny feeling because they had survived while all the cute villas and the farmhouses painted their Easter-egg colors, pinks and blues, had stopped looking like villas or farm-

houses in the one week of fighting while the war had gone
up this paved highway, and then at the gates of the city
when the guys could see it spread out on the plain in front
of them white and shining like a dream there had been
shelling and it turned out the city was being a little bit
defended after all, and then up the line they had begun
hollering for the bazookas and bazooka ammo and the bazookas went up the line while the guys lay there on the
shoulders of the highway saying, "Why the sons a bitches.
The sons a bitches said this was an open city. Some open
city." Then, finally, when the bazookas had taken care of
what turned out to be two Tiger tanks, it was Rome, and
somebody up in one of the windows began popping away
with a rifle which was a hell of a welcome, then it turned
out the sniper was a dame, it was a dame up there sniping
in the tenement house, some dame, and then when they
found out it was a dame sniping why they just hollered,
"Pass her down, Jack. I'll interrogate her. Let me interrogate her!" Jesus jumping crowfoot Christ were you tired.
A window went up in a house because all the windows had
been closed and all the shutters shut while the shooting
was still on and then a head came out of the window and
the head asked, "Inglese?" And they hollered, "Americano!"
And then it was the city, everybody cheering, flowers and
wine, handshakes and vivas, speeches and sigaretti, and it
was a city, a wonderful, a real city, clean, a city with streets
wide and sunny and lined with streets, bars in it and shops
with stuff in the windows and hotels with marquees, a city
standing up all in one piece, smelling and looking like a
city, a city after places like Capua and Venefro that weren't
even places any more just a name that used to be a place,
and Jesus jumping crowfoot Christ were you tired. All they
could do, the guys, was just lie there on their packs on the

sidewalks, dirty, gun and pack and uniform, all dirty, with their heads on a pack or on a machine gun, all dirty, and say, "Come here, you little ole cat," to the girls, "Come here, honey, I want to feel you," so tired they couldn't do anything but talk it out as they lay there, so tired they couldn't even lift a hand up to touch a girl's ankle as she went by. "Come here, you ole Maria," and the girls smiling so nicely, not understanding a word.

The old lady came up the street, in black, wearing on her head a battered old black hat like your aunt used to wear, in old-fashioned button-up shoes, hobbling on a cane, and she had a piece of bread in her hand, the kind of bread they ate that wasn't exactly brown and wasn't exactly gray, just a piece of it in her hand, hobbling up the street, and there you were, an American.

"I am an American, too," said the little old lady with the battered hat and a piece of bread in her hand on a street in Rome. "Are you from Buffalo?"

"No, ma'am. Hartford."

"Hartford? I am from Buffalo. Oh, it's a long time. More than forty years ago. Do they still have the steamers which go from Buffalo to Cleveland on Lake Erie?"

"I don't know, ma'am. I'm from Hartford."

"Oh, yes, Hartford. I remember the steamers from Buffalo to Cleveland very well. It's more than forty years ago."

On a street in Rome, and you were looking for a joint to drink in.

"This is what we eat now," the little old lady in the black dress said. "It is very bad with us," and she held up the bread. "The Germans have been very bad."

"Yes, ma'am."

"If I could only march with you," she said. "March. But I'm too old. I am an old woman. It's more than forty years since I've sailed on a steamer from Buffalo to Cleveland."

"Yes, ma'am."

You wanted a drink bad. You had only a couple of hours.

"God bless you," the old woman with the bread said. "I am too old to march but I can say God bless you."

Then she went up the street, hobbling on the cane, in the black dress, battered hat and high old-fashioned button shoes, and you found a bar, downstairs in a hotel, a bar right out of the Ritz, by God you didn't even think there were bars like that still in the world, dark, cool, and with leather stools, and little statues of cupids and girls who looked like they were stepping into a bath, and there was a lieutenant sitting on one of the stools drinking, and it was such a hell of a bar that you said to the lieutenant, because you couldn't see a bar like that being for just any joe, "This isn't an officer's bar, is it, Lieutenant?"

And the lieutenant said, "Not yet, soldier. But it will be."

So you had a drink down there, good cognac.

"Signorina," you said to the girl hurrying on the street. "Signorina, aspette un momento."

She smiled. She had nice teeth. She was wearing a thin flowered dress, very short.

"We want," you said, "the place Mussolini used to talk."

"Cos'è?"

"Mussolini," you said. "Dove parlate. Me and my friend want to see it."

"Chi? Il Duce?"

"That's right."

"Ma non c'è qui piu Il Duce."

"I know he ain't here. I mean where he used to speak. Il balcony." She thought it was very funny when you did an imitation out of the newsreels.

"E lontano," she said. "Lontano. La Piazza Venezia."

"She says it's far."

"Ask her how far," Stacey said.

"Molto lontano, signorina?"

"Si, si. Molto."

"She says it's molto. What do you say, we walk or we have another shot?"

"The hell with it. I walked enough."

"Grazie, signorina. Mio amico, his feet hurt."

"Cos'è?"

"What is this routine with the cose?" Stacey said.

"Stanco," you said.

"Ask the babe what she's doing."

"Lay off. She looks like a nice kid."

"I'm a nice kid, too."

"Scusi," she said, smiling. "Ma siete molto sporco."

"What?"

"She says we're dirty."

"What the hell does she think we'd be?"

"Camminato," you said. "Very far. E molto—how the hell do you say dust?"

"How the hell do I know?"

"Da Anzio?" she asked.

"Si. Da Anzio. "

"E terribile, la guerra, no?"

"What's that with the guerra?"

"She says it's terrible."

"She can say that again."

"Se vuole lavarsi . . ."

"What?"

"Lavare. Col aqua. . . ." And then the gestures.

"Oh, wash. She wants to know if we want to wash. You want to wash?"

"My throat."

"I think she wants us to go with her and wash."

"Ask her if she'll scrub my back."

"Lay off."

"You tell her she scrubs my back I'll wash my own teeth."

"Funny."

"Cos'è dice?"

"I've got a funny friend."

"Fun nee?"

"Comico."

"Oh," and a smile. She had a very nice smile. "Un comico teatro?"

"No. Un comico plain."

"Non capisco."

"That's all right. Come si chiama, signorina?"

"Francesca . . . E voi?"

"Harry."

" 'Ar-ree?"

"Harry. Don't go up, come down. And pronounce the h."

"Harree?"

"Hello, Francesca."

" 'Allo, Har-ree."

She washed your neck. She took the washcloth and got the dirt out, all the dirt in your ears and under your ears, all the dirt on your neck. "Tutti gli soldati sono come bambini." All right, but you didn't mind at all being a bambini, standing in the bathroom with your shirt off, and the gun propped up in a corner of the living room, all the neighbors coming in and out to tell how happy they were you had come at last from Anzio, they had waited so long, it was so bad under the tedeschi, this one with a relative in Brooklyn, that one with a son a prisoner, the other whose house had been bombed, then the wine and pasta. By God they were glad to see you. The liberatori, that's what you were, a jerk from Hartford, a liberatori.

"Francesca."

"Si?"

"I've got to go now."

"Go?"

"Via. I got to via now. Grazie for the pasta and the wine."

"Oh."

"What a look you have in your eyes, baby."

"Comè?"

"Nothing. Skip it. Non importa."

"Quando tornerai a Roma?"

"Who, me?"

"Quando?"

"Who knows, baby. Who knows."

"Qualche giorno?"

"Yeah, qualche giorno. I'll be back. You wait for me, huh?"

"Comè?"

"Aspette. For me." Pointing out who.

"Si, si."

"No kidding now. I'll be back. They don't knock me off in none of their wars. You wait, huh?"

"Non capisco."

"I'll be back. Returno. Capish?"

"Oh."

"You aspette. Don't you go off with some American now. You wait, capish?"

"Si. Aspettero."

"What a look you have in your eyes, baby."

"Comè?"

"I said what a look you have in your eyes, baby."

She smiled as though she understood.

"What's my name?"

"Har-ree."

"Arrivederchi, Francesca."

"Arrivederchi, Har-ree."

A kiss and a flower and a good-bye.

The flower you wore in your helmet marching out of town.

And the look you remembered in her eyes.

"That's right," said the soldier in the Bar Americano. "That's a day I'll never forget."

It had brought him back to this city, and back to this bar. He could remember the bar quite well, despite the length of time, for he had come here for a drink after leaving her house, the bead curtain, the tiled floors, the caffe espresso urn, and he could remember, too, the carnival that had been near here, and he had found both of them again, the bar and the carnival. But not her. He had not found her yet.

"You have been making the war?" asked the proprietor. The memories of the day the city had been liberated had warmed him, and he was willing for a short time to discontinue his reading of the crimes in Il Tempo. After all, they had liked the Americans then.

"Yes. Futa Pass," the soldier said.

"How is it? Bad?" asked the proprietor. He had an idea war, for the Americans, was never really bad because they had so many tanks and so many planes, and he always thought of it as a campaign in which each American had his own individual tank to protect him. Thus, the Europeans were dug in desperately somewhere, very poor in weapons, and then up came the Americans, like cowboys in the films, each with his own private tank. There was no end to the tanks, in his mind, and no end to the planes.

"Bad enough," said the soldier.

"Well, now you are in Rome you can amuse yourself. There are many girls. Beautiful ones."

"I'm looking," said the soldier, "for a girl now."

"It's a bad hour," said the proprietor. He was pulling back a little. This one, he thought, was going to expect him to produce a girl out of the cash register. They were very crude about girls, the Americans. About cognac and girls, they were crazy, and it did not pay to get involved with one on either subject.

"No," said the soldier. "I don't mean it like that." He had asked before, in the street, when he had first found the carnival, and they had looked at him, not liking the question. But somebody had to know. She couldn't just disappear. It was important that he find her again, and he had been waiting a long time.

"Look," he said to the proprietor, trying to make him understand the importance of it. "I'm looking for a certain girl I met once. I only met her a couple of hours and then I had to go away. Her name is Francesca. You wouldn't happen to know a Francesca around here, would you?"

"Her family name?"

"That's it. I don't know it."

"There are at least ten thousand Francescas in Rome," the proprietor said.

"I know. But I think she lives somewhere around here, in this part of the city. I thought if I asked, somebody might know."

"Vincenzo," the proprietor said.

"Yes?"

"Do we know a ragazzina who is named Francesca?"

"Francesca what?"

"He doesn't know."

"Maybe the da Luca girl. Isn't she called Francesca? The father is an avvocato."

"What's she like?" the soldier said eagerly.

"A ragazzina. Of no particular beauty."

"Does she sing?" the soldier asked.

"Does the da Luca girl sing, Vincenzo?"

"Who knows? They all sing. It's a neighborhood full of singers and arguments."

"She's about this tall," the soldier said. "I can't remember exactly how she looked. But she's pretty. She's like, well, she's like Linda Darnell in the movies."

"Who?"

"Linda Darnell."

"Vincenzo, what does she look like? Do you remember?"

"Who?"

"The da Luca."

"How would I know? I look at their legs."

"He's a big help, that hero," the proprietor said.

The soldier looked out of the window of the bar into the bright square. The six-story tenements, with their big doors, in the sunlight, looked all alike. He could go from house to house, asking in his bad soldier's Italian, if a girl named Francesca, about so tall, and with a nice smile, lived there. He had been walking all morning on this side of the river looking for her street. There had been girls on bicycles and he had looked after them as they rode by. He had looked down from the embankment at the girls lying on the decks of the boathouses in their very short, haltered bathing suits, and though he thought some of the girls looked like her they had not been her. On the Lungotevere there had been a big crowd of people outside the courthouse and it was a trial of some kind, some fascist, but he had not stayed except to look among the people for her. If he found her, she would look as she had looked on the fifth of June, and she would say: " 'Allo, 'ar-ree." And he would say: don't go up, come down. Harry. And pronounce the h.

"I asked about her singing," the soldier said to the proprietor, "because she used to sing Stardust."

"What?"

"Stardust. Polvere di stelle. It's an American song. She used to sing it."

"Who sang it?"

"Francesca," he said. "The girl I'm looking for." He hummed Stardust. "This is how it goes," he said. The proprietor listened. "I don't know it in Italian, but this is the tune. She knew the words in Italian."

"She sang that canzone?"

"The day I went to her house. She sang it to me to show me she knew an American song."

"No," the proprietor said. "I just remembered. It's not the da Luca. Her name is Fernanda. Am I right, Vincenzo?"

"What?"

"The da Luca. Her name is Fernanda."

"How would I know?" the bartender said. "Fernanda, Francesca, they're all alike to me."

The Marchese

THE MARCHESE ALDO ALZANI, blond, indolent, now thirty-three, lately returned to the capital from a Swiss exile and in magnificent health despite his recent experiences, lay on the terrace contemplating the delightful possibilities of the death of his father-in-law.

The terrace was boxed with flowers.

Below, the white villa was surrounded by a small private park, and guarded from the intrusions of the street by a stone fence, and protected from the changing political furies by an iron gate.

The wall of the bedroom which faced the terrace was made entirely of glass.

But the bedroom itself was simple.

It possessed a fireplace, a thick-napped rust-colored rug, a low ivory dressing table with a round glittering mirror, and a low wide bed covered with a blue silk coverlet.

It was a lovely bedroom.

Too bad the Marchese Aldo Alzani, whose ancestral portraits were all of dead Florentine gentlemen of a very splendid masculinity, and whose wife, the tall Maria, had such tremendously long legs, did not patronize the room. It was almost exclusively the Marchesa's bedroom.

On certain afternoons, however, when Aldo felt, for diplomatic reasons, that he could not postpone or any longer avoid Maria's demands, he would reluctantly enter the bedroom with the wide blue silk bed, and allow the slatted shades to be drawn on the glass wall facing the terrace. But he hoped not this afternoon. He sighed. Perhaps he should have stayed in Switzerland. It had been very nice in Davos, now the tourist trade was dead: the snow, the mountains, the few stray Englishmen playing passionate tennis right through the war, and then the Greek refugee boy, Pepi. But the Swiss were so boring: those thicklegged women in the awful stockings and the horrible wholesomeness. The neat vegetable gardens, where even the cabbages had a Calvinist look, and the dull postcard scenery full of quaint sanatoriums; my God, it had been incredible.

In a little while the gong would ring, shaking the villa, and he would go in to lunch. Aldo grimaced. The general, his father-in-law, would be seated as usual at the head of the long table. He would have to dress, despite the heat. The general liked his family punctual and thoroughly dressed. It was hardly a lunch; it was a bivouac, a campaign.

Eight years, Aldo thought.

Good God, had he actually endured eight years of that impossible drum-major, eight years of Maria? He picked up the highball beside him, drank, and thought: well, it is about to end.

"Aldo!"

"Yes, my dear?"

"Are you coming?"

"In a moment."

It was about to end. The situation had changed, and there were opportunities now in the general political chaos that had not existed before. It was an attractive moment in history for a man with—

A man with what?

Oh, say a man with a foyer hung with splendid Florentine ancestors, who had married for money, and who had been compelled, too many times, to attend precise two o'clock lunches, and to climb, too many times, into a low wide blue silk bed.

For such a man.

"Aldo!"

"Yes, my dear."

"It's getting late. You won't have time to dress."

"In a moment, my dear."

Because definitely the situation had changed. The drum-major was worried, quite worried. He growled, he rang gongs, he wore his decorations, but he was worried. He thought they would not dare to touch him because of his reputation. Yes, the drum-major was worried. Maria was worried. They were all worried but Aldo. Aldo pretended to be worried. Yes, the opportunity existed; it required now merely a push, the slightest kind of a push, oh say a push with certain documents, documents written almost a year ago. It was really an opportunity; delightful, he had not thought politics could be so delightful.

He drank.

Perhaps it had been wiser to come back from Switzerland, after all. Despite Pepi, whom he missed. But then one could not have everything. The phone rang. Aldo stood up, rather quickly, and went into the library. He closed the door. Then he picked up the phone and said, "Pronto. Si. This is the Marchese Alzani." He realized, as the voice came to him over the wire, that he had been quite right to close the door, although Martelli was being gratifyingly cautious. It must be their training, Aldo thought. They all had had to speak for so many years guardedly over telephones. It was one of their political virtues. "Yes," he replied, when Martelli asked the question. "Tonight." It was all settled. Martelli's voice sounded very pleased. He had probably doubted the Marchese's sincerity. Aldo did not have much of a reputation of that kind. He hung up.

He went into the bedroom.

"Who was it, Aldo?" Maria asked.

She was sitting at the dressing table.

"No one," he said. "A friend of Elena's." Elena was the Marchesa's sister.

"Don't you think you should dress?"

"Yes, dear."

"Oh," Maria said. "I forgot. Guido Cespa will be here. I have invited him."

"Who?"

"Guido Cespa. But you must know him."

"The Cespa of Poveruomo?"

"Yes."

Of course he knew him. Everyone in Rome since the liberation knew who Cespa was. It was Cespa's ambition to have everyone in Italy know who he was.

Aldo said, "How would you know him?" It seemed to him now that the Marchesa was faintly excited. At least there was a flush in her dry skin.

"I met him at the Di Capitanis. He's extraordinary looking. Besides, I thought he might be able to help Papa."

"I detest people for lunch," Aldo said.

"But Guido has so much influence."

"Hardly with the Committee of Epuration, my dear," Aldo said. "He has influence but hardly with the Committee."

"But I thought—"

The gong rang. The house reverberated with the imperial summons. The general was at table and awaiting his staff.

Aldo winced. Yes, he thought, it would be a pleasure to have them shoot his father-in-law.

Guido Cespa looked like what an actor is supposed to look like. His hair was cut long, it was graying, his features were strong and dramatic, and his eyes almost black. He stood and bowed as Aldo and the Marchesa entered the dining room.

The general growled.

Aldo saw that today the general must be feeling particularly uncertain: he was wearing almost all his decorations, the African as well as the Albanian ones.

Aldo shook hands with Cespa.

"You were in exile during the occupation, signor?" Cespa asked.

"Oh, exile. Switzerland. Not exactly a difficult exile."

"Ah, Switzerland."

"I detest Switzerland."

"Aldo escaped through Milan," Maria said. "It was very dangerous."

"I am most brilliant, my dear, during danger," Aldo said.

"It is so difficult nowadays," Maria said. "Aldo was telling me that in Pisa only last week they shot Leonardo Valli. He was only an actor but they shot him. Didn't they, Aldo?"

"He wasn't a very good actor. "

"I remember Valli," Cespa said. "He was one of our great talents."

"I thought he was an abominable actor."

"But, darling," Maria said. "That was hardly a reason to shoot a man."

"Why not?"

"Do you think, Signor Cespa," Maria said, "they will take any action against Papa?"

The general growled.

"Italy is indebted to the general, Marchesa," Guido said diplomatically.

"But will they try to arrest him? There are so many rumors. There is so much uncertainty."

"They would require proof, madame. They can hardly arrest a man of the general's reputation simply because they wish to. They would have to prove any accusation they brought against him before the world."

"Would they, Papa? Is Signor Cespa right?"

The general peered out at him from under his heavy eyebrows.

"Scum," he growled. "Political scum."

"Yes," Aldo said, quite lightly, "undoubtedly they need proof."

"Tell me, Signor Cespa," Maria said. "Do you believe in politics?"

"Ah, yes, madame. Unfortunately. We are no longer religious; we are only political."

"Does Poveruomo believe in politics?" Poveruomo was the newspaper Cespa edited. Some said it was the most influential paper in the country. It had very impressive circulation figures.

"Poveruomo believes in Italy," Guido said. "What Italy believes in, Poveruomo believes in."

Maria looked bewildered; she was not sure she understood.

"Yes, of course," she said.

"And what does Italy believe?" Aldo asked lazily.

Guido smiled sadly. He communicated to the people in the dining room a sense of his own unhappiness over the state of contemporary belief.

"Ah, yes, believe," he said, as though he were subjecting the word to a closer scrutiny, taking apart the sad etymology and semantics of it. "What does Italy believe? It is so difficult, isn't it, signori, to have a belief these days? The simplest conviction must be bought with a gigantic spiritual effort. I said in my article this week, have you read it, madame? that a scream of grief goes up from our country."

He looked at his little audience.

"A scream, signori, of grief, of pain. I said we of Poveruomo must answer this scream of grief."

"How?" Also said.

"With a scream of joy, signor. Yes: with a scream of joy. And why? Why would I, alone, be able to answer this cry? Why are the politicos so incapable of answering it? Why are all the committees and ministries of the left incapable of answering it?" He swept them with the black eyes, the strong, dramatic face. "Because, signori, Poveruomo alone understands the true state of the Italian soul."

Guido's eyes shone, his head was slightly reared as though he looked out, not at these three people, but on a square flooded with humanity, and beyond the square all the sunlit plains and the shadowed mountains of the peninsula, as though he saw, now, the unhappy provinces, the little towns in which the fishermen and the contadini lounged with empty hands in the bombed piazzas, the industrial cities of the north with their ruined locomotive works and stricken auto plants, on all the anguish, debris, disease, and bewilderment of Italy, and this vision was in turn shared by an invisible throng who were beginning to know, and to speak, with hatred or with fanatic affection, the name of Guido Cespa.

Aldo, listening, was unpleasantly aware of the man now; Guido was demonstrative, impassioned and crude, and Aldo winced. He was always helpless when he encountered such a combination in a man. Would he have dared to speak of the "Italian soul"? He had scruples even against using the word "spirit": he would have said perhaps "the mind" of the Italian people. But Guido was unassailable; he said soul, and a soul promptly took on a rhetorical existence.

"Yes, signori," Cespa said, "with a shout of joy I, and Poveruomo, respond. We are being strangled by the politicalism of the professional and the parasite. Ah, signori, they send me letters. A thousand letters every day!" He swung to Maria. "What wounds, signora! What moral, spiritual, and economic wounds! I wish you could see them, Marchesa—feel them, tremble and weep as I sometimes do! The hopelessness, the despair, the longing for salvation! To this they have brought us with their politics!" He held Maria's eyes. He wished her to see those letters that came to his office.

"Yes," Maria said. The flush was even deeper in the dark skin of her cheeks. Aldo was amused; it had really been dull in Switzerland, he realized now; really, so dull.

"Believe me, signora," Guida said. "We are cursed with timidity in our modern emotions. Our ideal is to be civilized Eskimos. But to read these letters! To see the contributions they send . . . twenty, thirty lire . . . Ah, those lire, signora! Poor, battered, assaulted, out of who knows what dirty pockets, taken from such empty pocketbooks! There are histories in those lira, signora . . . tragic histories, the fate of Italy."

"Come viviamo adesso," Maria murmured.

"Yes, signora: how we live now," Cespa said, looking into her eyes with an answering sympathy.

At the head of the table, from the bottom of his military abyss, the general said: "And what do you intend doing, signor? Politically."

"I am not a politician, Excellency."

"Nonsense," the general said. "It all ends up political."

"But we are not a party. We are a voice."

"I know, I know. But what do you intend doing with the sounds you make?"

"The experience with fascism," Cespa said, carefully, "and one is compelled to add, the disenchantment with the experience of anti-fascism, has made the people suspicious of all parties, all organizations. We are tired of them, Excellency; tired of the professionals who run them for their own profit, tired of the tragedies of power and the comedies of factionalism. The Italian soul is an exhausted soul; a soul which has been seduced, betrayed, and kicked out into the streets to whore." He looked now down into his plate as though, among the little strawberries of his dessert, the answers lay to so many difficult problems facing an ambitious man. "What do the people want? How do they want to live?" Aldo awaited the revelation.

"They want to live in peace."

Explosively, as though he had dragged the depths of human behavior to come up with this idea.

"They want to live in peace!"

The general growled, and looked as though his pocket had been picked.

Aldo himself had a faint impulse to giggle. But Maria was impressed. The people wished to live in peace; it impressed itself upon her with great force.

The gravest problem," Guido said, "for the Italian is that of honesty: honesty in public life, honesty in private life, honesty in business. That, signori, is the purge Poveruomo wants. Life has become profoundly immoral. We must make it moral again. The politicos think only of the inflation of their memberships. We think of the salvation of the nation. We have defeated Fascism: but which fascism, signori? Only yesterday's. Today we have the fascism of the left."

He smiled at Maria.

"They have changed the organist in the chapel," he said, "but the music remains the same."

Good, Aldo thought; that was better. He was beginning to see that Guido might have an interesting future.

"Ah, signor Cespa should be premier," Maria said. "Don't you think so, Aldo? It would be so different."

"Premier, signora? You flatter me. I am a journalist."

"No. Premier. He would make a wonderful premier, wouldn't he, Aldo?"

"Practically anyone would."

"Aldo!"

"What would *you* do with Italy, signor?" said Cespa.

"Oh," Aldo said, "sell it to Switzerland. The Swiss are so rich. They have so much loose change and nothing to spend it on."

"He's impossible," Maria said. "I married a wit. Do you know, signor Cespa, in eight years I've never been able to have a serious conversation with him?"

"Except about money, my dear. About money I make it a point never to joke."

Lunch was over.

Guido bowed.

"Madame," and he took Maria's hand and kissed it. He bowed to Aldo, to the general. "It has been a very pleasant lunch. But you should not make me talk so much."

"Not at all," Aldo said. "My wife delights in political conversations."

"At least one learns something."

Maria accompanied Guido Cespa to the door. Aldo could hear her talking with much energy as they crossed the foyer in which hung the portraits of all the splendid Florentine gentlemen who once upon a time had exerted, so they imagined, so much influence upon history. They were still, however, very splendid in their long dark frames, but so curiously unreal, so much part of a world one doubted had ever really existed at all.

Alone now, the general puffed on his cigar, sunken into a deep chair.

"What do you think of him?" he growled.

Aldo shrugged. "He might do something. I imagine the man believes what he says. All of it is false, of course, but he believes it, and that gives it a kind of truth."

"Eh? Don't be so subtle. Do you mean he's a charlatan?"

"As you like."

"What he says about the country has truth in it. I feel it."

"Oh, the state of the Italian soul? Of course, Papa," Aldo said. "There is truth in it when you hear it."

The general glanced up suspiciously under his heavy eyebrows.

"You're as corrupt as the rest of them," he said.

The general puffed on the cigar.

"I wonder if the fellow could do something," he said. "It would have to be political. How else can anything be done?"

Aldo looked at him: the short, heavy, broad-shouldered figure in the deep chair, the heavy face, the whole detestable immovability and heaviness of the man.

When he entered the bedroom, Maria was undressing. He watched her. Once, without the Marchesa's knowledge, he was able to have two simultaneous affairs: one with a Jugoslavian boy who had robbed him, and one with a girl from the Trastavere who had infected him. He had managed to conceal, from the Marchesa, both the loss of his health and of his money. But he had not been able to conceal from her quite his sexual indifference to her long, rather flat and bony body.

He noted, too, now with some alarm, that she looked somewhat excited. The excitement was in her eyes, in the energy with which she spoke. Under his blond mustache Aldo grimaced faintly.

"Don't you think Guido is exciting?" Maria said. "I had such a feeling while he spoke."

"I feel nothing but my salivary juices when I eat, my dear."

"Sometimes you can be absolutely intolerable."

"But why should you complain? I am amusing, I am witty, I am intolerable. What more can a woman ask in a husband?"

"Affection."

"But, my dear, we didn't marry for affection, did we? Or was I swindled?"

She had pulled the blue silk coverlet from the bed. Now she sprawled upon the sheets, her face toward the window, her long back to him.

After a while she said: "Aldo."

He had hoped she would not weaken; but she was weakening.

"Yes, my dear."

"Do you think there will be trouble for Papa? Do you think they'll dare?"

"We live in difficult times, my dear. We live among firing squads and Guido Cespas."

"Guido says he will do what he can."

"Oh," Aldo said. "I am beginning to think signor Cespa understands more than the soul of Italy."

"What do you mean?"

"Nothing, my dear. I talk. You know your husband: he talks."

"Come to bed!" She turned on her back. She was furious. She hit the pillow with her fist. "Come to bed," she said, "and stop talking. Stop, stop, stop that eternal talking!"

He sighed. It was so out of schedule. It would be even more of a distinct pleasure when all this was settled, once and forever. When Martelli would settle all this.

He went slowly toward the detested bed.

Carla

WHEN THE WEATHER was hot Carla liked to lie on the floor.
It was cooler, and when the shutters were closed the room
grew quite dark, and then you lay on the floor and dreamed.

Oh, magnificent dreams.

You are a great concert pianist. You have beautiful
clothes. You are very much loved.

This is because you are not yet eighteen years old, and
were only a child when the war began, and the picture of
the young, rather handsome marine officer on the wall is a
picture of your father who is now a prisoner of the English
in Bombay. The letters from him come very infrequently,
and it is difficult to understand why, now the war is over,
and the Italian fleet no longer exists, the English do not
allow him to come home, although in his infrequent letters he writes he is not too badly treated. But then, nobody
understands the English. Mama, of course, is lonely, you
know how lonely she must be, and she has all sorts of ambitions for you, she would like it very much if you were to

say that you will consent to marry the professore, but then Mama is so bourgeois. They are all so bourgeois in this palazzetta in which you live, with the Virgin in the hallway, and the little red devotional light under her tilted byzantine face, they are all so dull, so gray these neighbors, while you, inside, burn with such a great light. You are very thin, underweight, you have enormous black eyes, the small chin is rounded and firm, your hair you know is very pretty, Grigorio has said it is very pretty hair, but he has said too you are like a boy, you have no hips, and inside there is this light, this love, this longing to experience everything and to know everything, to be a cloud, a woman of fire and passion perhaps like Claretta Petacci or Tosca, a person of consequence and beauty.

Grigorio, of course, understands you, he has sympathy for you. Sometimes you think he has more sympathy than love for you, and in a way it is strange that you should find a foreigner so simpatico, and that he, a soldier, should understand about this light inside.

Besides, it has been so funny, the relationship with Grigorio.

In a little while you will see him, and until then you lie on the floor, in this house you detest, because it is cooler, although Mama thinks it is simply another insanity of yours.

Do you remember how, when you first met him, sitting in the courtyard below, on the green bench, distributing the colored pieces of hard candy to the children, you said to him: "What is a boy of the cow?"

And how blank he looked. A boy of the cow?

Then you said: "There is the red man, isn't there, in your country and the boy of the cow?"

When he had turned all the phrases about in his head,

Then she had said, because she had wanted to ask him this for a long time, "Are you married in America, Grigorio?"

He hesitated, and then he laughed and said, "Do I look like a man who marries?"

"But you must have a fiancee?" she said. "A fidanzata, no?"

"Oh, a girl, yes. Everybody has a girl."

She thought Grigorio, therefore, was very experienced, and was merely advising her to marry the professore because he was kind. It was very difficult for her to explain that she thought kindness was not really one of the important emotions.

One afternoon she had opened the shutter to look out again at the eternal trees, the everlastingly circling swallows, the sameness of windows and partly visible bedrooms and rooftops which hemmed in her life and never changed. Grigorio came to stand beside her, and that afternoon Antonio was away looking for work, and Mama was in the kitchen.

"It is so hot," he said. "You are beginning to get sunburned." He touched the thin brown arm on the window ledge. "But you are so thin."

"I am always thin," she replied.

"Thin and melancholy. You are the most melancholy little girl I have ever met."

"Why do you say I am a little girl? I am not a child."

"No. You are an old woman. With gray hair and false teeth."

"I have a friend," Carla said. "A woman friend. She is beautiful and she is much older than I. She is twenty-six."

"Yes. That certainly makes her much older. Does she use a cane and do all her bones creak?"

"She is also a very intelligent woman," Carla said. "I go to see her often. She is intellectual."

"I am intellectual, too."

"No. I mean she is of the intelligentzia. We talk very often, she and I."

"Of what?"

"Of the world. And of men. She is very experienced. She has lived in Paris and Venice. She says there are only two pleasures in life possible for a woman: to have a great art or a great love."

"Which has she?"

Carla smiled. "She paints but she is not a great artist."

"Yes," Grigorio said. "That happens very often with intellectuals. Which will you have, cara: the great art or the great love?"

"Both," Carla said.

"It is very difficult."

"You think of me as a child."

"No, I don't. I don't, really," Grigorio said. "I think of you as—"

"As what?"

"As Carla. Watching the swallows over the roofs in a wonderful and beautiful city called Rome."

"But I am a woman," Carla said. "Even though you do not think of me as one."

"Eighteen isn't exactly a woman, dear."

He was astonished. It was so young, so thin, this child's body against his, so undernourished, perhaps not even too clean, the business with soap being what it was in the city now, the war and melancholy had done so much to these little bones and this flesh in his arms, and yet such a warmth, such an overwhelming avidity for life flowed out of her, and through him, that standing there by the open window he began to tremble. "Carla," he tried to say, "You mustn't—" but the girl only kissed him more fiercely, and then with one hand he groped the shutters of the window closed, kissing her and thinking my God, my God, where did this come from? and thinking, my God, what if her mother walks in? thinking, my God, Carla.

He sat in the chair, then, and she knelt at his feet, resting her head and the lovely brown hair tied with a red ribbon on his knee, kissing his hand. The girl at his feet, and the gesture, the simple, incredibly loving gesture moved him as he had never been moved by a girl in love before.

"Grigorio," she said.

"Yes, cara?"

"I want you to have a place where I can come. I want to live with you."

"But, Carla—"

"Do you think it is bad that I said it? I am not a child. You think of me as a child. But I have shown you I am not a child. I want you to have a place where I can come and I want you to make love to me."

"But if your mother should know."

"Mama? Mama wants me to go to the Conservatory. Then I will graduate and I will be a musician. What will I do when I am a musician? I will teach or I will try to find a job with an orchestra, like the professore. But in Italy what orchestras are there now? Even the music is dying. There are no new orchestras and there are too many musicians now. That is what Mama wants."

"Carissima," he said, stroking her hair.

"You will find a place, Grigorio? A place where I can come and you can make love to me?"

"Yes," he said.

The place he found was in a street of tenements between

the Tiber and Monte Mario, a street full of children and little wine shops and salsamenterias, and the signora of the house who rented him the room insisted only there must not be many women. It was all right if his fiancee came to see him but there must not be a variety of fiancees. She asked, too, if it were possible to buy from him some American coffee or sugar, and whether he had for her husband any wool socks or cotton underwear to sell, but Greg said no, he had neither sugar, coffee, socks nor underwear, that the wealth of the American soldier was much exaggerated, and to corrupt her a little gave her a dozen cigarettes. The room was small. There was a long narrow Egyptian runner on the wall over the bed. The room had one window which opened on a big courtyard in which every evening at twilight the women of the tenement beat their carpets vigorously, and on Sundays when the operas were played over the radio the courtyard was full of magnificent song with all the radios in the houses tuned simultaneously to the music as though there were one gigantic communal loudspeaker set up under the dark and glistening sky.

The Egyptian strip gave them trouble. It was a souvenir of a trip to the Nile the signora had made in her youth. The hawk-headed gods and the angular brocaded animals turned out to possess an extensive mythology of bedbugs. But Carla proved more than equal to the crisis. She had the signora in, showing her the sheets, and demanding: "Is this a room to rent a stranger? Signora, in my house it is at least always clean."

The signora was genuinely upset. Down came the trip to the Nile, like the last illusion of her own youth. Greg brought to the house a bottle of benzina. The benzina stunk up the room for a week but the bedbugs vanished. Then the sheets were white, the room was quiet, in the evenings the women beat their rugs, in the afternoons he made love to her.

This had all been almost two months ago.

When she left the house on this particular day, and came out into the three o'clock sunlight, it did not seem strange or unreasonable to her that she should be so elated over what had happened. It was not something to be depressed about, or to think of as unnatural. To be a great musician, to despise a monotonous life, to have a child, these were the important things. It was sad, of course, that there was so much suffering now, even in this beautiful city of hers, and that to the south and the north so many villages which once had been pretty seaside resorts or prosperous little farming communities, were now destroyed. Her country was sad now, she herself was sad, the sadness was part of her nature and part of the history of her country, but she thought of the sadness as a significant thing, as something with depth and meaning. It was so important to do two things: to fill up the silence of one's life with music, and to fill the solitude with love.

She hurried down the narrow paved path between the green trees, some still flowering, and looked merely a thin brown haired girl, with a red ribbon tied in her hair, very simply dressed, stockingless, wearing wooden wedgies, a little white collar at the throat, somewhat childish, not quite eighteen, but extremely happy, full of importance, a Romanina on her way to tell a foreign soldier in a rented room that for two months now there had been no sign, and how excited she was there was to be a baby, how happy she was about this, how tremendously significant this was from the point of view of both art and life.

Rome is a city of broad streets, and even her poorest quarters, once one leaves the center of the capital, have an airiness about them, and a look of cleanliness. The airiness and the cleanliness may conceal the usual nests of hunger and human ignorance, common to the international poor, but it was nevertheless pleasant to see the sun lying so flat and white on the faces of these buildings, and to feel the airiness and the cleanliness. Grigorio, the intellectual, had once explained to her that the difference between Rome and the great cities of his own country was that here one did not feel the weight of the stone upon the human personality, one did not feel overwhelmed by the physical might of the architecture itself. But then, Grigorio always insisted he was a bad salesman for the virtues of his own country.

In the vestibule the wife of the portiere greeted Carla. She sat there, at the foot of the stairway, in the hall in which there was an elevator, but an elevator which did not run, just as there were electric bulbs but no electricity, knitting. She said, "Buon giorno, signorina." Carla smiled. The wife of the portiere thought of Carla as the fiancee of the soldato Americano who lived with the Bologninis. She thought of her a little jealously because it was well known that the fiancees of the soldati Americani lived well, and drank real coffee, and went to the military cinemas free. Carla thought of her as the wife of the portiere who kept chickens and rabbits in the backyard, and was always there in the vestibule, knitting.

It was cool in the room. When they lay on the bed together she thought the time had come to tell him. A fly buzzed in a corner of the ceiling. The room was very quiet. "Feel me," she said. "Feel me here."

He looked at her, and then he felt the small flat stomach. "Cosi?" he said.

"Yes. Do I feel different?"

"Is it a game, Carlaccio?"

"No."

"You feel like a stomach feels. On hot days, cool. On cool days, hot. Is that the difference?"

"No."

"Va bene. Tell me the difference."

Greg lay very still as she told him, then he got off the bed and went to the small table where he took a cigarette from the pack and lit it. Then he came back with the cigarette but he did not lie down again on the bed with her. Instead he sat in the chair beside the bed and looked at her.

"You are sure of this?" he said. "This is certain?"

"Oh, yes," she said.

"It has happened that a girl thinks she is like that, and then it turns out to be nothing. A cold, or something. It happens."

"No," Carla said. "I am a woman and I would know."

"Carla," he said earnestly, "listen to me. You are the loveliest girl I ever knew. I feel about you different than I have ever felt about any girl."

"Why do you say that?" Carla said.

"I want you to know it."

"But I know it," she said. "You have very deep feelings about me. But it is not simpatia? It is not because I am poor and a little Italian girl and because of the war?"

"Carla," he said desperately, "senta. Listen to me this once. This is a difficult world, and you are young, you don't understand it."

"Why do you say that?" she said. "I understand the world is ugly and stupid and how people suffer in it. I am Italian, and I understand that. But I understand too what happiness is."

"What is happiness, cara?"

"It is not a political thing like my brother Antonio believes. And it is not to be devout and respectable like my mama thinks."

"What is it? Questa felicita?"

"When I play sometimes I know what it is. And it is to be in love."

"Cosi simplice!"

"Is it not simple?"

"Yes, when you speak it is simple."

"Then what is it I do not understand?"

"Senta, cara. You must not have the baby."

"But I want it. I want it very much."

"Senta. The having it is easy. But afterwards? There will be many people starving in Europe afterwards. The children will grow up with bad teeth and bad bones. It was so after the last war."

"But I want it," she said. "I want it."

"Carla, you make it so difficult. You know so little about me, cara."

"You think you are old and disillusioned," Carla said. "But inside it is not so. You think because you have read a great many books you are difficult to understand but you are very simple to understand. And you think I am simple but it is not so. I am the difficult one and you are the simple one. I think," she said judiciously, "that when you met me you were in love with someone but now you are not in love with her. Does it make you unhappy now that you love me a little and not her so much?"

Greg looked at her, a little incredulously.

"O Christ," he said.

"But you will love me more," Carla said, "later."

"But there may not be any later, cara. Don't you understand that? I may have to go away. In the army one never knows, perhaps tomorrow, perhaps in a month. And I may not come back to Rome. Then what will you do? You are still going to the Conservatory. How will it be to go to the Conservatory like that? Then your mama, and the professore, he wants to marry you. Can't you see, Carla, how impossible it is?"

"Is it because you are afraid you will be tied to me? That you will not be free any more?"

"Tell me what you think will happen."

"Oh," she said, "you will fall very much in love with me when you understand my real nature. It will take a little time. I think you have difficulty loving. Sei un uomo chiuso."

"A closed man," Greg said to himself.

"But when you see that I am not a child you will fall in love."

"Will I come back and marry you?"

"You do not have to if you do not wish to but I think it will be better."

"And afterwards?"

"When the war is over you will want to go back to America. To see your parents. I will go with you. I do not think I will like America. It will be very impressive, but I think after I have met your parents we will come back to Italy. It is much nicer to be in love in Italy than in America, I think."

"I can't take you with me to America."

"Because I am so shabby?"

"No. Not because you are shabby, carissima. But because there is someone in America."

"Oh. That girl."

"She is my wife."

The fly buzzed angrily on the ceiling. He did not come

to her on the bed. He sat there in the chair, looking at her.

"Senta," Greg said. "There must be doctors. I will ask or we will find one. You must understand, Carla. Do you understand?"

What was there to understand? The trees outside the window would always be the same green, the swallows would always circle, one eventually became eighteen.

"Senta, Carla," Greg said. "We will find a doctor. It has all been a mistake and I am to blame for everything. I was cowardly and I would not tell you before. I should never have kissed you. I should never have made love to you. I knew you were a child. Are you listening to me? I am to blame for everything. I thought it did not matter. I thought nothing would happen. It was because I liked you so much and I thought if I were careful and if I joked nothing serious would happen. I am stupid. I am a stupid American like all Americans. We will find a doctor. There must be such doctors in Rome. They are in all the cities. It is not a terrible operation. It is very simple. Are you listening, Carla? Then we must not make love any more. It is because I was stupid and thought nothing would happen. Do you understand what I am saying, Carla?"

Only that the solitude would not be filled with love.

Pollard

CAPTAIN JOHN POLLARD had been, before he was attached
to the Rome command, and fixed behind an imposing desk
in the big public headquarters building which fronted on
the Piazza Venezia, a lieutenant in North Africa. He had
been blown up in North Africa after Kasserine Pass, and
among the experiences Pollard liked to tell the girl he
thought he was in love with, an American girl named Antoinette, and which Antoinette liked to hear, was the one
about the time the shell went *whoom whoom* just as he
had his head out of a foxhole and something slapped him
and it was a hand but there was no arm to the hand.

Pollard often had bad dreams because of North Africa,
and Antoinette had been awakened more than once, in
that luxurious "bed of matrimony" with which the apartment they had rented in the Piazza Mazzini was furnished,
by Pollard's hands clutched in her hair, and Pollard shouting. Those were the cliff dreams. In those dreams Antoinette was always falling off a cliff, and he, Pollard, was
always rescuing her, holding her away from the obscure
abyss over which she dangled by her long black hair.

Now Pollard sat behind the imposing desk in his office,

the first imposing desk he had ever sat behind and the first office, and read the sheet of paper in his hand again. The heavily built man standing so rigidly at attention on the rug in front of his desk must have been at least fifty years old. His hair was gray and grizzled, but this morning he had combed it with great care, and he wore a cheap striped shirt under his countryman's jacket. On his feet were a pair of thick army boots. The boots were evidently a gift, to judge from the letter.

The letter said briefly that this man, Sebastiano Forcella, had rendered valuable services to one Lieutenant Fred Maud when the lieutenant had been forced down behind the German lines during a flight in the vicinity of Aquila which was some forty kilometers to the northwest. Sebastiano Forcella had hidden the lieutenant from the Germans on his own farm at the risk of his life. Sebastiano Forcella was a friend of the allies, a democrat, and any services shown to Sebastiano Forcella would be greatly appreciated by Lieutenant Maud, and the letter was signed Fred Maud, first lieutenant, army air forces, with a flourish.

"Ask him," Captain Pollard said to his office interpreter, "what he wants."

The interpreter asked. Sebastiano Forcella, standing as rigidly at attention as he had done when he was in the army, explained.

"Work, signor capitano. He says the Germans later destroyed his farm and took away his two cows. He has come to Rome for work."

"Well, there isn't very much for him," Pollard said. "Ask him what he can do."

The interpreter asked. Sebastiano Forcella, with the dignity of a former military man in the presence of his superior officer, replied.

"He says he has come to work for the Alleati, signor capitano. He says he does not wish a reward for the aviator but merely to work and to support his family."

"Yes," Pollard said. "Ask him if he was a soldier. He's giving me the jumps standing there like that."

"In '14 he says, signor capitano. He says with the famous Bersaglieri Seventh he was a machine gunner."

"Well," Pollard said. "All right. Put him to work. I wish those air force boys quit writing testimonials, though. Do we have anything for him?"

"A cleaner, signor capitano."

"Yes," Pollard said. "Well, explain it to him. Tell him to report tomorrow."

The interpreter then explained to Sebastiano Forcella that commencing tomorrow he was to be employed by the Alleati here in their headquarters and that as a reward for the services he had rendered to the unfortunate lieutenant who had fallen near Aquila it would be his duty to see that the marble steps of the staircase were thoroughly washed, twice a day, and that the lavatories were kept scrupulously clean, and that each day, in the morning and in the afternoon, he was to empty the waste basket of the signor capitano in this office.

Sebastiano Forcella, rescued despite the loss of his two cows, clicked the stout heels of his army boots together, and executed a magnificent salute.

It was how they had done it, probably, in the famous Bersaglieri Seventh.

"Yes, all right," Captain Pollard said, and a trifle selfconsciously returned the salute.

Sebastiano wheeled and marched from the office. Tomorrow commenced the new life.

Pollard left the office, too. Downstairs, in the entryway,

the British sentries stomped and slapped their rifles as Pollard saluted. There was a great deal of saluting, going and coming, in this building. A motorcycle dispatch rider, dusty and goggled, chugged into the entryway as Pollard left. Outside, in the Piazza Venezia, his jeep was waiting.

"The Excelsior," Pollard said to his driver, "and slow."

The military car took Pollard down the Corso Umberto, turned up the Via del Tritone, went around the statue of the drinking Triton in the Piazza Barberini, moved up the Via Veneto and then parked outside the Hotel Excelsior. Pollard did not know why he never walked, it was such a short trip.

Outside the Excelsior, the MP's saluted and Pollard saluted. In June there had been British sentries at the Excelsior, too, but they had moved to the Ambasciatori: the saluting at the Excelsior was now less spectacular.

In the dining room, very white, very high-ceilinged, he saw Antoinette at a table, and she waved, and then he saw there was a Chinaman at the table with her.

"Darling," Antoinette said, "I'm starved. You know Dr. Wu, don't you?"

He didn't, but he could see that with Antoinette he most certainly would; just as he knew, because of her, a collection of war correspondents, a surrealist artist, a gentleman named Perrone he was convinced was a pimp, and the names of all sorts of chambermaids and waiters. It was an advantage she had of being a rare commodity at a particular moment in history, an American girl in an occupied city during a war.

"Hello," Pollard said.

"Oh, yes, this is the Captain," Dr. Wu said. Dr. Wu did not hiss. Dr. Wu was dressed in a cutaway, and a wing collar. Antoinette was still collecting, Pollard thought.

Pollard thought that he was in love with Antoinette and he thought that Antoinette was in love with him. But it was complicated. Pollard was just twenty-six, and he had been in the army four years, a lot of years to be in any army, and among the things he said the army had done to him was to ruin his career, although he had had really very little of a career to be ruined. He had been graduated from a small and not too well known college in upstate New York. After college he had come down to New York to be successful, leaving behind him a mother who was very fond of him and who thought, when he had become an officer in the army, that he was being successful. In New York he had lived for a time in a rooming house on West Seventy-ninth Street and he had worked for a small advertising firm on Madison Avenue and he had been earning forty dollars a week. This is what he meant when he said the army had ruined his career.

Antoinette, too, thought that she was in love with Pollard. She was quite certain that it was all finished with her husband, who was stationed in England with the Air Transport Command, and when she came to Rome to work for the Embassy she found her natural capacity for love very much enlarged. She loved the old churches and she loved living at the Albergo Olympia in the center of town and she rather loved the idea of being a rare commodity at a particular moment in history. She had done St. Paul's and had seen Keats' grave and had gone to Sunday mass at Santa Maria Maggiore and a Swiss Guard who worked on his off days as an official guide had taken her through the Vatican galleries. She had loved the Sistine murals but she had grown very tired in the galleries.

The bad dreams Pollard still had because of having been blown up in Africa somehow gave depth to the evenings

Antoinette spent in the apartment in the Piazza Mazzini in that "bed of matrimony," an Italian description of a large double bed which she found terribly funny.

In addition to the apartment in the Piazza Mazzini in which they made love, and Antoinette's place at the Albergo Olympia, Pollard had a large comfortable room, with an adjoining bath, here at the Excelsior on the Via Veneto, a hotel of magnificent proportions which had been a famous tourist hotel, then a German headquarters, and was now requisitioned by the Americans. So that, although it was difficult for an Italian coming down from a bombed city in the north, Genoa or Bologna or Milan, to find a residence in liberated Rome, and the popular comedies were full of hilarious situations in which people lived behind screens set up in a sala di pranza, Pollard and Antoinette were really very well housed. In a way, of course, the multiplicity of apartments was understandable. Pollard could hardly afford to come down to breakfast at the Excelsior with Antoinette on his arm. It would have been perfectly all right with an Italian girl, one of the nicely dressed amateurs with the hungry look in her eyes promenading on the Via Veneto in front of the hotel waiting for an invitation from the Americani to dine inside where there was much food. She would eventually wake up in some bed upstairs and if she had been particularly pleasant, she might get breakfast out of it, too. Everybody understood that, and the Excelsior, being American, had a more generous, as well as a more lurid reputation than the Ambasciatori, the English officers' hotel where there was an exaggerated tendency toward saluting. But with Antoinette, since she was an American girl, and working for the Embassy, and since, moreover, she had a husband stationed in England with the Air Transport Command, it was a

little out of the question. So they had to have the Piazza
Mazzini. Then, of course, there was the hot water at the
Excelsior. Antoinette would have felt positively filthy if
she hadn't been able to bathe at least three times a week
in Pollard's room at the Excelsior. The Olympia was very
nice and homey, but it was one of the smaller hotels, and
suffered the general afflictions of the city, one of which,
because of the lack of coal, was a plumbing system with
exclusively cold water. It worked out, then, that the Olympia was a nice place to hang one's things, and the Excelsior
was so accommodating for a good hot soaking bath, and
the Piazza Mazzini was lovely for the nights one wanted
to make love.

"Ah," Pollard heard Dr. Wu say. The doctor had something to do with the Vatican, Pollard gathered, the Chinese
legation there or something. "You have a very amusing
young lady, Captain."

"Who's a young lady?" Antoinette said. "Darling, the
man just called me a young lady."

"He's flattering you," Pollard said.

"Certainly," said Dr. Wu. "So young, so energetic, so
unintimidated."

"I'm no young lady," Antoinette said. "When you say
young lady to me, smile."

Dr. Wu smiled, literally.

"Shall I show him my scars, dear?"

Dr. Wu giggled. Evidently in China nobody laughed
outright.

"Look at the man," Antoinette said, "leering. My scars
aren't what you think, you Asiatic lecher. He is an old
Asiatic lecher, isn't he, darling?"

"Are you, Doctor?"

"Oh, yes."

"Young lady, he says. Come on, you Asiatic lecher, let's dance."

The band had begun to play a rumba. The little Chinaman was delighted with Antoinette. What a relief the Americans were from all those stuffy British. "With pleasure, my dear," he said, and followed the tall dark girl out to the dance floor.

Pollard watched them.

The Chinaman, university degrees and all, came up to about Antoinette's collar-bone. He was wearing a cutaway, morning pants, a wing collar, and his head was bald, glistening, and faintly yellow. The gown Antoinette was wearing was cut just about six inches below the level of the Chinaman's eyes. He was having quite a time, the Chinaman, out on that floor.

Pollard smoked.

Antoinette was looking down at the Chinaman, and smiling slightly, as she danced, a wickedly amused look in her eye. The floor was crowded with officers, all of them excellently tailored, all of them, as Pollard was, men behind broad flat desks in military offices in requisitioned buildings. They were the real governors of this city, these brushed and trimly turned out soldiers, and it was difficult to tell, looking at them, in whose interests they were here, the city's or their own. The little Chinaman, delighted with the rumba, which he danced perfectly, had begun crowding Antoinette a bit. He was crowding her, and giggling. Outside on the Via Veneto the city's morals were not at all what the Pope wanted them to be, and the city's politics not at all what the Italians wanted them to be, but here, in this dining room, under these lights, with these potted palms, and among these clean white tables, Pollard sat, smoking a cigarette, watching a tall dark American girl with whom he slept and with whom, he thought, he was very much in love, dancing with a Chinaman who had degrees from American and British universities, and who was giggling now as he slyly poked that little broad flat nose of his down the bodice of the black afternoon gown this tall girl wore. Then, as Pollard watched, he saw Antoinette, suddenly, with that little wicked smile, reach up and rap the good doctor three times, quite loudly, on the bald and naked top of his faintly yellow skull.

Pollard laughed.

After lunch, and the departure of Dr. Wu, Pollard thought it would be nice if they went for a walk. They could come back to the hotel later and Antoinette could have her bath. They went out of the Excelsior, Pollard saluting, and Antoinette, very gay and enthusiastic, on his arm. In the Via Liguria she admired a brooch in a shop window, something in dull gold. "Isn't it lovely? I love old things like that."

"I'll buy it for you as a wedding present."

"Are we going to be married, darling?"

"My mother says I ought to get married."

"It would be nice, married to you," she said, squeezing his arm.

On the Via Sestina there was a tea room, which she thought cute, and they must have tea there some day. A fur shop still displayed, mysteriously, some very expensive furs, and she admired the furs. There there was a wine shop, which looked so typical, bead curtains, flies and slab tables, that Pollard promised yes, he would take her in there for wine sometime. But the Pincio, at the church of the Trinity of the Mount, at the head of the great stairs which go down into the Piazza di Spagna, was loveliest of all. There was really a magnificent view of the city from here: the roofs, the gardens, domes, spires, palaces with old battlements, the column of the Madonna; Rome was quite a city from the Trinita dei Monte, particularly when one had eaten well, danced, and there was a hot bath waiting, and even love.

"Look, darling," Antoinette said. "Aren't those tomato vines growing on that roof?"

"I guess so," Pollard said.

"Isn't it wonderful, growing tomato vines on a roof? I love Rome."

"Well, it's clean," Pollard said.

"Oh, darling, don't be so American."

She sat on the stone wall which ran along the Pincio down to the Piazza del Popolo, looking at the wonderful view of the city. She really did like it. She liked the oldness of the churches, although at home she never went into one, and the idea of a city that had palaces, although if she had lived in one she would have rented the little studio on the top floor, and she liked the nineteenth century wideness of the boulevards and the seventeenth century narrowness of the alleys. She liked being so far away from the awfulness of New York, and the awfulness of her own life, and it was nice to be in a country which was not connected with one's own unhappiness. It was not exactly nice to think so, but the coming of the war had been very lucky for her. It had solved many problems. She looked at Pollard now, leaning on the wall, his clipped hair, youngish face, the very straight shoulders. Sitting at a desk in the Piazza Venezia had not yet taken the Fort Benning erectness out of them. "My God," she said, "I've been in love with you a long time. Two months."

"Bad?"

"Awful. Do you realize, darling, that in the two months

I know you I haven't broken a plate on you yet or run screaming through the corridors?"

"With or without clothes?"

"Oh, I'm respectable even when I'm having hysterics."

Pollard lighted her cigarette. "Don't burn your eyelashes again."

"I do burn myself, don't I?"

She had nice legs, a long throat, and being dark, people sometimes thought Antoinette was Italian, and then Pollard liked saying, "Hell, no. She's a white woman." The Romans, walking on the Pincio, or bicycling, looked at her sitting on the wall, the men at her long stockingless legs, the girls at her clothes and at her hair.

"You should let me take care of you," Pollard said.

"Would you, darling? I've never been taken care of. Would you bring me breakfast in bed? And paint my toenails? And crush an aspirin when I was having hysterics?"

"Uh-huh."

"Oh, darling, you're so dependable."

"That's me," Pollard said. "Joe dependable."

"You do love me, don't you, darling?"

"You're a nice girl," Pollard said, "that's why I love you."

"I'm not. Really, darling, I'm not."

"Sure you are," Pollard said. "I know a nice girl when I see one."

It had been a long time since anybody had thought she was a nice girl. Charles hadn't. But then, Charles was always much too busy thinking how nice, and how unlucky, he was. It was over now, the thing with Charles. It had been in the process of being over for years and then the war came along and settled it.

"I wonder what he's doing," she said, looking down at her cigarette, and her long bare legs.

"Who?"

"My husband."

"He's probably lonely."

"Charles? Lonely? If I know Charles he isn't being lonely. Not in England or any place else."

"I don't get it," Pollard said. "How did you go on living with the guy if you weren't in love? If the war hadn't come along you'd probably still be living together."

"Thank God for the war."

"If I were a girl, I couldn't see myself going to bed every night with a guy I didn't love."

"Couldn't you, darling?"

"No."

"You've got such a nice young face," Antoinette said.

"Thanks. I've had it twenty-six years."

"Oh, dear. Twenty-six years."

"All right, grandma," Pollard said. "But I still don't see it."

"It's complicated, sweet. I'm a complicated girl."

Pollard didn't know whether he should be jealous or not. He felt jealous but then, she was sleeping with him now, and not her husband, and it didn't stack up right for him to be jealous. "What's he look like, your Charles?" he said.

"Oh, a very pleasant looking louse," Antoinette said. But he had probably changed. She could remember how handsome she had thought he was when she was nineteen. That too, his being good looking, had stopped counting. He was good looking to so many other girls. "Everybody loved Charles," she said. "Only my husband rather liked to make sure I saw him being loved."

"What?"

"I was such an appreciative audience." It sounded sordid: but then, her whole life sounded sordid, when she thought of it. She made a determined effort not to think of it. She looked down at her hands, the nails painted, and the legs tanned from the Sundays at the Lido, thinking, well, she'd changed too in these two years. One thing Europe and the war had done, it had changed her; or so she thought.

"Do you know what that son of a bitch husband of mine once did to me?" She blew the cigarette smoke out carefully: it was funny being in Rome, during a war, telling it. She had thought she would never tell it. "He was having one of his big affairs then, with an actress. Oh, not much of an actress. Charles never got the big ones or the successful ones in anything. This was just one of the ambitious ones. Rather pretty, too, and blonde. It was a big affair. I mean big to distinguish it from the little ones, the one-night stands. I heard all about it. Trust Charles to tell me the glowing history, detail by detail, from barroom to bed." She looked at Pollard, smiling brightly. "You see, darling, I was supposed to share his triumph."

"Now, look, baby . . ." Pollard said.

"Sure I was. He brought the scalps home. Blonde scalps, redheads. I think the blondes were the most frequent. That was so I could appreciate just how charming a husband I had. Oh, I don't know—maybe he just had to tell me about them." She kicked her heels against the stone wall.

"What happened?" Pollard said. "I mean with the actress."

"He brought her home one night to dinner."

"And?"

"Oh, I was so elegant, so civilized, I could vomit I was so civilized. Do you know," she said, "I think Charles wanted me to admire his taste. Well, I admired it right through the cocktail and the entree. We used to eat on a bridge table in the living room, and she was so friendly, the little bitch, and Charles was being so pleased with it all it damn near made me scream. He was so surprised and so disappointed when I smashed the salad plate and began to cry."

"Lovely," Pollard said.

"I should have broken it on his head," Antoinette said. "But I was such a civilized girl!"

"What did he do?"

"Oh, he was outraged by his wife's behavior. He took his blonde home, in a taxi. I sat at the bridge table, bawling. Darling, I had a lovely marriage."

Pollard said, "You had a beaut. But why didn't you just pack up and go?"

"Oh," Antoinette said brightly, "didn't I tell you? I thought he was justified."

"You're insane."

"I thought that was love. Men were like that. I don't know, biology or something, I thought. He wanted beautiful girls and there I was, my nose too long and my hair too dark, not really what he wanted. The hours I put in looking at my crooked face in the bathroom mirror."

"It's not a crooked face," Pollard said.

"By the time Charles got through with me I thought it belonged on a freak."

"The guy didn't love you," Pollard said. "That's all. He just didn't love you."

"Oh, love. I got so I used to think love was what happened Sunday morning. He used to come into the bedroom sometimes Sunday morning and sort of roll me over. But quick."

"Baby," Pollard said, "I won't ever roll you over quick Sunday morning."

"I'm good now, darling, aren't I?"

"Good?"

"Sunday mornings and during the week."

Pollard was embarrassed. "Sure," he said. "I'll recommend you."

"Don't be so squeamish about it. Say it. God knows it took me long enough to think I wasn't a cripple."

"You're all right," Pollard said. "As a matter of fact, I think you're wonderful."

Maybe it was because it was during a war, and having a place like the Piazza Mazzini, but he thought she was. Looking at her, he thought, and got a little excited thinking about it, how long her body was, the long back and the long legs, and because of the time she spent at the Lido on the beach which had been cleared of mines, how brown it was. "Darling," he heard Antoinette say, "wouldn't it be nice if we went to the apartment now? I'll call Lois. I'll say I don't feel well. The Embassy'll survive."

"In the middle of the afternoon?"

"But it's wonderful in the middle of the afternoon. The Romans do it then. It's so nice when you feel relaxed and sleepy in the middle of the day."

"I just ate," Pollard said.

"Oh, God, men and their stomachs," Antoinette said.

"Okay," Pollard said. "Let's."

They began to walk back to the Excelsior: Antoinette would call from the hotel. The sun was hot in the sky, and on the newsstands the papers carried the headlines of the big trial in the Palace of Justice. Turning off the Via Sestina, Antoinette said, "I wrote Charles."

"Wrote him what?"

"That I was in love with somebody."

"When did you write?"

"A few weeks ago."

Pollard stopped. "What did he answer?" he said.

"I haven't heard. Oh, it won't mean a damn thing to him. He'll be glad to get rid of me."

"That's what you think."

"That's what I know, darling. He'll console himself. He's probably consoling himself right now."

"Okay," Pollard said.

"Now don't you get moral, dear. You haven't anything to complain about, you know."

"Haven't I?"

"After all," she said, "you do have me. Right in the middle of a war. It's sort of comfortable, isn't it, darling, having me right in the middle of a war?"

The lobby of the Excelsior was crowded. Field officers were checking in and departing, the bellhops carrying their heavy dusty green val-packs. The orchestra was playing after dinner music, and there was the kind of activity in the lobby a bus station might have. In July it had been a little scandalous: there was the legend of the officer, checking in, who opened his room door and there was a girl in the room, and the officer checking out said, "I don't know her name. She goes with the room." The officer checking in never did find out her name either, but she was still there when he checked out. Antoinette laughed at the stories, and was curious about the girls, and was surprised so many of them were really pretty. The hotel manager, thin, in a hard starched collar, called to Pollard as they entered the lobby. "Captain Pollard. There is a telephone please." Pollard went to the desk phone, and somebody said, "Hello. John?"

"Yes. Who is it?"

"Lois. Is Antoinette there?"

"Yes. Hold on. For you, baby," he said to Antoinette.

She went to the phone, and later Pollard remembered the whole thing as sort of incredible, her standing in the lobby at the desk phone and the officers checking in and departing, talking to Lois at the Embassy, and then Lois switching the call over, and Antoinette letting out the damnedest shriek he ever heard right in the lobby.

"Charles!" she was saying into the phone. "Charles—my God, where are you?" At the airport, that was where he was, Charles. He wasn't in England at all. It was that letter and he wasn't in England at all, he was here, in Rome, at the airport, on leave, twenty minutes from the city.

PART TWO

The Prosecution

SIGNORI:

Where the road forks, on the Street of the Seven
Churches, near the catacomb of the chapel of St. Cecilia,
there is an indescribable odor in the country air. The
campagna is green there on the Street of the Seven
Churches; the eucalyptus dark and tall; and although the
fruit trees are each beginning to bear their own fruit, and
the gardens behind the trattorias are very bright with the
enormous roses grown by their gardeners, nevertheless one
cannot escape first noticing and then being profoundly dis-
turbed by the odor. Since the twenty-sixth of June those
who have gone up the white and badly paved road that
leads from St. Paul's to the catacomb of the chapel of St.
Cecilia have smelled suddenly this taint, this infection.
The contadini in the carts under their striped umbrellas,
the pilgrims in black, the brothers of the holy order of Don
Bosco at their prayers or the brown Dominicans in their
sandals, the police at the traffic control point, all breathe
this odor and all know what its source is.

And we, too, signori, know what has corrupted the natural odors of the fruit and the roses, the fresh winds of the campagna.

And he, too, the accused, knows.

If one follows the right hand fork of the road for a distance, one comes, as I have come, to a high wooden fence, and a door in this fence. The fence surrounds what was once a sandpit but what is no longer a sandpit. And if one enters, as I have entered, through the door in the fence, there is an open space in which certain disused machines lie rusting, and then, some thirty paces from the door, the mouth of a cave. A cave which interconnects in a series of caves and galleries but which is actually one cave. Here the odor becomes overwhelmingly strong. There may have been, as we came up the Street of the Seven Churches, many unimportant thoughts in our minds: we were uncomfortable because of the heat, the morning has been a failure and the evening promises to be dull. But the cave will change you: I tell you it changes all who enter it. No one can follow that odor to its source and not be changed.

It is first the darkness, the odor and then the darkness. The earth is damp, mottled, the roof scooped out and hollow, and here it seems as though everything gives off that sickening taint: rock, sand, clay, and dirt, so that one's whole world becomes foul, the infection personal, the decay intimate. Then one begins to see in the darkness the shapes of the earth and of coffins. There are many coffins. They are simple coffins lined neatly against the rough walls and the lids are covered with flowers. There are photographs, too, standing in small frames on the lids of the coffins among the flowers or pinned to the wall of the cave. They are photographs, if one examines them, of many different kinds of men, and of some who were not yet men, some who were boys of thirteen and fourteen, and who are all now dead. The photographs do not any longer resemble what is in the coffins, although at one time what is in the coffins and has been recovered from the earth looked like these photographs. It was, signori, difficult to identify what was recovered from the earth. For one must remember: there was first the machine gunning, then the hand grenades were thrown into the cave to complete the work of the machine guns, and then, later, there were the great rats. I have seen what is in those coffins; I have lifted the lids.

I did not weep, for somehow one does not weep.

I turned, after the coffins had been opened for me and I saw what was in them, and I went out into the sunlight because the odor was unendurable; and when I was out in the sunlight, on the white road, I looked across the fields and beyond the walls of the old villas, and there in the valley I could see our magnificent city.

But there was that taint on the air. Even in the sunlight, even looking down into the valley. And I thought: how long will it be, O my country, before we cleanse our skies of this odor?

Signori:

Today we are here to do part of this cleansing.

There sits the accused, and being citizens who understand the quality of justice, I am profoundly convinced that in this case, as in all cases, you will judge him as you would yourselves wish to be judged. I propose therefore, when I speak, to speak objectively, yes, even to restrain myself from the pity or the indignation which one might so easily feel at the thought of the tears and the spilling of so much blood which this man has caused. I think of myself as a just man, although perhaps I, too, in circumstances beyond my control would be compelled into injustice; and yet I will restrain myself. Yes, in spite of all the tears and all the blood, I will restrain myself, because in a time when justice is in disrepute and truth hardly believed in, I find myself oddly believing in justice and in truth. Our understandings have been crippled by twenty years of tyranny and six years of war, our sympathies debased, the natural instincts of the heart distorted. And he who would today put together his broken world must mend more than his house and repair more than his garden.

The defense has conjured up for you the life of the accused: "the life of a mediocrity" in the attorney's words. How, forty-five years ago, he was born in a small city of the South; the father, a professor in an intermediary school; the mother, religious, but of small culture—and the family itself, a history compounded of poverty and misfortune; a brother confined to an institution for the paralytic; an embittered sister; an elder son dead in the war. At the age of sixty-five the implacable father dies (you know the towns of the South, those solemn processionals of the dead, the black plumed horses, the hearse gilded at the corners, the swinging censers) and the son, the youngest, is left fatherless, a schoolboy of doubtful abilities, morose (so many of these childhoods, signori, are full of this commonplace strangeness) learning in the sunlit, quiet classroom what must have already appeared to him superfluous and burdensome: the gestures for a lyric of Alfieri's, the tenses of a Latin verb.

A small village, an obscure beginning, a struggling family—with such fragments of a sociology we start. What the boy thought (sitting sleepily in the sunlight watching his mother pound the tomato paste, lying awake in the winter cold hearing his brother's snore and the indistinct voices out of his sister's dreams) we can only guess: the figure emerges more clearly only in his late adolescence as the sky of 1914 darkens to war. In June, 1917, we know he volunteers for the Bersaglieri, puts on his country's uniform (and is thereby no longer the provincial or the indifferent scholar of Latin verbs) and disappears, transformed, into the trenches, eventually to suffer a minor wound in the left temple.

When he reappears again (you will note how our narrative flickers like a primitive film) he is changed and older. War has pushed him into an awkward military maturity. The past, father, mother, native village, has begun to subside, and now the future takes a more violent hold upon him. He is being shaped (by what, signori? fate, history, the disbelieved in devil?) for his own destiny; he is being secretly prepared for some as yet invisible denouement. Demobilized, Naples claims him, postwar, turbulent Naples of the cafes, the tourists, and the robbed strangers picked up in the back alleys. He is ambitious (a common vice) confused (a commoner one) and anxious to be rich, admired, known, obeyed (the most common of all). Here we know a little and can reconstruct more: how, for example, he is fascinated for a time by a scheme which involves the invention of a perpetual motion machine, and how his soldier's pay is invested with two gentlemen who are the authors of this scientific marvel—a pseudo-engineer and a lawyer of a most doubtful legal background. He, of course, loses his money; the fantasy of a quick fortune collapses; other schemes (an automobile engine which runs without a carburetor) bordering on the illegal, dreamed up by unscrupulous men, all eventually come to nothing. In addition, he suffers at this time a curious malady: his eyelashes, his eyebrows, his hair (so tightly crisp, so black and curled) begin to fall out, and he endures six months of dermatological agony; but finally this, too, passes, he is cured and he recovers. He is poor; he is discouraged; he is bitter; he sleeps badly. He is ripe for politics.

How he drifts from perpetual motion and carburetorless automobiles into politics, at what climactic moment the decision is made, what crystallization of his ambitions takes place on what street corner or at what public meeting or under what circumstances, and how he confronts at last the shaping course of his own destiny—again we do not know. It is possible that even he himself no longer remembers, for so much of what we do and have done in our lives remains obscure and hidden, the motive lost, the intensities forgotten, and we are left in a continually liquid present we cannot truly explain, recalling a continually receding past we no longer understand.

So once more he comes into our vision, changed, wearing the latest of social disguises, not now the soldier or the get-rich-quick speculator in the shadier bourses, but a figure of more menacing potentialities: the squadristo, the fledgling blackshirt, illuminated by the flames shooting out of a burning union hall. We see him everywhere now, multiplied; in the square where the socialist mechanic is dragged and compelled to kiss a dishonored flag; at night on the lonely country road where the peasant returning from a meeting is ambushed; in the raided apartment of the editor of the liberal weekly when the expensive vases are smashed, the music albums stepped on, the paintings ripped. He sings now with a violent choir: *O youth, youth, springtime of beauty!* Is photographed, smiling, with his favorite blackjack. Feels his stale provincial blood race at such heady events. Is known and greeted in the notorious cafes. Acquires the vocabulary of a bloodthirsty idealism. And life now seems to him full, signori: ah, how full violence makes life seem!

So the fatal career is begun. He discards forever the backward boy in the sunbaked village. He moves upward and onward, from squadristo to police official, the violence is translated to new levels, the years go by, the years of our national agony, and Naples knows him, Livorno, Verona, he marries, fathers children, becomes respectable. His deeds lose their accidental character, and become for him the very maxims of law and order, and he achieves a certain reputation among the people for implacability: implacability, that trait which is crossbred from moroseness and ambition. His very defects as a human being contribute to his success as a fascist. And all these years, signori, he is being prepared, he is moving obscurely toward his minor calvary, and it comes, finally, on the night of the twenty-third of March.

You all know how on that night, after the incident of the bomb, he was, having been sent to pacify our rebellious city, called to the office of Colonel K., and how furious the colonel was that evening. You know too of the reprisals which were planned: for every dead man in that patrol ten hostages were to be executed; and the list of these hostages was to be drawn up by the accused. You have heard how on that evening Colonel K. declared to the accused: I am depending upon you. And, assuredly, he was one such men could depend on. And later that evening, the Minister of the Interior declared: What can I do? It is necessary. Yes, yes, give them the list! Whereupon the accused states that having thus received his authorization from both his masters all guilt was lifted from his spirit.

A list, signori: names, one writes a list of names copied from the dossiers. Names of not too important an identity.

One has one's job, and besides, one has the authorization —the wonderful absolution of authorization! And twenty years have been spent preparing for precisely this moment, twenty years are culminating in this final task, this last of all one's orders. The village, the war, the perpetual motion machine, the burning union hall, the ambushed peasant, the raided apartment, Verona and Livorno, have gone into the making of this moment. It has all been for this; it has led, by intricate paths, to this; to this night where under the desk-lamp he sits painfully copying from the dossiers a list of those about-to-die. They will be taken without warning from the dark cells of the Regina Coeli. They will be driven through the pale streets of the sleeping city to the fork in the road on the Street of the Seven Churches. Men see them: a butcher's truck loaded with soldiers and prisoners. Who are they? No one asks. There are so many trucks driven through the city now, loaded with so many prisoners.

And he? He returns late to his hotel. Crawls into the matrimonial bed. Prepares for sleep. It is rumored he was troubled that night. By what, signori? He had the authorization. If he had the authorization, why should he be troubled? What more can a man ask than the authorization? But the rumor says he was troubled. A flicker of something undefined. But not very distinguishable from mild indigestion or an unpleasantness because of the late hour. He is troubled, and troubled he crawls into bed, and sleeps, by his wife's comfortable side, while in the cold dawn the butcher trucks move toward the fork in the road near the catacomb of the chapel of St. Cecilia.

And while he dreams, the machine guns begin. . . .

And when he turns over on his side, in the wide bed, the grenades are thrown. . . .

And then eventually they are all asleep, equally, and in the cave the last shower of earth falls. . . .

Ah, signori! they tell you that in his cell now he reads the Bible. Most devoutly. That he thinks much of his dear wife and of his loved children. And that he begs often for the holy intercession of the very Mother of God. But it is tardy, signori: is it not a trifle tardy, this remorse? This late conscience dashing up like a man about to miss his train? Surely, the authorization should have been enough. And I confess these sketches of his humble spirit leave me singularly unmoved. Still, still, on the warm wind, where the road forks on the Street of the Seven Churches, I smell that terrible odor, and still I see, among those pitiful flowers, the photographs in their small frames.

Twenty years, signori: twenty years we have endured these careers. Twenty years we have bled from such authorizations. *O youth, youth,* they sang, *springtime of beauty!* But this is the harvest of their age; from Istria to the Gulf our country lies irreparably ruined. And who knows what terrible surgery may be needed before we are healed? Who knows what medicine, bitterer than the illness, may be necessary before we are well again?

And now I have finished: you have been patient, and my speech has been long.

For him: I ask what justice herself in her own cold voice would ask: death, and in this manner: to be shot in the back.

The Liberated City: II

EVERY EVENING at five o'clock the American army in Rome stood retreat. Retreat was a beautiful ceremony. The band played and the color guard stood at attention beside the flagpoles under the French tricolor, the Union Jack, and Old Glory. Old Glory was in the center. The MP's went out on the bridge and stopped all the bridge traffic when the band played retreat. The drivers in the sixbys got down from their cabs and stood at attention. The boys who were going to town in the town army bus got out of the bus and stood at attention. The Italians were not compelled to stand at attention or to salute, but in June and July when the city was freshly liberated some of them stood at attention and saluted the French tricolor, the Union Jack and Old Glory. By September none of the Italians were saluting. The traffic stopped and the soldiers stood at attention and the band marched across the yard and the color guard waited for the band to halt in front of the flagpoles. As the band halted in front of the flagpoles, Warrant Officer Seligson executed a sharp flank and marched to the head of the band. The sun glinted on his horn-rimmed glasses. He raised his pencil or a stick because he was always losing his baton and then the band played the anthems. They played the French anthem first and the color guard hauled down the tricolor. Then they played God Save the King and they hauled down the Union Jack. Then they played O Say Can You See and they hauled down Old Glory. The soldiers saluted all three anthems and retreat was very beautiful. Then Warrant Officer Seligson executed another sharp flank and the band marched away and the bridge traffic moved and everybody piled back into the army town bus and the bus went to town. There were too many allies with too many anthems, everybody thought.

Giorgio

COLD, SWEATY, Giorgio opened his eyes in the disordered bed, and saw that during his sleep Maddalena had undressed him. She herself lay sleeping heavily beside him. His armpits, and the inside of his thighs, were damp, and under his head the pillow was damp, as though in his sleep he had cried into it. He lay there, exhausted, for these days sleep did not refresh him.

His world reassembled itself: a clock, the papered walls, light from the slats of the shutters.

From the street the sound of motors and of people.

If it were only possible to lose one's identity, to awaken with another face, in another country. But he was Giorgio: he awoke, and he was still Giorgio, the owner of this face, the victim of these headaches, the possessor of such a life.

Sleep was, at best, the briefest of kidnappings.

Beside him, Maddalena breathed heavily. She wore a pink nightgown and in her sleep it had crawled up about her hips. Her face was slack and she had even less beauty in sleep. Her breath came and went between the dry pale lips. The lungs worked to keep the tired flesh alive between her lying down and her waking up. Her skin was full of imperfections and there was a slight down on her upper lip.

But she was warm and he crept close to her warmth.

It was as though despair made love to inertia. He put his hand on her thigh as he would if he were about to coax an old and much-used machine into life. He did not so much caress as begin her, and when at last she stirred, turning toward him, it was as though an engine made these little moans, and shuddered in these quick spasms.

She did not open her eyes. It was all done in darkness. Perhaps it seemed to her only another sort of dream.

"Mi prende, mi prende," she moaned.

The clock audibly ticked on the dresser. He lay by her inert body as though he had been wounded in this encounter. Inside him, where he had hoped love might slacken the tensions, there was no relief. Then he saw that she had already fallen asleep again.

He got up quickly and went into the bathroom.

The man in the mirror was the partner of his soul. He looked at him and said: What have they done to you? Why are they punishing you?

The man in the mirror did not know either.

When he was dressed, he closed the door quietly not to awaken her, and then almost ran down the stairs into the street. From the street he would escape into the house, and then he would escape from the house to the street.

On one of the sidestreets off the Piazza Fiume he went into a trattoria. It was a family eating place of the neighborhood. It was called La Bocca. The tables were wooden and wine came from two wooden spigots in a barrel near the wall. A spiral of flypaper hung from the string on the electric light. The tables were covered with the sort of paper that is used to wrap bread in a bakery. Enrico's married daughter, whose husband had been killed in the explosion of a ship at Bari in the south, was suckling a child. She was still a young woman and the breast she gave the child was white, smooth and veined.

She nodded to Giorgio, and called: "Papa!" and then Enrico came out from the rear of the trattoria where the kitchen was. Enrico was an old friend, though Giorgio had not seen him in some time, mainly because he had wished to hide himself from all the people he knew. Now Enrico, clapping him on the shoulder, made him sit at one of the wooden tables, and filled a fiasco with white wine. It was almost like the old days though Enrico looked older and thinner.

"So," Enrico said. "How do things go?"

"Bad. And you?"

"We live," Enrico said, and looked at his daughter suckling her child. "How is Maddalena?"

"I left her where she belongs: in bed."

"Eh, but they don't stay there."

"Mine would live there if I let her."

"Taste the wine," Enrico said. "I had a barrel brought down from the Castelli."

Giorgio tasted the wine.

"And the guide business?" Enrico said. "I heard you had become an authority on the ruins."

"Eh, it's all soldati," Giorgio said. He brooded into the tumbler Enrico had given him. "When you tell them the price they complain. But it isn't the ruins they want to investigate. It's the women."

"Soldati and signorini," Enrico said.

"Even the boys on the streets are pimps."

"I know, I know," Enrico said. "Povera Roma. What has happened to our city."

"Senta, Enrico," Giorgio said. "I have something I want to talk about. Tell me: do you think I should go back to the Tivoli to work?"

"Hmm," Enrico said, glancing into Giorgio's face. "Have you spoken to Mario yet?"

"Not yet."

"I hear the Tivoli is making a fortune these days."

"But, listen," Giorgio said. "You know how I left. I insulted him. I threw my apron in his face."

"Well, it was in anger."

"But you know Mario La Pina. You know what he would do to his own mother if it was a question of money. You know what a fascist he is."

"Drink up your wine, Giorgio."

"Tell me, Enrico: you know what sort of man I am. I always wore the best, I was a spender. I never went down on my knees to anybody."

"A man does what he has to do, my dear friend," Enrico said.

Giorgio looked across the trattoria at the daughter suckling her child. There was happiness: possibly the only innocent state we knew, when what one needed was given in the mouth and one's only world was the loving nipple.

"Why should I lie to you?" Giorgio said, looking at the daughter. "Listen, Enrico. Last week suddenly in the Piazza San Silvestro when I was on my way home I found myself crying. Crying, for no reason. I stood there, full of shame and helpless. I couldn't even go from one side of the street to the other. I stood there, yes, like a child, and I cried."

Enrico looked at his friend with concern.

"You should go to a doctor," he said.

"Then all day," Giorgio said, staring but not seeing the daughter, seeing only himself, "I want to sleep. But at night

I lie in bed and I can't sleep. I'm afraid to go to sleep. Listen, Enrico: do you know how I feel? I feel as though something terrible is waiting to happen to me. As though there were a shadow over me. Do you know what I want to say?"

"Yes," Enrico said. In a way, he knew. These were not so uncommon sensations now.

"So today I made up my mind," Giorgio said. "No matter what it cost me I will go and ask Mario La Pina for the job again. If I could work again at the Tivoli!"

"Well then go, fool," Enrico said. "Of course go. Why did you delay so long? Here, first finish the wine."

The daughter smiled sympathetically at him as he left the trattoria, and Enrico watching him go thought to himself: Eh, poveraccio. How changed he is. How we are all changed. Che brutta vita.

The daughter said, "Giorgio looks so bad, Papa."

"He's a sick man, "Enrico said, touching the soft cheeks of the child. "But who isn't?" The child seized his long forefinger. "Except you," Enrico said to the child. "Except fat you."

Giorgio hurried through the twilight: what would he say to Mario La Pina? Ah, Padrone. Come va? With a smile, as though things were as they had always been. Who still comes of the old crowd? He searches, guarda! Isn't that a familiar face? But of course: Bertoli, the avvocato. He smiles and he is recognized in return.

Senta una cosa, Mario: remember how I used to demonstrate to the customers how one peels an orange? Ecco: thus, with the knife. Thus, with the fork. You see? It is not necessary at all to touch the orange, madame. So: he cuts swiftly and expertly around and around, the peel unwinding in a brilliant coil. Afterwards it is possible to take the coil, close it and fill it wth a raspberry ice.

Besides, he is the author of the Giorgio, the best cocktail in town. The faces may change, times may change, but the Giorgio does not change. And it was he who introduced it. At this bar.

If the gentleman would care to, he, Giorgio, would prepare one now. He goes behind the bar; he wears the white jacket, the black tie. He shakes the silver shaker. It is a magnificent moment, a triumph, the reestablishment of the king on his throne. How could Mario La Pina deny him this?

Yes: one must recognize that certain compromises are necessary. Events do not turn out as one supposes they will. There are unforeseen difficulties, unsuspected obstacles, life is not simple, justice is not always served. Deep inside him, however, despite the shifts to which necessity forced him, he would continue to despise these people. He would keep his political integrity, he would be still a true son of the people. But what was one to do? So many things crushed even the most determined to the wall. Each, finally, must look out for himself. They all did, the Bonomis too, the Nettis, the Togliatis, all looked out to see that their pockets were lined and there was meat on the table and a cigarette in the pack. Who was he? An ant rushing furiously from anthill to anthill: how could they demand from him what they themselves were not capable of?

As one entered the Tivoli one came first to the cash register, and then across from the cash register there was the bar. Then two steps led down into a circular room in which there was much glass. There had always been a great deal of glass in the Tivoli but as Giorgio entered the cafe he saw that Mario La Pina had since changed the scheme of decoration. The colors had been changed and there was much more glass than there had ever been. The ceiling had been painted an ivory tone, and the chairs and tables carried out the motif of ivory. The lighting was now concealed in long glowing tubes and was blue-white. But it was the quantity of glass which impressed Giorgio. For now the three walls of the cafe were lined solidly with continuous mirrors. And in these mirrors everything in the Cafe Tivoli was duplicated and infinitely extended.

Giorgio stood uncertainly in this luxurious and changed Tivoli, looking down into the circular room and the inexhaustible mirrors. The Tivoli was more crowded and noisier than it had ever been.

The daughter-in-law of La Pina was still, however, behind the cash register. When Giorgio entered she gave him a quick suspicious glance. But he had come to let bygones be bygones, and he nodded to her, and said: "Buona sera, signora."

There was also a new man behind the bar.

He examined the new barman critically.

He did not know him, and if he did not know him he was not a good barman. Giorgio knew all the good ones. He could tell this was the kind of a barman who would put too much sugar into a cocktail and who would squeeze the lemon peel.

Giovanni came up the two steps from the room below and saw Giorgio standing there.

"Eh!" Giovanni said. "Look who's here."

He was no longer a busboy. He was a waiter now.

But he did not shake hands.

"Come va?" Giorgio said.

"Bene, bene. And you?"

"I live. Is Mario around?"

"In the kitchen."

"So, I see the boss has promoted you."

"Magari," Giovanni said. "Some promotion. It's not the old Tivoli any more. It's an asylum from five to eight."

"Yes," Giorgio said. "I hear Mario is making a fortune these days."

"Scusi, Giorgio . . . I have an order."

He ran off.

Well, what had he said to Giovanni? Italy should not get into the war. That was the cause of the quarrel with La Pina. But it was yesterday's story. Now, Giovanni was a waiter, and he was ready to forgive, he was ready to put the white jacket on again and go behind the bar.

Cigarette smoke, the sound of glasses, the sound of laughter and talk, the waiters hurrying, the orders given and the orders taken, this was his world, this was life.

The mirrors fascinated him. It was as though each of the customers at the ivory tables was duplicated and duplicated in a silver space. There was not one gentleman leaning forward across the table, balancing between his thumb and his forefinger the long cigarette holder, and offering to obtain a permit from a colonel of the Alleati he personally was well acquainted with, a permit that would allow a vehicle to travel from Rome to Florence where one could buy wholesale gloves or jewelry to dispose of retail in inflated Rome—there were a dozen of them, equally groomed, equally thin-lipped, with just such a cigarette holder, extending into space, all personally acquainted with a colonel of the Alleati.

There was not one British major describing to an attentive table how he had acquired an electric refrigerator for the villa which he had requisitioned on the outskirts of the city, and how in addition he had secured a military generator to supply both the villa and the refrigerator with power—there was a column of British majors, with as sandy a mustache, and with just such a complexion, all being at the identical moment the proud confiscators of refrigerators and generators.

There was not one blonde, in her middle thirties, with her arms clacking because of the heavy silver bracelets, talking to both the Italian dottore and the American captain, and playfully slapping the captain as he touched her thigh under the table and saying: No, no. La porta è chiusa, nor one captain saying: I'll open the door, honey—there were a multitude of blondes in their middle thirties saying: No, no. La porta è chiusa, and a multitude of captains saying: I'll open the door, honey.

And a multitude of Italian dottores to laugh at just such a joke.

But Giorgio, too, was duplicated. On each side of him stood other Giorgios, their collars frayed and their shoes in such bad condition, waiting painfully for some Mario La Pina. They too went on indefinitely into space. The sound of laughter, the smoke of cigarettes, the noise of a hostile festivity rose all about them.

Mario La Pina came up from the circle of glass and tables. He was short, broad, bald, with a hooked nose and a black mustache, dark skinned, and looked in his tight suit like a prosperous Turk. Giorgio smiled, and in the mirror his duplicates wore as unhappy and as forced a smile.

"Ah," Mario said. "The agitator."

"Hello, padrone," Giorgio said.

La Pina examined him. "You look—well, the king wouldn't pick you for his bodyguard."

It was a joke. But one must perforce endure the jokes.

"Business is good, eh, padrone?" Giorgio said.

Mario turned, short and broad and dark, to look down at his good business. "The conquistadori: guarda." He turned back. "So, agitator—whom do you insult now?"

"I?"

"I thought by now you would at least be Togliati's secretary."

Another joke. Except Mario did not smile. He did not smile and he did not look at you when he spoke. He talked to you but he watched his daughter-in-law at the cash register, his waiters, his glowing blue-white lights.

"No," Giorgio said. "I've reformed."

"Eh, you?"

"Senta, padrone," Giorgio said. "I've come—"

A waiter interrupted.

"Padrone—"

"Yes?"

There was trouble with a check. It was a lieutenant. He insisted he had given the waiter a thousand lire. The waiter insisted it was five hundred. Mario knew the truth depended on how drunk the lieutenant was. If he was very drunk it was probably a thousand. The waiter would have tried it if the lieutenant was drunk enough.

"Is he drunk?"

"Of course."

"An American?"

"A South Africano."

"All right. Give him the change for a thousand. If he comes in again tell him there's no table."

The waiter went away.

"Padrone—" Giorgio said.

"Yes?"

"I want to go back to work."

"Work?"

"I want to come back to the Tivoli. I want to go behind the bar again."

It had been said, finally. The whole right side of his head ached. There was a pain as though he had not slept or had read too many hours under a bad light.

"And aprons?" Mario said. "You don't throw aprons in the boss's face any more?"

"No."

"And speeches? No more speeches?"

"No."

"The fire cools off, eh?" Mario said. "We're not such big heroes as we think."

"Listen, padrone—" Giorgio said.

"Eh, what do you want?"

It was Giovanni. There was a complaint about the fruit. A worm had been found in an apple.

"So? Bring her grapes."

"Va bene."

"Who was it?"

"The darkhaired one down there."

Mario looked. It was nobody of any importance. A woman some officer had probably brought in off the street.

"Bring her grapes. She'll have enough worms of her own soon."

Giovanni went away.

"Padrone," Giorgio said. "What do you say?"

"No," La Pina said.

"But, padrone—"

"No. Not even as a dishwasher," La Pina said. "I make it a rule never to hire a man again once I've fired him."

"But, padrone—"

"Listen, Giorgio: don't beg me. I don't like to be begged."

"I was a good barman, wasn't I?" Giorgio said. "In the old days I made money for you."

"The old days are dead."

"Mario, listen—"

"Look, Giorgio," Mario said. He turned at last to face him. The big dark face was squeezed out of the starched collar. "Nobody throws an apron in my face twice. Once—but not twice. Not to Mario La Pina."

"Padrone, listen," Giorgio said. "It was a mistake. You know me. I do things. Ten minutes later I'm sorry. You know me, I lose my head."

"Don't ask me to find it for you."

"Listen, Mario. I'm sick. I have terrible headaches. Half the time I think I'm going crazy."

"No."

"Let me show you," Giorgio said. "Let me go behind the bar. I'll show you I have forgotten nothing. I'm still Giorgio."

He went behind the bar, and all the Giorgios in the glass followed him.

"Excuse me," he said to the barman.

He took the shaker out of the barman's astonished hands. The barman looked at Mario La Pina.

"Giorgio," Mario said. "Get out of there."

But Giorgio was looking at the row of bottles. One began with Napoleon cognac, a jigger, carefully measured . . .

But there was no Napoleon. There were many brands but not the old ones, not the ones from before the war.

"Padrone," Giorgio said. "Where is the Napoleon? I need first the Napoleon—"

La Pina came behind the bar. He took Giorgio's arm, furiously.

"Get out of there," La Pina said. "I knew I would have trouble when I saw you. Get out."

"But, padrone . . . there's no Napoleon."

"The devil take you and the Napoleon," Mario said. "Get out!" He pulled. "I knew it," Mario said. "I knew it. You're crazy. Go away. When you came in the door I knew there was going to be trouble."

Giorgio felt himself being pulled from behind the bar. His right eyeball hurt as painfully as if he had fallen on it. Looking up he could see in the mirror all the Giorgios being dragged from behind the bar. The liquor was false and bad, the Napoleon was gone, there was only glass and blue-white lights in the Tivoli now. It was all cheating, it was all being done for the money.

"Take your hand off me, fascist," Giorgio said.

"What?"

"Fascist!" Giorgio said, loudly.

He pushed La Pina away.

Below, in the circular room, there was quiet. They turned at the tables to look up at Giorgio standing between the cash register and the bar. The major asked what the bloody row was now? There was always a bloody row with these excitable johns. All the blondes in the mirrors glanced up, a vague apprehension in their blue eyes. Dio, what was it now?

It was Giorgio.

Behind her cash register, the daughter-in-law wavered between a scream and a quick effort to call the carabinieri. Giovanni, seeing and knowing Giorgio, debated whether he should interfere. Even for La Pina he was not going to get himself punched by a crazy Giorgio.

Giorgio went down the two steps into the circular room.

"Do you know whose liquor you are drinking?" Giorgio said. "Do you know whom you are making rich?"

It was not important now which one in this room he addressed. They were all equally guilty, they were all equally involved in his shame. The colonel, the major, the blonde, Giovanni, the man with the cigarette holder. He addressed them all.

"I was once barman here. Senta: what right has the man to refuse me my job? Believe me: he's a fascist! I know him —the whole family! An exploiter, a fascist. Ask him what he did in forty. Ask him how much money he is giving to the Party now. Ask him how many behinds he has kissed!"

"Giovanni!" La Pina shouted. "Stop him."

"They should call the carabinieri," the blonde said to the captain.

"Ask him what he did for his country!" Giorgio said. "Ask him what sacrifices he has made!"

"Mario," the American captain said. "What's the matter? What's he blowing his top for?"

"The man's crazy," Mario said.

"Si, si! I'm crazy!" Giorgio said. "But who's made me crazy? Who?"

"Need any help?" said the American captain.

"If you please," Mario said. "I've had trouble with him before."

"All right, pal," the American captain said. "Let's go. You're just disturbing the party."

"Giovanni," Mario said, "help him."

Now that there was an American officer holding Giorgio by the arm, Giovanni was inspired. The Americans were the source of justice.

The American captain was strong, amused and invincible. He propelled Giorgio up the two steps, firmly convinced that what he was doing was for everybody's mutual good. There was a good deal of clucking as Giorgio disgraced everybody in the Tivoli by his behavior. But it was part of the disorderliness of the entire capital now. The blonde said as much, and the dottore agreed with her.

In the street, La Pina said, "Now go, please. Before I call the carabinieri."

"Fascist!" Giorgio said.

"All right, fascist," La Pina said. "I spit on your politics." He turned to the captain. "Thank you, sir."

"That's all right, Mario."

"Come," Mario said. "Have a drink with me, Captain."

They went back into the cafe.

Giorgio ran. Suddenly, he could not endure the streets, the sky, the people. Fragments of the twilight spun past him. He would go some night and set fire to the cafe. He would break every window in the place. He would kill Mario La Pina. He was cold, he trembled. Mama, mama mia, he whimpered to himself. Terrible abysses of shame and humiliation opened in him. He must go somewhere, he must hide in some hole. But where? Where could he possibly hide? To be dead. Ah, how they would weep on his tombstone in the cemetery of San Lorenzo.

He ran, knowing how the street stared. It did not matter. At the Piazza del Popolo he turned toward the river. The cobbled streets were patched with little wineshops and groceries. He ran down the Via delle Penne, across the Walk of the Ripetta, across the Lungotevere, and climbed down the bank of the Tiber.

Why hadn't he said all the truth?

One day, gentlemen! Ah, one day, all the accounts would be settled.

We live in darkness. We whimper: we have exhausting dreams :we assault the inert bodies of our wives.

But one day, gentlemen!

Yellow, narrow, deep, the river listened.

We will come out of this darkness. I, too, Giorgio. Holding our sick hearts. Full of gall and bitterness and shame.

Without pity.

For who has pitied us?

He snarled down into the yellow water. But he did not really believe what he said to the swirling river.

The truth withered up in him, the anger turned to tears.

He began to shake.

The sweat turned cold.

He was more wretched than ever.

Harry

HARRY STOPPED many times on the street. Sometimes it was a store that sold watches. He thought he would buy one of these big calendar dago timepieces. Sometimes it was a store that sold pigskin ladies' handbags. He thought he would send home to his sister one of those elegant bags with the shoulder strap. Sometimes it was a store that sold jewelry and he thought of buying another silver ring like the one with the mounted lion's head. Once an MP in a doorway said, "Put the lid on, soldier," and he put his sweaty cap back on his head. The movies were Italian, and in one theater they were playing Il Capitano Blood. There was no place to go; it was twilight; it did not look as though he would ever find Francesca. Then coming into the square he saw Schulte. He hadn't seen Schulte for God knew how long.

"Harry!" Schulte said.

"Why you old son of a bitch," Harry said.

They were glad to see each other.

There was a newsstand on the corner, and in the center of the piazza there was an old powerful Triton drinking waterlessly in the dry water fountain. There was a cafe triangling the corner, and there were small tables outside the cafe, and under the chestnut trees. There were girls of all possible professions walking from the piazza up the street under the chestnut trees. Some of the girls smiled when the soldiers whistled and some of the girls walked on indignantly. But you could not tell in advance which girls would smile and which girls would walk on.

"Christ almighty," Harry said to Schulte, "I haven't seen you, man, since when? The depot, ain't it?"

"That's right. The depot."

"Wasn't that depot a crock of something?" Harry said. "What happened to you after the depot?"

"I went up with an engineer outfit. Then I got transferred after the Liri Valley."

"Transferred? You get hit?"

"No, I didn't get hit. The medicos found I got water on the knee."

"How do you like that."

"And you?"

"The 85th."

"Rough, huh?"

"Man, rough."

They sat at one of the green tables on the sidewalk and Schulte ordered cherry brandy and the shoeshine kids bothered them about their boots. An old man with a violin came out of the cafe. Harry looked out into the center of the piazza at the stone Triton bent backwards to drink from a sea horn. Sometimes as a girl came down the street under the chestnut streets he would hope it might be Francesca but as she came nearer it would be just a girl. The hair would be a little like hers or the shape of the face but that was all.

"Listen," Harry said. "What became of Beeker?"

"Beeker?"

"You remember."

It wasn't even a year ago they had shipped from Hampton Roads. Harry could remember calling off the names of the ads on the walls of the warehouses as the train moved through the back streets of Norfolk. Good-bye, Armour's ham. Good-bye, Aunt Jemima. Good-bye, Zonite. Good-bye, Lipton's New Tomato Vegetable Soup. Even the looey up front in charge of the car had grinned.

Good-bye, Hotel Baltimore. Good-bye, Armstrong's Linoleum Floors.

"Beeker," Schulte said, "got half his ass blown off at the Garigliano, I heard."

"Half?"

"You know Beeker: he'd get half."

"Man, his old lady'll blow her cork. Remember how she used to send the cookie boxes in the states? What'd they have, a one arm lunch joint in Philly, wasn't it?"

"That joker used to eat the cookies after lights out. He had the bunk next to mine. I used to think the joint had mice."

"It had mice."

"Well, he'll nibble cookies on half a butt from now on."

They drank the cherry brandy. The twilight imperceptibly deepened.

"What about Minelli?"

"Little Red?"

"Yeah. The iceman. He was always telling Driscoll the hell with the hikes he wasn't going to kill krauts with hikes. He was going to kill them with a gat."

"Driscoll used to say it ain't a gat. It's a rifle."

"Red used to say to me all guns is gats."

"Remember Driscoll came in tight one morning after a shackup. He threw Red and the goddam bunk together half across the barracks."

"What became of Red?"

"The bastard got in pigeons."

"Pigeons?"

"He's flying pigeons with some pigeon outfit up near Montecatini."

"What the hell's he know about flying pigeons?"

"Ask me. Used to breed them for pigeon soup in Sheepshead Bay."

"Ain't that a crock of something. Pigeons."

"Well that's how they fall."

"They should ask me to fly eagles. I saw an eagle once. What about Cunnerdy? Fat Cunnerdy. You remember: with the wife. How we never could figure a broad goodlooking like her marrying a fat slob like him."

"Ack-ack I heard. Down around Bari."

"Ack-ack? For Christ sakes. Cunnerdy? But he got basic in heavy weapons."

"His brother was in ack-ack."

"Ain't that the mother lovin' army for you. Fat Cunnerdy gets out of the infantry, I don't. Who else?"

"Remember D'Agostino?"

"Tony? The hot shot from Syracuse?"

"I saw him in Naples."

"He all right?"

"They don't kill Tony. He says so himself. He says they are saving him to run the dice tables back in Syracuse."

Then Schulte said: "Remember Melofsky?"

"Hymie?"

"Yeah, Hymie Melofsky."

"Sure I remember Hymie. What's he in?"

"He ain't in nothing."

"What do you mean he ain't in nothing?"

"He ain't in nothing."

"Oh," Harry said. Then: "Where did it happen?"

"Near Piemonte."

"That poor bastard," Harry said.

"Well, that's how they fall."

"That poor bastard," Harry said. "Of all the guys."

"Well," Schulte said, "that's a mother lovin' war for you. Let's see if we can get the ginzo with the violin to fiddle something from the hit parade of 1912. Hey, Jack: veni qua."

The old man with the violin touched the edge of his hat and smiled. He was an old man who played this cafe at the same hour every evening. The violin was wrapped in newspaper in the violin case in which he also carried usually a piece of bread.

"Si, signor," the old man said to Schulte.

"Listen," Schulte said, "do you know an American canzoni, Pop?"

"Si, si," said the old man, tucking his fiddle under his chin. "I play Oi Marie."

"O Jesus no," Schulte said. "In every mother lovin' joint you go they play Oi Marie. Or Pistol Packing Mama. Play another canzoni, Pop. Cinquanta lire you play."

"Is nice Oi Marie," the old man said, timidly.

"Pop," Schulte said, "I heard Oi Marie. I heard it in Naples, I heard it in Capua, I heard it in Venefro. Do you know Paper Doll? Do you know Down in the Red River Valley?"

"Oi Marie," the old man said, scratching on his fiddle.

"He knows Oi Marie," Harry said.

"O Jesus," Schulte said. "All right, Pop: send me with Oi Marie."

The old man began to play Oi Marie in the soft twilight while the Triton bent backwards for the water that did not flow and the blue fumes climbed out of the exhaust pipes of the traffic in the piazza. The leaves on the chestnut trees stirred with a little papery sound.

Harry thought: she could come down the street now. It was possible. He was so damn lonesome. Everything looked different and felt different. Now when a girl smiled she was hustling. Nobody shouted viva. Nobody threw roses. Nobody asked you into their house and washed your neck. But she could come down this street: it was possible. They said if you waited in one spot long enough in this city the whole world went by.

"What are you in now, Schulte?"

"Ordnance."

"Where?"

"Cecchinoglia. It's outside Rome."

"That's a deal."

"Well that's how they fall, kid."

I was I were in a town like Rome, billeted here, Harry thought. A break, that's all one wanted out of the army, a break now and then. In the mornings when it rained the rain fell into your oatmeal, and they floated, the raisins, in the canned milk and the rain. Every evening in the spring and fall the rain fell in the mountains, then in the mornings the earth froze, then in the afternoons it thawed. The mud caked on your boots, weighing them like grotesque snowshoes. Sometimes you stood, early in the morning when you woke up, out in the cold blueness of sky and mountain, looking sleepy-eyed at some white beating star fading and fading, full of sadness, thinking that you would see such a star, as white, as large, if you were home. But home faded, too, eventually, like the star faded; faded away, and one remembered less and less as the days of heat and rain and dust and the eternal feel of the weapons on your body went on unchanged, and there was no hope, no end to it, the odds always getting smaller and smaller, and then soon it was hard to remember telephone numbers, hard to remember the names of streets you knew so well, hard to remember when you had been anything else but what you were now, for all of it faded, the mind could not keep two worlds equally alive.

But Schulte, he got out, water on the knee, he beat the army. To be in a city like this, Harry thought, to be billeted here. He could find her then with that kind of a break. To sleep in a bed again, Harry thought: a bed with sheets. Christ, the places I've slept.

I slept in a hole in the ground. I slept in a cave. I slept in a blanket in a grove of olive trees; in the bushes on the shoulder of a road while the convoys went by; under the altar of a church where there was only half a roof on the church.

I slept in the kitchen of a pink villa that had a garden full of fig trees in the back, but nobody lived in the pink villa any more.

I slept on the earth when it was wet and when it was dry; when it was cold and when it was hot; when it was stony and when it was soft.

I slept everywhere but in a bed in a room with four walls and a window open like people ought to sleep.

Christ God.

He looked at Schulte: what a lucky bastard Schulte was, having a bed to sleep in, having a city like this.

"What do you hear from home?" Harry said.

"Home? I don't hear," Schulte said. "Hey, Pop: basta with the Oi Marie." He took out a fifty lire note. "Here, buy yourself a piano." The old man touched his hat. "I play ancora?"

"No ancora," Schulte said.

"Grazie, signor."

"Home." Schulte said. "Who hears? I don't write no more. I bust up with my wife."

She writes, and then the letter comes. It comes in the afternoon, with the second mail, and it's a V-letter; the words all microscopically reduced. She even claims she cried as she wrote it, and the tears, too, microscopically reduced. Everything down small enough so a plane can carry it across the ocean, your letter among the other letters, like this, with somebody's microscopic tears. "Hell, man, I don't believe she cried at all. She just says she cried." The letter begins darling, as they all begin, but you had felt funny all day, that feeling you get when something is about to happen. Why think it shouldn't happen to you? Who are you it shouldn't happen to? "I think I told you once I was in the vegetable business in Chicago." Darling, darling, darling, I know I shouldn't tell you this, I know it's not fair but I know you want me to tell you the truth, and there is darling standing, wearing his fatigues, his hands with car grease on them, getting told. "Nice, huh? A beaut. She just had to tell me. Who the mother lovin' hell asked her to tell me?" All microscopically reduced, letter, tears, a life.

"Aw," Schulte said, "what's the diff?"

He wasn't going home to Chicago, not now, he wasn't going home to Chicago back to the vegetable business. He was going to get demobilized here. "I figure I can buy a sixby from the army after the war and go into Transportation. The eyeties they don't have no trucks now. You could make a pretty good dollar in this country after the war."

He fingered the cherry brandy glass.

"After the letter I went out and I got a dose. A pip of a one." His fingers tightened around the thickness of the glass. "A real pip."

No, he had sweated out three cures now, and the CO had busted him once for it, the first time it showed and he reported in, but it was one of those doses that came back. He shouldn't be drinking at all or smoking, but he smoked, he drank. What difference did it make?

"They cure it now," Harry said. "Penicillin—"

Schulte waved it away: "What difference does it make, dose or no dose?" he said. He looked at Harry, his lip lifting off the yellow teeth. "I'm giving it back where I got it. I'm redistributing it," he said. His fingers curled murderously around the jigger of cherry brandy.

In the center of the piazza the powerful Triton stood, naked and muscled, and Harry thought: she could come now around a corner like this, smiling, or appear under these chestnut trees burdened with dark burrs. To say: hello, Francesca. Do you remember me, Francesca? I wore it in my helmet the flower you gave me marching out of the gate. To say: gee, baby, am I glad to see you. To say: aw, honey, you don't know the amount of time I spent thinking about you. To say: I came all the way back to Rome just looking for you.

"Let's go," Schulte said. "Take the bottle. I'll get the tab."

Somewhere in this city. A look in the eyes of a girl remembered from a day when everybody thought they were at last free.

"Come on," Schulte said. "Let's blow."

They slouched together up the Via Veneto, the bottle

making a bulge inside Schulte's woolen shirt. Their uniforms were too hot, their boots too heavy. They moved, with that long unmilitary gait, past the entrances of embassies, shops, cafes, hotels. The sentries did not slap their rifles for them, they were not saluted, they were the concern only of the hustlers, the shoeshine boys, the women selling maps, the peddlers selling mosaic bracelets. They had no share in the life of the country, only in the destruction of it. They looked enviously and bitterly at the officers of their own army and country who sat, with women, in the cane chairs outside the cafes. The officers were clean with a cleanness they could not achieve; their women were invariably pretty. They seemed, to the soldiers whose armpits were stained with their own sweat, to possess a whole world of privileges they were denied. They looked at the women, at their legs and at their breasts; they looked at their floating hair; they looked at their tanned and naked arms lying on the tabletops. They looked at them with the hard obscene stare of convicts. They moved, carrying with them through the early evening crowd on the Via Veneto a private atmosphere of pathos and menace. They did not belong to this relaxed and chattering evening world. This language was not their own; they could not sit down at these tables, as they wished to, and talk easily to these attractive women. The few ugly phrases they had learned in broken wineshops or in the back alleys of Naples would have been quickly exhausted. Time would have pressed heavily on them, their twelve hours or their twenty-four hours or their thirty-six hours; there was never time enough to eat or to sleep or to make love. They were neither enemy nor friend, neither tourist nor businessman. They were soldiers to whom all countries not their own were hostile provinces populated by those who wanted their money and those who wanted their lives. So they slouched up the broad cosmopolitan avenue in the warm twilight, drunk now, nursing a bottle of sugarless cherry brandy, a little narrow-eyed and slack-mouthed because they wanted to be sitting at ease at these tables outside the cafes and they wanted to belong to this alien but attractive life and could not, and had not come from a country which had ever taught them how they could.

They crossed the Via Porta Pinciana, going under the old wall and through the old archway into the Villa Borghese, a green park through which ran a wide highway. They moved on, into the leafy coolness, following the quiet paths, until they found a little circular stone place with stone benches and a dry fountain full of leaves. Then they sat on the stone benches and took the bottle of cherry brandy and drank.

The first stars were out. It promised to be a full moon.

It was at this hour, in the cool and the greenness that Pierino Caneva and Assunta Venturini had also chosen to walk through the pleasant recesses of the Villa Borghese. Pierino was employed by the Ministry of Finance and he was in love with Assunta. It was a beautiful love complicated only by the fact that Pierino was a husband as well as Assunta's lover, and the father of two children, neither of them Assunta's, the youngest already displaying great vocal gifts. Despite his fatherhood and husbandship, Pierino always referred to himself as Assunta's fidanzato, and it did not seem at all to him a complicated series of relationships to be borne at the same time by one man.

They walked, Pierino and Assunta, and when Pierino spoke to Assunta he called her "dolce mia." His arm was about her waist so that it ever so discreetly touched the

fullness of Assunta's breast, and when the longing over-
came him he would stop and, taking Assunta in his arms,
kiss her with great passion. Assunta returned the kiss with
as great a passion and allowed herself to be troubled by
the thoughts of Pierino's wife only when the kiss was
thoroughly completed. So they walked under the trees, admiring the freshness of the stars, and Pierino hummed the
verses of "Ho un appuntamento colla luna" until they
came to a little circular stone place with benches and a dry
fountain full of leaves.

They heard Schulte say, from the stone bench: "Hey,
amico: aspette. Veni qua." Then Pierino stopped uncertainly, his arm about the waist of Assunta.

"Veni qua," said Schulte, from among the trees.

But Assunta knew instantly what was to be done. She
looked into the place where the dry fountain was, and saw
two soldiers, and the almost emptied bottle of cherry brandy. For Assunta, in a quiet place like this, even two soldiers
were two too many.

"No, no," she said. "Pierino, non fermiamo ci."

"But they are only two soldiers, my sweet," Pierino said,
as though one did not become alarmed in the recesses of
the Villa Borghese until one was halted by two orang-
utangs.

"Ma, sono ubriaco," Assunta said.

"Be calm," Pierino said. "I know the Americani. They
are not dangerous like the Polacchi or the Indiani."

And he smiled, the smile which had reduced the defenses
of Assunta in the very beginning when the thought of the
wife had troubled her much more than it did now. Besides, he was in the employ of the Ministry of Finance,
and therefore, in an obscure way it is true, had a political
duty toward the Alleati.

"Say, Jack," Schulte said, coming toward them, "I want to talk to you."

"Okay," Pierino said. He was proud of his knowledge of such a vital American phrase. They were drunk, the Americani, but always the soldiers were drunk. Witness this one, how much difficulty his legs were already giving him. It was a thing of great amusement, the drunkenness of the Americani. He had often observed it; they were like children drunk, the Americani.

"Listen, amico," Schulte said. "Me and my friend are lonely. No signorini. See?"

Pierino understood.

He nodded to show he understood and smiled to show he was in sympathy with such a need.

"Pierino," Assunta said.

"Have a cigarette, Jack," Schulte said, offering one. Pierino was flattered. It was as he thought: the Polacchi now, they would be dangerous, and besides, they would not offer cigarettes.

"Pierino," Assunta said, "let us go."

"But why? They are only a little drunk. They want to talk."

"I am afraid," Assunta said.

"Calm yourself, my sweet. They are lonely and they wish to have a little conversation. It is understandable."

"She your girl, Jack?" Schulte said.

"Cos'è?"

"She your fidanzata?"

"Oh, si. La mia fidanzata."

"She's sure stacked for a fidanzata," Schulte said.

"Pierino," Assunta said. Among the many stories current in the city she recalled one in which a girl of the streets had taken to bed with her for three thousand lire a drunken

American. The three thousand lire, although a vast sum
for such a thing as love, had not been too dear, for the
drunken American had bitten both her breasts so severely
that she was forced to spend a week in the hospital of San
Giovanni. "Pierino," she said, "please. Let us go. I am
afraid."

"Listen, Jack," Schulte said. "Ask your girl if she wants
to come with us and have a party. Understand?"

"Comè?"

"A party. With the signorini. We drink, we dance, we
make love."

Pierino understood now that perhaps Assunta was, after
all, justified, although she was a woman and naturally exaggerated a situation. Although it was an evening of much
charm, and one would have liked to continue the walk
through the leafy recesses of the Villa Borghese perhaps
it was wiser to postpone such a pleasure. They were, of
course, children, the Americani, but here by this dry fountain and among these trees it was not the proper moment
to play.

"Scusi, signori," Pierino said, and gave them the best of
his smiles. He took the arm of Assunta and wished to move
away.

"What's the matter, baby?" Schulte said, and he took
Assunta's arm also. "Look at the moon. Bella, no? That's a
pretty moon and you don't want to walk away when there's
a pretty moon up there like that."

"Si. E bellisima, la luna," Assunta said.

"Why don't you go take a walk, Jack?" Schulte said. "Go
take a passegiata for yourself around the park."

It was a problem for Pierino, and one that the Ministry
of Finance had never prepared him for. The terror in the
eyes of Assunta was very real. He did not wish to lose his

dignity and he did not wish to have Assunta scream. She would scream soon, he knew. Pierino looked at the other soldier, the taller one, who held the bottle. He did not know which was to be more feared. This one, the shorter and uglier, seemed more dangerous. This had never happened in the days of the regime, and despite his democratic nature Pierino had a longing for the quiet and the order of the dictatorship when one could walk and make love to Assunta in the Villa Borghese without such difficulties as he was now experiencing.

"Scusi, signori," Pierino said. "Dobbiamo andare," and once more he attempted to move on.

"Listen," Schulte said. He put his other hand flat up against the thin chest of Pierino. "We walked up here from Anzio, see?" He pushed Pierino. "For what? Tell me for what?"

"Schulte," Harry now said.

"Tell me for what?" Schulte said, not taking the flat of his hand away from the chest of Pierino, and pushing him, while Pierino still maintained his chivalrous and desperate grip about Assunta's waist.

Pierino still wished to settle this all in peace and in mutual satisfaction. "No, amico," he said. "If you wish a signorina go to the Piazza Colonna. There are many there under the galleria. They are girls for the soldiers. Assunta is of a good family."

But it was in another language, and perhaps it would not have mattered even if Schulte had understood.

"Listen, you," Schulte said. "When I was getting shot at what were you doing? You and your goddam white teeth. You and your goddam hair oil."

"Schulte," Harry said.

"You and the goddam vino we drink. You and the goddam broads we get doses from. You and your goddam country."

Assunta had understood, as she tried to pull Pierino away, only two words: Anzio and signorina, and now, in her terror, she screamed: "You should have perished on the beaches at Anzio before we let you into our gates!"

Schulte understood only the word Anzio.

"What did she say about Anzio?" he said. For Anzio was sacred, Cassino was sacred, the beachhead at Salerno was sacred. Assunta could have said, with more safety, that he was guilty of incest.

"Listen, sister," Schulte said. "Do you want a rap in the mouth too?"

"All right," Harry said. "Cut it out."

"I'll rap her teeth in," Schulte said. "What did she say about Anzio?"

"The dame's scared."

"I'll scare her. I'll cripple her she opens her yap about Anzio."

Harry took Schulte's arm which held the arm of Assunta, and pulled it away. "Go on, stupid," he said to Pierino. "Andiamo. Beat it."

Pierino recognized the moment as one in which questions of dignity were no longer involved, and taking Assunta quickly by the hand he fled with her away from the dry fountain full of leaves. Assunta, running, sobbed: "Che bestie, che bestie!" because she had been frightened and disgraced. Pierino knew, as they ran past the quiet trees under the freshness of the stars, that after they were safe he would face a genuine crisis in their love. He knew that the problem of the wife would now be almost insurmountable. It would be a long time before she would walk in the Villa Borghese with him again and he would call her dolce mia and they would stop on the path to kiss each other with such passion.

Behind them, Schulte struggled to escape from Harry. Harry held him. Harry said, "Schulte, for Christ sakes."

"I'll kill the bastard," Schulte said. "Let me go. Let me go I'll bust both of them."

Harry held on.

"Harry, I'll clout you."

"Go ahead clout."

Schulte swung. They fell over together into the wet evening grass. Then Schulte lay still on the grass.

"You crazy son of a bitch," Harry said. "Look." His lip was cut and bleeding.

Schulte turned over so that his face was in the wet grass. Harry saw he was crying.

"Listen," Schulte said. "After the war I was going to get a vegetable wagon. I was going to put a sign on my vegetable wagon. We served you in time of War and We serve you in time of Peace. I was going to put it on my vegetable wagon."

Harry dabbed with his handkerchief at his cut lip. He wanted to lie down on the stone bench and think of Francesca. Maybe he would remember some other detail he had forgotten about the street she had lived on.

"Listen," Schulte said. "I used to think after the war I'd get a break. I could go peddle in the residential districts. No cop would give you a ticket because you're a veteran."

He wanted to lie down on the stone bench and think of Francesca.

"Oranges," Schulte said. "In Chicago they like to eat oranges. That's what I was going to do. Before I got dosed. Before I got that letter. Now I ain't never going to leave this mother lovin' country."

He got up from the wet grass and went toward the dry fountain full of leaves. The wind moved among the trees and it was colder now. Schulte leaned over the fountain and Harry could hear him bringing up the cherry brandy. He put his face down in the wet grass. He could hear Schulte yawking. Under him it seemed as though the whole earth heaved.

Pollard

POLLARD THOUGHT to himself, what are you lying on the bed for? All right, Pollard thought, her husband is here. Husband got a plane in dear old England and flew across the Mediterranean, the blue blue Mediterranean, because she wrote him a letter. Letter said I love another, letter said. Oh the hell with it, her, him, all of it, Pollard thought. It's not important, Pollard thought: why should I lie here pretending it's important? Know what she is don't you? Pollard thought what she was. It was biological.

Josepina, the maid, came into the room, a change of towels slung over her arm, and saw Pollard lying there. She saw, too, the bottle on the end table beside the bed.

"You are sick, Giovanni?" she said to Pollard.

"No, I'm not sick."

"To me you look sick."

"Josepina, do me a favor."

"Si."

"Shut up and go away. Change the towels and go away."

"Va bene."

Josepina went into the bathroom and changed the

towels. She was fond of Antoinette. Josepina, too, thought Antoinette amusing. She herself would not have dared even in her youth to take a bath in the room of a man, but with the Americans all sorts of curious things seemed to be permitted.

She came out of the bathroom. Pollard lay, staring at the ceiling. He had had another drink out of the bottle.

"Are you going to lie there all day?"

"All day."

"Che uomo."

"All right che uomo. Now go away."

"Because he has come?" Josepine said, folding her arms across her flat breast. "The husband?"

"You know everything, don't you? Is there a goddam thing happens you don't know?"

"God gave me ears," Josepina said. "I listen. A big door has a large keyhole. Also, I saw him in the lobby. He is very handsome in the face."

"Who asked you?" Pollard said. "He can be handsome in all departments as far as I'm concerned."

"He is a soldier, her husband, no?"

"He is a soldier, her husband, yes. Now go away. Take your towels and andiamo."

"To have come here from Inghilterra and make such a surprise he must love her."

"Will you go away?"

"Va bene. And you? You will lie here, like this, drinking?"

"I'll lie here like this drinking."

But when she had gone he could not. He said: what am I going to do? He got up off the bed and went to look at himself in the mirror. Did it show? He thought it ought to show. Something. The nausea, perhaps.

He went down the elevator. There was the usual crowd in the lobby: officers, messengers, women, the hotel people. Going toward the mail desk there was a thin dark man in the dark green USO uniform, carrying a sheet of music. Pollard recognized him. He was famous. He walked nervously ahead of what must have been his manager, and he wanted an envelope large enough to mail the music sheet in, and the music must have been the number about the beachhead, the one they were singing now, the one with the arithmetical lyrics. Pollard went on into the bar and asked for a gin.

In the mirror behind the bar looking at himself he thought he needed a shave. Tie tucked in, double silver bars, a captain, by God, that's what he was, a captain.

Lieutenant Lord came up to the bar.

"Move over," Lord said. "Let a man in."

"Hello, Lord."

"What are you drinking?"

"Gin."

"That, and a trainwreck, is what killed Father."

Lord was a medical first lieutenant. He used to tell how he became a medical first lieutenant. After he hit the induction center back in Illinois in the early days of the war a man from Classifications and Assignments came into the barracks and said: All right you guys, start running across the drill field. The guys lit out across the drill field. The first forty guys who hit the barracks on the other side of the drill field went into medics. The others made general service. Lord said that was Illinois and that was how he became a medical first lieutenant: he could run.

"Hey," Lord said. "What's with Antoinette?"

"Why?"

"I saw her with some joker on the street and she intro-

duces the guy as her husband. Where did she dig out a
husband this late in the calendar?"

There it was again: the nausea. It must show. Pollard
found himself using a bad smile to cover it. Double bars,
tie tucked in, a captain, that's what he was.

"Oh, they dig one out eventually."

"I thought you owned her."

"Well, you thought wrong."

"Oh. Excuse me, Mac. I was looking for the men's room."

"You ask a hell of a lot of questions for a little boy," Pollard said.

He went out, not returning the MP's salute, crossed the
street and walked toward the Via Sestina. There must be
something he could do with his time. There must be something to get the sickness out. Good Christ you would think
it hadn't happened to him before. It had happened to him
before. It happened to everybody at least once, and it had
happened to him at least once before. The time it had happened he had made a goddam idiot of himself. Now he
knew better. He was a big boy now, a captain in his country's hup-hup army, in a foreign country too, overseas, in
Africa he had been blown up and had knifed a man all in
a real war, and if you wanted him to he could sit down and
describe all his experiences. He could write a book about
his experiences. He had all kinds of experiences, blue ones,
black ones, red ones. He could even sit down and tell them
to a war correspondent, he had that many. No biological
was going to throw him and his experiences. When a broad
doublecrosses you, the prescription is simple, you do what
the book calls for; you tank up and you go out and get laid.

Pollard went into a barber shop.

He got himself shaved, powdered, his hair combed and
his shoes shined, and he even let the barber put a towel

packed with ice on his face and the only thing he stopped at was hair oil. When he came out of the barber shop no time at all seemed to have elapsed and his stomach had undergone no appreciable change whatsoever. He still felt kicked there. He went into a moviehouse where in addition to the French film with the Italian subtitles there was a vaudeville come-on featuring a team called the Three Bonos. He took about a half hour of the Three Bonos who would have been great on Mulberry Street, then he went out of the moviehouse the way he had come in and, shaved and shined and kicked in the stomach, he headed for the Albergo Olympia.

There are times in a man's life when the best thing he can own is a pokerface. Everybody was going to look at him and they were all going to know that the cuckoo had been evicted from the skylark's nest because Mr. Skylark had just flown in, and he was going to have nothing at all to protect himself with but this face he carried around above the tight collar on which gleamed those two bright silver bars. That wasn't much to have in an emergency, and Pollard knew it.

But at that he was lucky. The first person he saw at the Albergo Olympia was the dago driver whose family sedan had been converted into a taxi to pick up and drive about the city whatever visiting military firemen were in town and staying at the Olympia. Pollard had found out in a sympathetic moment that the driver and his family sedan were about to be de-requisitioned. His tires were gone. It appeared that military regulations allowed the giving of gasoline on a buck slip to dago civilians but did not permit an allowance of tires. The visiting military firemen had used the dago's car until the tires were shot, and now they were de-requisitioning him and his car. The dago now had no tires, no benzina and actually no more car. He was de-requisitioned all right and he hung around the Olympia waiting for justice.

Pollard said buona sera to him and went on into the sort of sitting room with the radio and the writing tables the Olympia had downstairs. There was nobody there but little Eddie Stern, who ran the hotel, writing letters, and, in one of the easy chairs, her legs stretched out and her shoes off, Lois Cauley, talking to somebody from the Red Cross. All he had to face from Lois was a "Hi, John," as he sat down.

"That's ten nice toes," Pollard said.

"Honey, I'se so tired," Lois said. "I walked and walked."

The somebody from the Red Cross was telling Lois the lovely silver serving set he had picked up from some Countess. "Dear, you should see it. Antique design, hollow silver handles, all engraved. I know the people who made it, you know: wonderful silversmiths in Milano."

"In where?" Pollard said.

"Milano," the somebody from the Red Cross said. "Oh. I see. You say Milan."

"This is Roy Cramm," Lois said.

"How do you do," Roy Cramm said.

"Roy picks up the most wonderful bargains," Lois said. "Lace and old silver, and all he gives for them is his PX stuff and some coffee."

"My dear," Roy Cramm said, "you can pick up fabulous things in this country now. They haven't a button, you know. They'll take anything."

"Coffee and soap and cigarettes," Lois said. "Isn't it wonderful?"

"Yes," Pollard said. "Wonderful."

"I've my eye on a painting now," Roy Cramm said.

"Beautiful little thing."

"Not a beautiful little Michelangelo?"

"Oh, no. You really couldn't trade in on that, you know. No, this is a modern thing I saw. Some young artist on the Via del Plebiscito. You don't need money, you know," Roy Cramm said confidentially. "They'll take anything you have."

"How about socks?" Pollard said. "You think there's a solid gold carving dish I could trade in on for some socks?"

"Socks?" Roy Cramm said. "Oh, I see."

"Don't you listen to that old John," Lois said.

"Well, I don't see any point in not taking advantage of an opportunity. Do you, dear? I didn't make the war, you know."

"Don't you listen to that old John," Lois said. "You just go right on picking up your bargains. I think they're wonderful."

When Roy Cramm had gone away to see what he could do about the beautiful little painting or perhaps the fabulous piece of ducal lace, Pollard looked at Lois and said:

"Where is she?"

"Upstairs," Lois said.

"Is he with her?"

"Of course."

"Well, that's nice. What made me think he wouldn't be? Coming all that way from England he wouldn't want to waste time, would he?"

"Now don't be nasty, dear."

"I wasn't being nasty, honey. That was me being realistic."

Lois looked at him. She had a redhead's fair skin but she always looked as if she were going through her first sunburn. "Bad, honey?" she said.

"Bad," Pollard said.

"Do you want to talk?"

"Is that good for you, to talk?"

"That's what the man says."

"All right, let's talk. Let's go talk and drink. Do you have anything to drink?"

"Some scotch and there's a half bottle of gin."

"Where?"

"In my room."

"All right," Pollard said. "Let's go to your room."

They went up the flight of stairs past the lister bag in the lobby of the Olympia, and then Pollard remembered that Lois' room was the room next to Antoinette's. Christ, he was whipping himself good, wasn't he? He was trying to get as close to it as he could.

Lois saw him looking at the door.

"Now, John," she said.

"I wasn't going to break it down," Pollard said. "I was just thinking how many times I've gone through it." He looked at Lois. "What I need, baby, is a good orientation film. Six reels, restricted, for what ails you."

"Honey," Lois said. "I don't think it's such a good idea you're coming up here."

"Honey," Pollard said. "Open that door."

There was about a half bottle of gin but no juice and Lois called Eddie downstairs and Eddie said he would bring up some juice. Lois had the scotch, but Pollard thought he couldn't wait for the juice and he had some of the gin without it.

"That, and the trainwreck, killed my daddy."

"Lord said that," Pollard said. "Only he said father."

"Who's Lord?"

"A lieutenant. A medical lieutenant."

"Well, we all in Texas say daddy," Lois said. She stretched back on the pillow. "Ain't this war a scream?" Lois said.

There was a door to the bathroom, a connecting bathroom Antoinette and Lois shared. He was that close. He could have put his ear up against the wall and listened. The thing to do was to stop the pictures forming in his head. He knew from the time before the worst thing that happened during it was the pictures which formed in your head. That was why you tanked up and went out and got laid, because of the pictures. If you tanked up enough they stopped. He had not been able to prove yet that anything really made the pictures stop.

He drank the gin again, straight.

"Lover," Lois said, "don't you think you better wait until Eddie brings the juice?"

"Oh, I don't get drunk no more," Pollard said. "I try, but nothing happens."

"Well, drinking like that," Lois said, "you won't get drunk. You'll fall down dead." He was sitting at the edge of the bed, his back to her, the gin bottle hanging down between his legs. "Are you really that much in love with her?" Lois said.

"What do you think?"

"Oh, I thought maybe it was a long war and a short memory."

"You got a husband, too, someplace, haven't you?"

"Someplace. Australia."

"Miss him?"

"Uh-huh."

"Everybody's got one," Pollard said. "And they're all sleeping around. Ring around a biological rosie."

"Keep it clean, Captain."

"Husband and wives," Pollard said. "Why don't they

figure out another combination? Husbands and something else. Or wives and something else."

"Listen," Lois said. "Would you tell me something? I'm dying of curiosity."

"Tell you what?"

"Antoinette," Lois said, "is she really that good?"

"What are you collecting, statistics?"

"Honey, I'm just curious."

"Scientifically?"

"Uh-huh."

"Yeah," Pollard said. "She's good. That I'll give her. She loves him, doesn't she?" he said, jerking his head toward the wall.

"I guess."

"She wouldn't be with him if she didn't love him, would she?" Pollard said. "And in the same bed. That's what gets me."

"Oh," Lois said, "we do funny things."

"Listen," Pollard said. "I'll tell you what hurts. She was just using me. Because when they were married he two-timed her and made her bawl in restaurants and gave her an inferiority about how lousy she was in bed, she used me to beat his brains in. That's all it was. Ring around a rosie."

He drank the gin again.

"I think she likes you, honey," Lois said. "I think she likes you very much."

"Sure," Pollard said. "Why not? Me any my bars. Me and my hot water."

"Now, honey," Lois said.

"Listen," Pollard said. "I'll tell you another secret. Top drawer." He looked at her. "What am I doing in this uniform?" he said. "What am I doing giving guys orders? What is this I got into?"

"A war, lover."

"It's no war," Pollard said. "It's a masquerade ball. That's what it is. What am I doing with bars on me? An officer, by act of congress. It's a masquerade ball: orders, regulations, salutes, insignia. Look: I'm a guy off the street. I'm nobody from Nowhere, North Dakota. Who are they kidding—me running Europe? I can't even run myself."

"Somebody has to be the officer," Lois said. "Why not you?"

"Because I can't make myself believe it," Pollard said. "I look in the mirror and I don't believe it. We're an army of phonies, baby, that's what we are. An army of jerks playing soldier. And Christ be good to me if I'm any better than any of them."

"Oh, I don't believe that," Lois said. "We're not as bad as all that. We have a fine lot of men in our army."

"Honey," Pollard said, "wait until midnight. Wait until the masks come off this halloween dance."

Eddie came in with the juice. Pollard lay back on the bed thinking: this isn't helping. I talk but it doesn't help. I've got X-ray eyes and they go right through that wall. It's been a long time for him. What's it like when you haven't seen your wife for a long time? Do you look to see if the mole is still there, do you watch for any new tricks she's learned? He was clouding up now, and he could hear Eddie talking to Lois. Lois was all right. She had a husband in Australia. He wondered if she had been getting any. Lois was saying: "My God, I don't see how you stand the hair on their legs." And Eddie said: "The Roman girls don't have hair on their legs, Lois." And Lois said: "Well, they certainly had hair on their legs in Naples. The least they could do is shave it off. Don't tell me they don't have razors." Then it clouded up again, and the pictures came back, worse than before, the details, and the nausea welled up in his stomach. When he came out of it he heard Eddie describing to Lois how to learn to speak Italian. "You just empty your mind," Eddie said. "That's all. You just empty your mind."

"Honey, you feel bad?" Lois said.

"No, I'm all right."

"You sure now?"

"Yes, I'm all right."

He closed his eyes thinking it might be better if he closed his eyes, but all of it would come back, and he said to himself: O you bitch, O you bitch, you're doing this to me. Then when he opened them again, because the pictures were too vivid with his eyes closed, Eddie was saying: "Well, you know what they say about Texas: it was attached to the Union for rations and quarters."

"Is there any more gin?" Pollard said.

"You had enough, honey," Lois said.

"Don't take care of me, please," Pollard said.

"I'll go get some grapefruit juice," Eddie said. "The juice is all gone." He went out and then Lois said: "You know, baby, you shouldn't drink any more. Really."

He lifted his head up off the bedpost, shook it to clear the clouding up out, and Lois said: "My God, you men." Then he looked at Lois, lying back on the pillow, and he put his head down on her breast. Lois said: "Don't—"

"Why not?" he said.

Lois said: "Don't." Then he turned his head and he kissed Lois where her blouse was open on the faintly flushed skin that always looked like it was going through the first stages of sunburn, and Lois shivered as though she were cold and put her hands to his head to push him away, and then he said: "Don't—" and she said: "Stop it, stop it." Then he tried to put his arms around Lois, under her, and kiss her again, and Lois said: "Pollard, stop it, I'll hit you," and he said: "I'm only kissing you," and she said, "Stop it. If you don't stop it, so help me I'll crown you. I mean it," Lois said. Then Pollard, still trying to kiss her, said "Why?" and she said: "Don't take it out on me. I don't like it. Now please, stop," and Pollard stopped. He stood up. The room lurched and he had to hold the bedpost and he said, a gentleman of the old school, to Lois: "I was trying to, wasn't I? God, I stink. Excuse me, baby," and letting go of the bedpost he went carefully across the room and opened the bathroom door and went into the bathroom.

The Marchese

THE BUILDING WAS enormous, old, gray. It had the look of
a police station, but a violently overgrown one. Outside, in
the driveway, the big black sedans used in the special raids
were double-parked. Aldo, mounting the broad unclean
wide staircase, was halted under the archway by a guard in
a sentry box. Whom did he wish to see?

"The signor Martelli."

His papers, please.

Aldo frowned; he did not wish to show his papers. He
did not wish any rumors later on. Would the guard phone
from the sentry box? The guard, smoking, picked up the
phone; what name would he say?

"The Marchese," Aldo said. "He'll know."

He waited, under the archway, looking curiously at the
gloomy structure. The Questura was hardly a pleasant
place. He would not have liked coming here involuntarily,
flanked by two plainclothesmen of the Security Police. The
phone was put down. "All right," the guard said.

The corridor was inadequately lit, lined with doors, and
absolutely deserted. The tiled floor was pocked with cigar-

ette stubs, ground under heel, and evidently the walls were
spit on frequently. Aldo thought: the politics change but
not the Questura. The stink and the gloom were inherited,
along with the file cabinets.

He debated which of the mysterious doors to try: this
oak one or that frosted glass one. He opened an oak one
and he confronted a roomful of men in unpressed civilian
suits, dealing cards, reading newspapers, and discoloring
the air under the unshaded light bulb with cigarette smoke.
It was, Aldo guessed, a detectives' retiring room. The smoke
spread in wavering layers under the suffocated light bulb
and a battery of police eyes examined him.

He was most polite: could the gentlemen tell him where,
in this mysterious corridor, he could find signor Martelli?

"Who?"

"Signor Martelli."

"Why do you want to see Martelli?"

"I have an appointment."

A big one, in a black suit, balancing a hefty buttock on
the desk edge, picked up the phone. Aldo thought there
was perhaps too much of picking up of phones here.

Looking at the men, in this room that was so much like
the detective rooms in every *roman gello* he had read, Aldo
was quite sure they had no difficulties with their pasta ration. There was not the remotest indication here of a hollow cheek or a sunken eye. It was obvious that whatever
else the Government might change, the quality of the police had survived almost untouched. As a matter of fact,
Aldo thought, while he waited, he would bet any quantity
of occupation money that some of these gentlemen had
graced this room under other dispensations. They looked
much too proficient under the unshaded light bulb to have
mastered this trade in the four months of power of the new

government. Après moi, Aldo thought, not the deluge at all, merely the same detectives.

The big one put the phone down.

"Yes?" Aldo said, politely.

Signor Martelli was waiting for him in an office down the hall. Aldo followed the big detective out, closing the door on the *roman gello* and preoccupied card players. The corridor, again; and then a door, which was Martelli's —and Martelli, in the room, nodding to him as he entered, and a girl. There were bookshelves, Aldo saw, which he found a little surprising, a file cabinet, which was to be expected, and a long dark table, behind which Martelli sat. Against the wall, standing, there was what Aldo supposed was a guard, a man in a pair of infantryman's badly cut green trousers, wearing a slung carbine. But it was neither the guard nor Martelli, sitting behind the table, who held Aldo's interest—it was the girl, sitting on the other side of the table, looking, Aldo thought, like a martyred coal miner. It was the combination of the dark skin and the naked scalp. For the hair had been more than cut; it must have been shaved off the scalp, literally. There was nothing, in Aldo's opinion, more obscene looking than a bald woman, and this head, in the light, seemed incredibly bald. The interview, the questioning, if there had been an interview or questioning, seemed over, and Martelli did not speak, he sat there, very tall, behind his table, merely looking at the obscenity of the girl's head.

"That is all, signorina," Martelli said. "Buonanotte."

The girl stood up. She wore a dress of red wool, short, belted, and Aldo was startled as he realized that not only was the girl's figure good, but that she must have been, although it was impossible to tell with that naked skull, pretty. Now everything seemed exaggerated; the nose lengthened, the eyes too far forward, the nakedness of the head contributing an unnaturalness to the whole face. As she stood up, now, she took out of the pocket of her red dress a blue dotted kerchief, shook it, and rigidly, her face unchanging, put it over her naked scalp, tying it under her chin.

The guard waited until she had finished tying the blue kerchief under her chin. When it was tied, and the obscenity hidden, her face, with the kerchief, dwindling normally, the guard reached over and pulled the kerchief from her head.

It was as though she had been stripped, and she stopped, going to the door, some faint emotion at last rippling over that terribly controlled face. She half put her hands up again to adjust the kerchief, the guard not moving, watching her, but she did not complete the gesture. The hands went down stiffly at her sides, the face again hid its emotion, and she went out, not turning, not looking at the men, her head like some ravaged monk's.

The guard followed her into the corridor.

Martelli nodded at a chair: "Sit down, Marchese." The room was warm, the window filmed with dust. Aldo saw the girl, sustained by some deathlike pride, walking down the corridor, badly lit, the cigarette stubs ground on the floor. Would she put the kerchief on again in the hall? Martelli, looking across the table, smiled; it was neither kind nor hard—a smile: and said, "It will grow back in six months. Meanwhile—" he paused. "Well, it will save her money at the hairdresser's."

"Yes, I imagine it will."

Martelli looked, to Aldo, like a consumptive athlete. He was tall, big in the shoulders, and his front teeth were broken. But the face itself was thin, the cheekbones high

and colorless, the eyes very narrow and black and capable
of looking at you without squinting or wavering. Aldo did
not like men who made a virtue of a direct look. "She had
long hair," Martelli said, meditatively. A drawer was coming open; he lifted a bottle of what seemed whiskey to the
table. "She wore it like this, down to her shoulders. I remember once I sat in a beauty salon, watching her while
she was under the drier."

"You knew her?" Aldo was surprised.

Martelli held the bottle over a glass. "Marchese?"

"Thank you. English, isn't it?"

"Yes." The smile again. "I have it from a colonel. With
the whiskey came a bit of advice on the advantages of having a monarch on the Italian throne."

"The English are fond of kings."

"One thing the English have, good whiskey." He set
the glass down. "The girl—yes, I knew her. I was once a
little bit in love with her." Aldo must have betrayed his
surprise again. "But she was responsible for this," Martelli said. He touched, not too happily, the broken teeth in
his mouth. "They do not make me very handsome, eh?"

"No."

"I had such a clumsy dentist in the Via Tasso."

"Oh."

The Via Tasso had been Gestapo headquarters, a for-
bidding building, now shunned, its windows nailed up. "I
had eight days in the Via Tasso because of her," Martelli
said. "The Germans—" He shrugged. "Well, it doesn't matter now. But she was pleasant. If she hadn't become a little
informer, I might still be in love with her. Not much, but
a little."

"Did she inform on you?"

"Yes: it was after I was back from Milan, in October,

one night when I went to what I thought would be a comfortable supper at her house. The money, I guess, was too attractive. They paid five thousand lire, you know." He poured the whiskey again, carefully. "I promised myself I would find her." And fingering the tumbler: "She had hair down to here. Well, in six months it'll grow back." He drank. "It was equitable, no—her hair for my teeth?"

Aldo looked curiously at the man with the broken teeth. Martelli was the only practicing socialist he knew. There had been others, the literary and the parliamentary ones, and now there were a great many of them and much talk about a federated Europe. He did not despise socialists any more than he despised monarchists; a political passion, of any sort, whether for a king or municipal equality, were equally fantastic to him. He thought briefly of Cespa: the new nationalism the man, consciously or unconsciously, represented; and, as always, the personality overshadowed the politics. Cespa was so obviously playing in a political opera—how was it possible to take his rhetoric seriously, when one heard continually the basso pumping wind into his lungs and saw the artifically induced effects? But Martelli—well, he had been in the Via Tasso. It was a distinguishing thing. Whatever the validity of his politics, the experience was real, and Aldo could not possibly conceive of himself in similar conditions. He could, conceivably, have been Cespa; he could never have been Martelli.

"You were in Switzerland during the occupation, Marchese?"

"Yes."

"The Swiss are lucky. A country, like an oasis, in a desert of wars."

"I found it dull."

"It's better to be back in Italy, eh?"

"Yes: it's not dull."

"No," Martelli said, smiling. "Italy is not dull." He moved the papers on the table. "The occupation was strange, an undeclared civil war. I had a friend who lived in a chicken coop the entire time the Germans were here. In a chicken coop. But then, he was a Jew. He says it was an incredible experience."

"Well, he survived."

"Yes, but he cackles a little, he says."

Aldo said politely: "It must be interesting, the life of a policeman." He meant because of the experience of the Via Tasso, and because now Martelli had triumphed. They had all triumphed, those who had been in the Lipari Islands and in the Via Tasso, all of them, except, of course, the dead ones, who never triumphed.

"Is it?" Martelli paused, smiling at a private secret. "Do you know, Marchese—sometimes it is hard to get used to myself sitting at this desk?" He indicated all the room. "Sometimes I feel I should be on the other side of it, standing, waiting to be questioned. I feel, what is the word? An imposter."

"But it is more interesting from this side."

"Interesting? Well—" He turned slightly, looking at the window dark with night and filmed with dust. "I do not so much mind it when two American soldati are perhaps accused of rape. One expects that. Or a report comes in that some Pole has backed a truck up to a jewelry store on the Via Nazionale and hooked his tire chains to the iron shutters, and then pulled the shutters very efficiently off. One expects that, too, including the eventual emptying of the jeweler's window. No, I don't even mind when some ignorant carabiniere arrests one of the leading members of the Soviet delegation because he can't distinguish Rus-

sian from German, and all big blondes with clipped hair-
cuts are tedeschi to him." He paused, smiled again, showing the bad teeth. "But the Indiani. The gentlemen with
the beards and turbans. What is one to do when they begin molesting little boys on the street? After all, they are
the Alleati—our friends. . . ." And sighed: "The Indiani,
they make it difficult."

"Yes," Martelli said, "that is being a policeman." And
then, with an almost imperceptible eagerness, "You
brought them?"

"Yes, of course."

Aldo took the long envelope out of his pocket. It contained all the correspondence. The proofs were quite defi-
nite, enough to satisfy even a socialist. The general had
been foolish, of course, to commit so much to writing, but
then he had probably thought that an Allied victory was
impossible. The Germans had seemed so invincible then.
The documents involved the capitulation of September
eighth. There was army information of a very specific kind.
There were suggestions on how best to disarm those units
which might have been inspired to defend the city. There
was proof that an artillery battalion stationed in the hills
had never received its orders to resist the German advance
on the city. It was all there, all the necessary proofs, all the
evidence. He hardly emerged, the general, from those
documents as a savior of his country. It was not difficult to
imagine what the press would do with such billets-
doux.

Martelli slipped the documents back into the envelope.
"Do you mind, Marchese, my asking you a question?"

"Not at all."

"Why are you doing it?"

"Oh, perhaps the money," Aldo said.

"I don't think it is altogether the money."

"My dear Martelli," Aldo said. "Money is one of the few relics whose authenticity is not disputed."

Martelli considered him. "You know, of course, what this will mean to your father-in-law?"

"Of course. At least imprisonment, possibly death, certainly disgrace."

Was there a flicker of contempt in Martelli's cold eyes? He would, naturally, despite the Via Tasso, have such moral scruples against the betrayal of the father of one's own wife. Underneath, all these iron personalities had such conventional scruples. "Well," Martelli said. "I suppose it does not matter. But I was curious."

"As a socialist?"

"No, as a policeman." He held up the colonel's excellent whiskey. "This, and the Bible, wasn't it, conquered an empire?"

"Yes, but not ours."

"We'll be happier without one. Your family is very old, isn't it, Marchese?"

"Ancient," Aldo said. "We go back to the time of Dante. Is it impressive?"

"No," Martelli said. "Italy is mostly a past, a first-rate past with a third-rate future."

"Poor Italy. Have you been in Tripolitania, signor?"

"No."

"It was a country I liked. The heat prevented anything from happening. The women sat in their gardens, under large straw hats, fanning themselves, and the men drank."

"And the natives?"

"They worked, naturally."

The smile, that was neither hard nor kind, appeared. "I think it would not be difficult to dislike you, Marchese."

"Yes?"

"I am sitting here, wondering if in another society you would be a different man."

"Who knows?" Aldo looked engagingly into Martelli's eyes. "Paradise must have its snake." He leaned forward, confidentially. "As a socialist, signor Martelli, you look forward optimistically to the future, no?"

"Yes."

"Can you see mine?"

"The aristocrat has no future," Martelli said. "I'm talking generally. It is a dead social type."

"Really? And I feel so much alive." He disliked, now, Martelli's calm dogmatism, and somehow it irritated him to think of himself as a sociological fossil. "The future . . ." he said. "After all, signor—we were somebody's future once. You and I are what our grandfathers promised their children. I imagine the children were disappointed."

So Martelli did not like him—he shrugged; it did not matter. To Martelli, despite the atmosphere of political manipulation he moved in, each discovery of man's infidelity, pettiness, and dishonesty, those permanent veins in the rock, must come as a kind of continual shock; he suffered, Aldo guessed, a series of perpetual and unacknowledged disillusionments. And disillusionment, Aldo remembered, was a favorite Italian experience: his countrymen were being eternally disenchanted. "Yes," he said, "I imagine the children were very disappointed."

He stood up; the envelope lay on the table, and Martelli touched it with his fingertips. "You know, of course," Martelli said, "that when the documents are published, it may effect the entire family."

"Yes."

"Your wife, too."

"She will recover," Aldo said. "I'm sure she will recover."

They shook hands. "Well, buonanotte."

"Ciao."

He went out of the office, closing the door behind him carefully. The corridor was as badly lit; and, as he descended the steps of the Questura, past the parked raid cars, he thought of the girl: had she put the kerchief on her head as she came down these stairs? He felt taller, more expansive, better than he had felt during the air-raids which had turned out to be quite dull, even better than he had felt with Pepi. He thought: politics seem to agree with you, and then, suddenly, he wanted a bright, noisy place to sit in.

The wineshop was small. It was a wineshop of the neighborhood, a place with barrels and shelves racked with bottles, and in the wineshops a boy was singing to a gypsy. Aldo listened to the boy sing, his head tilted on one side, his eyes mockingly half closed, and his voice singing to the gypsy as though he were making love to her. She was an old gypsy, in a yellow fortune teller's costume, with ear-rings, and a face like a man's, strong-nosed, dark-eyed, and with a growth of hair on her upper lip thickening almost to a mustache at the corners of her mouth. She had big pendulous half visible breasts. The boy wore a striped jersey, his hair sleek and combed to a point on his neck, his feet in white canvas sandals, his ankles brown and smooth. He straddled a chair, now, in the wineshop, and he laughed at the gypsy as he sang, and called her Mama Spagnola and Aldo, listening, thinking now and then of Martelli, heard the boy say he worked in a bicycle shop down the street. A bottle of vino bianco was on the table in front of Aldo, and he listened to the Neapolitan song the boy sang, looking at his brown throat and brown arms in the jersey, the long narrow feet of the boy in the canvas sandals, and the boy's voice was very good and he sang with much feeling.

The boy laughed.

"Like my song, Mama?" he said.

"You're all right," the gypsy said, nodding. "Go sing to some girl. Why don't you go down to the river and sing to some girl?"

The boy laughed. He had very white, strong teeth.

Aldo was delighted with the boy. He sat, drinking his wine, in his white tropical suit, delighted with the boy's brownness. The boy was darker than Pepi, and stronger, but not as tall. He must spend so much time in the sun, Aldo thought, to get brown like that.

The gypsy looked at him.

"He's pretty, eh?" she said to Aldo in French. "He's a pretty boy, no?" Aldo was surprised.

"Yes," he answered, in French.

"He has a girl. Don't you have a girl? He takes her down to the river. Every night he goes down to the river with her."

The boy laughed. He put his hand under the gypsy's huge loose breast.

"Feel them," the boy said. "My God. Feel what they weigh." He balanced the breast on his palm, weighing it. "My God. Is that how a woman gets when she's old?"

The gypsy looked down incuriously at his hand.

"My God," the boy said. "If my girl gets like that I'm finished with her."

"She'll get like that. She'll get worse."

"Not my girl," the boy said. "You should see my girl. They fit in my hand like an apple. I can put my little finger on one and my thumb on the other."

"He goes down to the river with her every night," the gypsy said.

"Down by the sailors' barracks," the boy said happily. "It's too bad you're all worn out, Mama. It's too bad you're not young and small like my girl. What a time we could have."

"You and your girl," the gypsy said. "Some night a fly will bite your rump and you'll both fall in the river."

He would offer the boy a drink, Aldo thought. If the old gypsy would go, he would offer the boy a drink, and he would sit, looking at his white teeth smiling. They were wonderful teeth. What was Martelli doing now? You are a dead social type. Really? Dead social types sometimes enjoyed curious resurrections.

"What does my hand say, Mama?" the boy said. He held his palm out. The gypsy stroked it, with her thumb, slowly.

"You'll kill somebody."

"Who?"

"Yourself."

The boy laughed. "How, Mama?"

"Going down to the river too much."

"She reads palms, signor," the boy said to Aldo. "Ask her to read yours. She'll tell you how much money you'll win and what kind of woman you need."

Aldo extended his hand. "Everybody is predicting my future tonight," he said. He smiled at the gypsy. "Tell me my future, signora."

"What kind of a woman does he need, Mama?" the boy said.

"He doesn't need a woman," the gypsy said. "Give me a cigarette, pollicchio."

Aldo withdrew his hand slowly. "Do you always predict such accurate futures?" he said in French to the gypsy.

"What do you want?"

"I was going to offer him a drink. He's very charming. I've been sitting here admiring his teeth."

"Admire someone else's teeth."

"Hey," the boy said, looking at them happily. "What are you talking about? What is she saying, signor?"

"Nothing." Aldo smiled winningly at the boy. "We were discussing the future."

"She's an old witch," the boy said. "Don't let her talk you into nothing. I'll bet she's a hundred years old."

"You see," Aldo said in French. "He thinks of you as an old woman. Hasn't he beautiful feet in those white sandals? They are so narrow."

"He has a girl," the gypsy said.

"I won't take him away from her."

"I know your kind."

"Do you?"

"Yes," the gypsy said. "I've seen everything. I know your kind. You'll dirty him."

"What is she saying, signor? She talks five languages. She drinks wine and smokes cigarettes and tells fortunes. She's told everybody's fortune in the neighborhood."

"Aristocrat," the gypsy said.

"Yes?"

"Leave the boy alone."

Aldo looked at her: the huge breasts, pendulous and veined and chocolate-colored, the ear-rings, the strong nose like a man's, and the mustache thickening at the corners of the mouth. Perhaps she was, as the boy said, a hundred years old. He stood up. "He is pretty though, isn't he?"

"Yes."

"I envy his girl."

"You would dirty him."

"Buonanotte, signora."

"Good night, aristocrat."

"Hey, Mama," the boy said. "Shall I sing you another song? This is a song my girl likes when we're down by the river."

"You and your girl and the river," the gypsy said. "Well, go on, sing."

Carla

MAMA SAID: "Why don't you eat, Carla?"

There was a soup in which some green vegetables and some carrots had been boiled, a plate of chestnuts, and the ration of bread on the table. For Antonio, who liked them, there were some watery brownish vienna sausages which Grigorio, who hated them, had given to the family.

"I am not hungry," Carla said.

There was, of course, a great deal of talk about food in the city: what one had eaten in the past, what one was compelled to eat in the present, and what one would like to eat in the future.

"Ah, madonna," Mama said. "What a child. What blessings have been showered upon me."

"Please, Mama," Carla said. "I am not hungry."

"But you are always not hungry. I don't know what you live on," Mama said. "Look how thin you are."

"I'll be fat enough when I'm old," Carla said.

"One needs strength," Mama said. "Even to sit at the piano and to play one needs strength."

"Food has nothing to do with music."

"Brahms got his belly on air?"

"Oh, Mama."

"Mama," Antonio said, "I beg you. One night let's eat in peace."

Mama sighed. She spooned her soup. "When your Papa comes home I'll retire and let him control you. I'll take a vacation."

"All right," Antonio said. "We'll all take vacations."

"Antonio," Mama said. "Did you go to the Bureau for War Prisoners? Did you ask them why there's been no letter?"

"Yes."

"For a month now no letter."

"There's been no ships."

"No ships?" Mama said. "Why should they have no ships? There are enough ships for the soldiers. They go every day to India. Why should they come back empty?"

"I don't know. That's what they told me."

"Eat," Mama said. "Eat the chestnuts."

There was a radio but the tubes had been burned out six months ago and it was impossible to find or to buy radio tubes. And it was better to eat early while there was still light, for later it would have required candles, since there was no electricity, and candles were thirty lire apiece. The disadvantage of eating early however was that one got so hungry during the night.

But Mama consoled herself.

"Ah," she said, "when your father comes home we'll make a festa. Then we'll dance."

"Mama," Carla said suddenly. "Mama, I want to go out and go to work in a hotel or a restaurant."

"In a what?" Antonio said.

"I want to go out and go to work in the orchestra of a hotel or a restaurant."

"And the Conservatory?" Mama said. "You'll graduate in June."

"You'll go to the Conservatory and graduate," Antonio said.

"Why should I? Look how I dress, look at my shoes. Look how I go into the street."

"It's my fault," Mama said.

"No," Antonio said.

"I'm talking to Mama not to you."

"You listen to me," Antonio said. "You don't know anything. I know what working in those restaurants and hotels is. The girls who work there are no good. My sister isn't going to work in any hotel or restaurant."

"Why do you let him speak to me like that?" Carla said.

"Your papa is not here. Antonio is the father in my house now. The son must be the father."

"Oh, Mama."

"Eat," Mama said. "How is it possible for a girl not to eat?"

"I don't want to eat."

"When Mama tells you to eat why don't you eat?" Antonio said. "Why do you make so much trouble? Why don't you ever think of somebody besides yourself?"

"Antonio, let her be."

"Do you know what they sing in the streets now?" Antonio said. "I heard the children singing it." He sang:

Caramelli, bambi
Ciocholatta, segnori
Washie à mama
Sigarett' à papa . . .

"That's what the children sing now," Antonio said. That's what they learn in the streets."

"Ma è carina," Mama said, amused.

"It's not funny. I don't think it's funny."

"Children," Mama said. "The disgrace is not important. The Virgin take care of us and permit us to survive until your father comes home from India."

"If she listened to me," Antonio said, "she would get engaged to the professor."

"So you wouldn't have to worry about me?" Carla said.

"If you get in trouble—" Antonio said.

"What would you do?"

"Something," Antonio said. "You'd see."

"Antonio, basta," Mama said.

"I'll never get married," Carla said. "Do you hear me? I'll never get married."

"Carla, basta," Mama said.

Carla stood up from the table.

"What are you doing?" Mama said. "Where are you going?"

"To the moon," Carla said.

"Go to the North Pole," Antonio said.

"Antonio, basta," Mama said. "Madonna, that's enough." They heard the door slam.

"Eat," Mama said. "Eat the chestnuts."

The sky was darkening now and the children were gone from the streets. Her city had lit, as the last glows went out of the sky, its meager supply of wicks, and in many kitchens they cooked over charcoal fires or even wood fires. The primitive forms of existence were much more complicated than the modern. Even for the peasants. Carla had seen one morning on the Ponte Milvio an old woman with her bare hands picking up the steaming horse droppings after the police cavalry had cantered across the bridge. She put the horse droppings into a wicker basket. It was because there were no horses left on the farms. What horses were left were in the police cavalry.

The wounded mechanical body of the city drew labored breaths. She knew how angry Antonio would be, and how Mama would wring her hands if they knew, but it was necessary that she talk again to Grigorio. It was so urgent. Because he did not understand. She had been too upset this afternoon. But she would go to him now and she would make him understand.

Below her, as she crossed the bridge, there were shadowy forms on the banks of the Tiber. Perhaps soldiers, or the children who waited to rob the soldiers when they were drunk. The political slogan of the Christian Democratic Party painted on the walls of the embankment was like the writing on the wall at the feast of Belshazzar. It was fading, too. But the effect was less spectacular.

In the piazza she found several camionettas waiting. The camionettas were small vehicles of peculiar manufacture. Sometimes they were little trucks which at one time had probably hauled wood or vegetables; sometimes they were converted motorcycles. A platform on which there were three wooden benches accommodated the passengers. There was a ladder propped against the tailgate. The latter was homemade and none too secure. As Carla mounted it, the driver said, "Careful, signorina." The ladder ricketed under her.

She paid her twenty lire and sat in a corner of the bench behind the tarpaulin-covered rear of the cab.

There were many jokes about the camionettas. One often felt, as they rattled, coughed and exploded their way through the town, that their official destination was the guillotine. They would have made fine tumbrils. More than half the seats were now taken. The driver, a fat square man in shirtsleeves and a cap, stood beside the camionetta counting a thick mass of lire. The driver was always assisted by a boy. The boy's duty was to prop and to unprop the small ladder by which one climbed into the camionetta. During the ride he squatted on the tailgate, with his feet dangling down, admiring the city, or if he was a musical boy, he sang.

A man in a bleached raincoat climbed the ladder. He took out a handkerchief and carefully dusted the bench in the middle before he sat on it.

"Is it dirty?" the friend asked who had come into the camionetta with him.

"Probably."

"Well, a little dust won't hurt the patches in my pantaloni."

They sat down. It was quite crowded now in the camionetta. It was very difficult for those in the middle bench to find a polite place to put their knees.

"Scusi, signorina."

Carla tried to shift so that their knees were not directly touching.

"What a way to travel," the man in the bleached raincoat said.

"It's better than nothing."

"Not even a bus. Not even a trolley left."

"It's better than walking," the friend said. "Autoista," he called, "when does this thing move?"

"Pazienza," the driver said, with the wad of slightly unclean lire in his fist. "We'll go."

"He guarantees it," the man in the bleached raincoat said. "Look at that sack of money."

"A hand of gold," the friend said.

"Yes," the man in the raincoat said. "Behold the new millionaires."

Once, in the summer, Carla had gone to the farm of her Uncle Luigi in the mountains near Grosseto. There she had felt free. She had liked the hills and she had liked the marketplace in the town, and the town square full of men on a Monday morning. Mama said she dreamed her life away, but what life was not dreamed away? And what was there to a life without dreams? The imagination redeemed life. Without it, things sank into a stony nothingness: a wall was a wall, a street was a street. Things must have shadows and depths as well as sunlight. You do not know the world, darling, Grigorio said. Oh, what was the world? What was it they wanted her so much to accept? Dullness and hopelessness, that was the world. A camionetta in a dark piazza, that was the world. Benches on which the knees of strangers touched and were withdrawn. A man in his shirtsleeves counting his unclean money. Grigorio did not love her. He had said he did not love her. In some other country of impossibly tall buildings and doors which opened by electric eyes there was a woman to whom he was married. There was an ocean between them, but despite the ocean he was still married to her. She tried to imagine the other one: was she beautiful? Was she taller than she was? Did she have the clothes that she could not have? If she had such clothes, if her own country were not so poor, if she could make him understand the kind of fire that burned in her, he would fall in love with her.

There were so many places they could go if they were in love.

Paris. In Paris she was very much admired. They lived in a hotel with lace curtains on the windows. All day and all night they kept on the electricity. The rooms blazed with light. It was wonderful to have the rooms full of light.

T'amo, she said in the blazing light. T'amo per sempre.

New York. She gasped as they skyrocketed up the elevator. Ancora, ancora, she said. They rode down again in the elevator and then they rode up. It was wonderful in a city where the power worked. So many things in the restaurants. Gleaming silverware, white tablecloths. The meal began with little pastries. They were full of a yellow cream, and powdered with sugar. There was real coffee. May we have more? she said. There was no limit to the pastries one was permitted to eat. Grigorio insisted she take soup. You are like my mother, she said. I am like your mother, he said, but different. Over the bowl of chicken soup she said: T'amo. T'amo per sempre.

A pretty girl in red sandals and red elbow gloves climbed the ladder. She sat down at the very end of the bench by the tailgate. There was hardly any room at all now in the camionetta. The benches were all crowded, the knees were all interlocked. Opposite the girl in the red sandals and the red elbow gloves a dignified elderly gentleman tried to read a newspaper in the failing light. The girl with the red sandals glanced at her wristwatch and tapped the red polished handbag she carried. She was in a great hurry.

"Why doesn't he go?" she said. "What is he waiting for?"

The friend of the man in the bleached raincoat explained:

"He has to fill the camionetta, signorina."

"Fill it? But it's filled now."

"He doesn't think so."

The girl in the red sandals examined the condition of the camionetta. "Dio," she said, "where he will put more people? Look: they are in each other's laps now."

The driver leaned forward.

"Signori," he said. "Stringere un po'."

"Stringere!" the girl said. "But how can we squeeze? There is no place left to squeeze in."

"There must be twenty-two passengers," the driver said.

"Without twenty-two, signorina," the friend of the man in the raincoat said, "he doesn't budge an inch."

"Even if we were on our way to Paradise," a woman said across the aisle, "he would not start without his twenty-two passengers."

"Twenty-two," said the man in the raincoat, "at twenty lire. That's four hundred and forty-four lire a trip."

"Each way," his friend said.

"I forgot. That's right."

"Eight hundred and eighty-eight lire the complete voyage," the friend said.

"Eh, a profitable load to Paradise."

"Ti prego," the girl in the red sandals said to the driver. "Begin. I have an appointment."

"He'll wait," the driver said.

"I didn't ask your opinion," the girl said.

"Signori," the driver said. "Un po' stringere. There lacks still two places."

"Guarda," the girl said. "We're like cattle now."

"Scusi, signorina. But who is the driver, you or I? You want to drive? Go up front."

"Asino," the girl in the red sandals said, tapping her red pocketbook fretfully. The gentleman reading his newspaper permitted himself the slightest of pressures upon her stockingless knees.

"Scusi, signorina," the driver said. "But if you don't like my limousine, go ride in a taxi. There are taxis. Why upset yourself with my poor truck? Go ride in a taxi."

The girl in the red sandals flounced a little and bit her very pretty underlip.

"She has an appointment," the driver said. "Because she has an appointment, I have to go charging off with half a load. Listen to her! An appointment. With whom? The Pope is waiting on his knees to bless you? The king's only son?"

"Oh, go, go away," the girl said.

"I am an asino because I ask her to squeeze in a little and make a little room!"

"Save your speeches for the elections," the girl said. "Tomorrow there's a big meeting in the Piazza del Popolo."

"Per favore," the driver said furiously. "Non mi rompeva i co'l"

The girl flushed.

"Dirty mouth," she said.

"Dirty or clean," the driver said, "please! Don't tell me how to drive and don't break my balls." He walked off indignantly.

Silence and the fading light.

"Eh, dio," said the friend of the man in the bleached raincoat, "that was some buon viaggio."

The dignified gentleman pressed gently on the round anonymous knees.

Finally, two passengers climbed into the camionetta. There was a great deal of shifting. It appeared that if one did not breathe too strenuously or did not move one's legs there actually was room for two more passengers. The boy unpropped the ladder and hooked up the tailgate. "All right?" the driver called. "Si. Va!" the boy said, and swung himself up on the tailgate. The little truck shuddered and roared. A mechanical malaria shook all its springs and axles. Then, exploding fumes into the deepening twilight, it chugged slowly out of the piazza, bouncing the twenty-two passengers on the wooden benches. The boy, however, was not one of the musical assistants: he was one of the cigarette smoking ones.

Grigorio, Grigorio, Carla thought. They went together to the Piazza Clodio. There was a carnival. He wished to take her on the mechanical horses, but the horses were not running. He wished to ride with her on the Chute-the-chute, but there was no power. Only the games at which one threw quoits and the distorting mirrors were still capable of giving pleasure, but the distorting mirrors were not popular now. So they had sat, drinking vermouth, an aranciata for her, in a gelateria, and watched the soldiers and the girls.

Grigorio, Grigorio, Carla thought. The swallows flew from the chimney pots. Slowly she undressed. She wore a safetypin in her underclothes. She was ashamed. How thin you are, he said. So thin. We must fatten you up. We must make you fat and healthy. A pint of cream a day and then all the soldiers will turn around and stare at you when you walk down the street. Will you stare? How can I, when I am walking beside you?

Grigorio, Grigorio, Carla thought. They went to the opera. It was Tosca. Gigli sang. The soprano was traditionally big. Little Gigli knew it was a joke when he gave a small hop to kiss her: he smiled at the audience. They sat in the last row. There had been trouble about the seats. They had sold for the performance more tickets than there were seats. At the torture scene he laughed. Because of the red spotlight and Tosca singing to the governor. But it was not just to laugh at the suicide of Tosca although the leap from the castle was obviously no higher than three feet. She had killed herself because of love and the last aria was very beautiful. But he laughed at it.

Grigorio, Grigorio, she thought.

The camionetta rattled and shook. It was very difficult to rid oneself of the foreboding that at any given moment it would topple over, blow up or fall to pieces. Only absolute necessity held it together.

"Scusi, signorina," the man in the bleached raincoat said. He wriggled a bit. "It is very uncomfortable, isn't it?"

"Yes," Carla said.

"It is a sin, believe me, to make human beings ride like this."

Grigorio, Grigorio.

"If it would rain," said the friend, "at least there would be a good harvest."

"What has the rain to do with it? Even if there is rain how will they cultivate the fields? They are full of mines."

"That will be a job, clearing the mines."

"There will be a harvest all right," the man in the raincoat said. "A harvest of explosions. There are the magnetic mines, the bakelite ones, the glass, the cement, the wooden ones. One thing Italy has more than enough of: mines."

"Our problems," the friend said.

"Scusi, signorina," the man in the bleached raincoat said and readjusted himself again on the wooden bench.

Then one goes to a doctor, Carla thought. It is killed, taken out of one, the darkness comes in. No, she could not, she would not permit it. Even if he did not love her and she could not conquer the other woman on the other side of the ocean she would have the child as a memory. She would take it to Grosseto, there in the mountains. Uncle Luigi was kind. He was an old man who loved horses. He was kind; he understood her a little; he, too, hated the city. She would take the child there, in the moun-

tains. She would name him Grigorio. He would be very
beautiful and gifted. It would be a child of love, of passion,
and of sorrow. Such children are the gifted ones. They
would be together, she and the child, in the mountains.
She would teach him the names of animals and trees. She
would teach him music, only the great music. Uncle Luigi
was kind. He would take the child with him to watch the
communal harvester painted yellow and red and explain
how it worked. The golden chaff would dust his hair. He
would be strong. He would not be a bourgeois like the
rest of them, thinking only of safety and comfort. He
would love music and be an imaginative child. When he
grew up they would go together to Venice or to Genoa.
They would live near the sea. If he wanted to she would
let him be a sailor. Her father was a sailor. A sailor and a
prisoner.

Grigorio, Grigorio, she thought.

She would not go to a doctor. Grigorio would understand. She must make him understand.

It was quite dark now. The camionetta chugged through
the darkness. It wheezed, it labored, but it moved. Above
all, it moved. The miracle was in the moving. The boy sat
with his feet hanging over the tailgate and smoked his
American cigarettes. The heads, the faces of the twenty-
two passengers floated obscurely in the darkness. Her
shoulder, her hip touched despite herself another human
shoulder, another human hip. In the narrow aisle between
the benches her knees, too, touched.

He would say it was romantic. He would say it was because she was a romantic little girl. He would say what her
mother said, what Antonio said. He would say it better
and with more sympathy but in the end he would be saying only what her mother and what Antonio said. He

would say: no, give the child up, graduate from the Conservatory, marry the professor. I am a soldier: I have a wife: I will not see you again.

Never, never, never.

Non ti vedro piu. Non ti vedro piu.

Mai. Mai.

"What I think of sometimes," said the man in the bleached raincoat in the darkness, "is Europe without cities, without streets, without work. A desert of mountains and rivers full of dead bodies and broken tanks and empty burned plains. . . ."

"It is better not to think," the friend said.

"Asia is rich," the man in the raincoat said. "America is rich. But Europe is always poor."

"War," the friend said. "It's like cocaine; with it or without it the victim kills himself."

"It's not a question of war any more," the other said. "It's a question of a biscuit for breakfast and a can of sardines . . ."

How distant that ocean would be which would separate them. He would write. Then he would stop writing. The piano stood in a corner of the room, the vase on top of it, the music open. She sat and played. Mama came in and was satisfied she was practicing. Mama was in the thin green cotton kimono. Her face was thin; her hair was untidy; her hands were red. Outside the trees did not change, nor did the sky change. In the summer it was hot and the grass grew green again and again the shutters were closed against the sun. In the winter it was dark and cold. Only the light from the Virgin illuminated the hallway. She went up the stairs, she went down the stairs. She was a thin unimpressive little girl not yet eighteen in a brown dress with a white collar at the throat. She went down to the Tiber to walk near where the ship of the boys' naval club was. From the bridges they fished, but the fish were diseased. Under the bridges were the soldiers and the women of the soldiers. There were many murders, there were obscenities everywhere. Life was mottled and sick. There would be no letters. She would wait. She would say: he has forgotten. Now he will remember. Now he will write. But he would not write. He had promised but there would be the other woman. She could not conquer the other because of the marriage and because of the distance. She would fade perhaps slowly but she would fade. He would remember the swallows longer. He would remember the trees longer. She would become an invisible obligation. He would have nothing to say. The letters would be a burden. The other woman would have him both in bed with her and in his mind. There would be only Mama and Antonio. There would be the professore. They were eternal. They were eternal and dull like the trees and the grass. If she had a child. If she had. She went up and down the stairs. She was a thin unimpressive girl of perhaps not too great a talent dressed in a brown dress with a little white collar at her throat. The hallways were dark and the city was dark.

Non ti vedro piu. Non ti vedro piu.

Mai. Mai.

"In Europe," the friend said to the man in the raincoat, "nothing is believed without blood. Nobody believes in a cause unless they point to the blood as proof that it means something."

"But what does the blood prove?"

"Niente. It proves they have veins."

"What will be the end of it?"

"Who knows? Maybe we'll drown in the blood proving what great bleeders we are."

This was her city, tree-lined, splendid, lightless, sick. It was mortally sick. The stupid still hoped. Little dreams flickered up in their dead eyes, and then guttered and went out. The reality was the hopelessness.

The reality was Mama and Antonio.

The camionetta coughed, exploded, wheeled clumsily into the square and stopped. The assistant spit into the street, leaped off, and unhooked the tailgate. Then he propped the narrow ladder up against the hanging tailgate.

"L'ultima fermata," the assistant called.

The passengers unlocked themselves. Slowly. They began to descend. The dignified gentleman at last reluctantly withdrew his knees. The girl in the red sandals did not wait for the courtesy of the ladder but leaped off, holding her red handbag, and disappeared into the darkness. She was probably quite late. The driver came out from behind the wheel and kicked the tires of his vehicle. They were all still there.

"Careful, signori," the assistant said, giving each passenger as they descended his hand.

"Scusi, signorina," the man in the belted raincoat said. He extricated himself from the knees and went out, too. The friend followed.

Carla stood up and slid between the benches, smelling on the dark night the fumes of the exhaust pipe, thinking that no matter how far she traveled she would not ever now come close enough. The reality was the hopelessness. Grigorio, Grigorio, she thought.

T'amo. T'amo per sempre.

But the room, in Paris, would not blaze with light. There was darkness, the city was in darkness. The darkness was the reality.

"Careful, signorina."

She fell so that the ladder turning with her as she fell was beneath her and the upper part of the ladder was violently thrust into her stomach.

But the only sound she made in falling was a scream almost without meaning or fear.

PART THREE

The Defense

HE FELL ASLEEP in his cell with the small weak electric bulb burning and the Bible, opened, on his chest, and in his dream it appeared that once more he was in a courtroom, but it was a courtroom enormously enlarged and it was difficult to see exactly who the judges were.

He knew, however, that he was being judged, and that it was necessary for him to prepare some defense. The judges, whoever they were, would not interfere with his preparations and he would be allowed to call whatever witnesses he wished and to submit whatever testimony he thought favorable to himself. All the testimony would be carefully heard and the evidence submitted would be fairly judged in accordance with the laws by which this court abided. His feeling was that the session at which he was now present had been sitting for some time, for perhaps a longer time than he himself knew, and that no adjournment would be made or any recess called until he himself was satisfied with the procedure of the trial and felt that all the circumstances bearing upon his case had been fully presented. When he was satisfied there would be an adjournment and a recess during which a decision would be considered although he might not know the decision immediately. He understood that much was already known about him in this court; yet if he wished to, he was free to repeat any or all of the evidence already in possession of the court. His lips felt very dry and he wished desperately that those to whom he was to plead were visible.

"Excellency," he said, and then he paused. For he considered, on the basis of his limited understanding of the nature of the court, that it might be wiser and more politic to assume the authorities were plural and that the higher judiciary powers were divided.

"Excellencies," he therefore said.

Once more he paused and hesitated, for this did not seem altogether wise either; perhaps there was, after all, only one magistrate. A court of this importance might have, though it was difficult to be certain, only one judge.

So that, finally, he said: "Excellency," and began to speak.

He wished His Excellency to understand first, the sort of a man he was. It was necessary, before any subsequent evidence should be introduced, that his nature be understood.

"The public prosecutor, Excellency," he said, "declared this afternoon, and you may have heard, one is compelled to assume there is little you do not hear, that I was stupid."

He hesitated, licking his dry lips.

"It is true, Excellency: I am stupid. I am a stupid man."

Was he being heard? It was impossible to tell. And yet one had to assume that one was being heard.

"But there is a difference, Excellency, between being stupid and having a knowledge of one's own stupidity."

Was he being understood? It was very important that this question of his stupidity be understood.

"My stupidity, Excellency, was of another kind. It was

a heaviness. Inside me there was this heaviness, this lack of
something, always. Things reflected themselves in me with
only a feeble light. They shone dully and I did not respond.
It was not that I did not wish to respond; it was that I
could not respond, ever. It was difficult for me to feel or to
penetrate an existence that was not my own; a flower, an
animal, another being. It was not that I did not wish to be
curious; it was that I felt no curiosity. Yes, I would feel,
the way a slow and disfiguring bubble swells in the mud,
now and then a certain desire to know the nature of others;
for there was a knowledge, small and rudimentary, how
different we must all be and yet how alike; but it was too
difficult. There was my heaviness, and the bubble would
break. So that I was alone inside my nature, always. I told
myself: it was enough, and that this was my burden. I
moved about heavily; and in the end, I accepted this separation of myself from the others."

Had he made it clear? Yes, of course: it was not so difficult. Why should he assume he was more difficult to understand than others who had come here to be judged? It was
in the nature of this court that understanding was part of
the judging, and the sentence, since there must be a sentence, was involved with the laws of understanding.

He took the pocket handkerchief from his breast pocket
and wiped his slightly sweating hands.

His father. . . .

"You see, Excellency, when I was young, there, in that
village in the south, I knew that they thought I was both
stupid and morose. How was it possible for them to see
that lack of something which was in me and which condemned me to be what I was? Only my father perhaps understood, for I often think the heaviness was in him, too,
though less of the slowness which I had. So that, no matter

what I was, my father would say: he is my son. And besides, one is small and has an excuse in one's childhood for one's own impotence. One has a father who says: he is my son, and who accepts the responsibility for what one is."

And then the death. . . .

It had rained that day his father died and it was in the fall. That could be seen, of course: how it rained that day, and the terrible unreality of the hearse, the great frightening plumed horses, and himself, a child in that processional, among the relatives and the friends, seeing his mother's tears, hearing the lamentations of the relatives, and not quite believing, not quite understanding. And in the rain, the grave diggers, and the descent into the earth of the coffin, the slow unbelievable lowering, and then, his alienation.

For who was to say: he is my son, and I am responsible? Who?

"Is it not so, Excellency? Is that not what one wishes? Not to be responsible?"

The piazza. . . .

It was so much later, when the lowered coffin was almost forgotten, and he was already a man who had been a soldier and had killed; in the piazza, later, there had been the bleeding man. He had been very badly beaten. Even now he could remember quite distinctly that sensation of the blood of the man; for it was early then, when the question of the responsibility for the blood had not yet been entirely cleared up. In the war it had been different. In the war one assumed that others were responsible: the king, the general staff, the mystical nation. The dead in the mountains during the war were obviously not one's own responsibility, and besides, one was always in the war so near death oneself. It was only that soldiers did not like to see the man they shot fall. The falling was for a brief moment uncomfortable. But in the war it was different, and the responsibility was clearly theirs during the war, but here, in the piazza, the responsibility was not yet clear.

So the orator had to make it all clear.

They lived, he and the others, and the bleeding man, in a time of great historical change. History, the orator wished them to understand, was beyond good or evil, beyond scruples, beyond questions of conscience. The nation was the conscience. And since history, which demands of us only the noblest of acts, the greatest of devotions, the profoundest of loyalties, the most rigorous of disciplines, is born out of violence, the Party (a noi! a noi!) itself, that great instrument of history, would assume the responsibility.

Violence, a bleeding man, was necessary. The necessity, and the Party, absolved one. He saw that, did he not, His Excellency? It was not so difficult: it was not even unusual. Why should he be burdened with a guilt which was not even an unusual guilt?

Did not the Party say: I am responsible? And when they sang, did they not sing: *O Sons of Italy?* So that one was again a son and not responsible.

He knew that the court was probably not unaware of this argument. Perhaps, for a long time now, this had been the most frequent, the most common of all the defenses made here, and whatever extenuations were claimed by the accused, they were probably claimed on these grounds.

He felt more confident. This was, after all, no mystical plea. It was solid and factual and demonstrable. Certainly, it was known to all.

There had been, then, the night of the dossiers.

"Believe me, Excellency: I sat in my office with a heavy

heart. Yet what was I to do? You have heard how, on that evening, when I had received my instructions, I approached the Minister of the Interior. I questioned him. He was my superior and it was right that, in a moment of such great importance, I go to him and question him. And he replied: 'What can I do?' "

He paused.

"There was a moment, then, of panic," he said. "I remember it very exactly, that evening with the Minister of the Interior. He was, I remember, lying in that large, clean bed of his, and so much was at stake, and I had gone to him as my superior, and yet he replied: 'What can I do?'

"You see, Excellency? It was not the reply to make," he said. "I was the subordinate and he was the superior. If I were to accept his reply, that he, too, in reality, did not know what to do, then he also would become a subordinate. It was impossible. That is how our life is arranged: there is a dynasty of superiors to whom one is answerable, who give the orders and who accept the responsibility. That is how it must be. That is how we have arranged our lives. If, in a crisis, as this was, they deny they are the superiors, but are in reality only subordinates too, what shall the subordinates, who all their lives have been subordinates, do? It was a moment of great panic for me. For after so long a time, how was it possible for me to accept the knowledge that it was only subordinates who are in command of subordinates, and they are only made to appear as superiors?

"I was furious," he said. "He is a fat man, the Minister, and looking at his fatness and his cowardice I was almost driven to striking him.

"To lie there, in that hotel bed, and to dare to say at such time: 'What can I do?'

"I wanted to smash him.

"But I controlled myself. For you see, Excellency, he had no right to deny he was a superior. It was quite clear, our relationship: in the room, I was the subordinate. Because he was afraid, he wanted to climb down to my level. And I could not permit it. It was his place in the dynasty to take the responsibility and to free me. If both of us, in that room, were to be freed of the responsibility, then neither of us would be in reality freed: we would both be guilty. And it was his duty to take the responsibility."

He breathed deeply. That was how it had been that evening. It had required tremendous control, for he could not, now that all his life threatened to fall in upon him, allow the Minister to escape.

"So I insisted," he said. "I made it clear. I took the orders. He lay there, fat and asthmatic and frightened, and tried to shift out of it.

" 'What can I do?' he kept repeating. 'What can I say?'

" 'Give me the authorization,' I said."

" 'It is a terrible thing,' he said.

" 'Give me the authorization,' I said."

" 'So many,' he said. 'So many names. They will kill so many of them.'

" 'Give me the authorization,' I said."

"And finally he succumbed. He knew what corner I was forcing him into. But I would not let him escape. Had he not enjoyed the privileges of a superior? Now let him take some of the burdens. He squirmed. He would not say it directly. 'One must do as they say,' he said finally. It was a reluctant answer.

" 'Does that mean,' I said, 'that you are authorizing me to do as they want?'

" 'Yes,' he said.

" 'You are giving me the authorization,' I said.

" 'Yes,' he said, and I was triumphant. I had kept him a superior in spite of himself."

There remained then only one other point to be cleared up. Now he had come this far he did not think that what he intended to prove about the other point would be too difficult.

It was the question of the dead; the dead, and whatever justification they thought they had.

The witness who appeared then might have been a man of any age. It was hard to tell. The experience had been very trying, and his last moments had obviously been violent ones, and then they lose so many things once they leave: age, the particular features they once possessed, identifiable characteristics. There had been men of many varied occupations in the dossiers, and he could not distinguish which of these the witness himself had once followed. By his erectness he might have been one of the executed army officers, though some of the young men who had been shot had also been excellent athletes, so that the erectness might have belonged to either. Then, again, he might not have been an army officer or one of the young athletes; there had been printers shot, and lawyers, as well, and several students; it was difficult to know. He knew that the witness seemed very erect, that he was featureless, that the clothes he wore had suffered terribly, and that the stains on the clothes were earth, and that the smell was that of the earth, too.

Curiously, he seemed to hear:

—Your name?

—I have none now.

—Occupation?

—It is no longer important.

—Did you know the accused?

—Yes.

—When?

—When he compiled the list from the dossiers, I was on that list.

His witness. If he were to achieve some sort of acquittal, this was the moment. He understood that he was free to ask what questions he wished, make whatever point he thought necessary, regardless of the relevancy.

To the witness then, he said:

"Signor, what would you have done were you in my place on the night when the orders were given to me? What would you have done were you the Questore of the city, and if you had been summoned, as I was, and compelled, as I was, because of my position, to do?"

The witness looked at him, and the court, at that moment, seemed full of a formidable silence.

—I am not you, the witness said.

"But what would you have done?" he insisted.

—I am not you, the witness said. I could not have been you.

"But you envied me," he said. "Can you deny you envied me? I was rich. I had power. I was safe. You envied these things. You, too, wanted them. To have them you would have done, and been forced to do, what I did."

The witness did not answer.

"Then you would have been me," he said, "if you had had these things. It is terrible to be poor, it is terrible to be ignored. What we do we do because of our natures and because it is terrible to be poor and to be ignored. No one foresees what he will be compelled to do eventually because of these things. No one knows. No one can say this would not have been forced upon me. So I would have acted, so I would have behaved. Who knows what horror they will eventually become the innocent authors of? Or how the small unhappiness of a childhood may in time become the huge crime of the man? For, as you might have been me, I might have been you. I, too, might have stood in the cave, in that darkness, and known, as you did, that smell of the earth, and heard, interrupting my prayers and my terror, the machine guns, and fallen, as you did, among the already fallen.

"Ah, signor," he said, "that is the penalty of being human: there is nothing one can say one is not capable of, or anything one can say one might not have been."

He waited.

Then reluctantly, forcing it from himself:

"Even such a crime. Even what I did."

The court must have waited, too, as he did, intensely for the answer, and yet the court must have known what the answer would be even before it was given.

—I was not you, the witness said. I could not have been you.

And vanished

Again he was alone.

The answer was bewildering, at first, for it was not an answer he had expected, or the nature of which he entirely grasped; but he understood, after the answer, that it implied that judgment on him was inevitable. Even though the substance of his crime was unclear to him, and it was difficult, imprisoned as he was inside himself, to feel any genuine guilt, and even though it seemed that he must go on and on explaining and explaining himself until at last the court understood, after the answer of the witness it was obvious that judgment was inevitable.

They would hold him responsible for the dead.

Panic and terror seized him. Was one to be held at last responsible here? Had he, all his life, calculated wrongly, and did they here, these cold and immovable and silent judges, hold one finally responsible? He found himself sweating, and his heart constricted, as though it were being squeezed, for it was impossible for a man to come finally before a court such as this, and accept whatever he had done, in a long and violent life, as something done out of his own choice and with the exercise of his own will. It was not just; it was not true. The court understood that; the court must understand that.

The darkness was hostile and condemnatory; he sank down upon his knees, because of his fear, and it seemed to him he had never been more alone in his life. Holy Mary, full of grace, he said; and then he imagined he heard music, a music announced by measured trumpets; and then vapors drifted across the darkness. Light, like turned jewels, flashed, and while he knelt, contrite and desperate, it seemed to him a splendid retinue, full of the glitter of benevolent power, bringing with it a music of boys' voices, entered; and there, borne in a golden sedan, mitred and merciful, hugely forgiving, he saw the Blessed Vicar, and he said, out of the agony of his uncertainty (for he knew he was lost) and his fear (for he could not endure the weight of the meaning of his own life) —

"Forgive me, Father."

"Intercede for me."

"Absolve me of my sins."

The golden chair shook. Purely the voices of young boys sang. The censers flung their sweet smoke. Low, solemnly, the ecclesiastical orders chanted.

Then the Holy Father (what remembered face was that? what gesture, out of the past?) leaned, blessed him, forgiving him, and called him: My son. Trembling, he held out a rosary, and that, too, was blessed, and he pressed it to his lips, tasting his tears.

Absolution, like a cloud, spread through the darkness, now luminous and shot with the glint of papal jewels. The enormous weight of his own life lifted. He wept against the rosary.

And heaven opened: there, rank upon rank, with all their transfigured faces, stood the blessed armies of the subordinates, each forgiven identically, each washed clean of his sin, each at last having transferred the burden of his humanity to the Son, and each, while choirs sang and doves plunged through the humming air, celestially and eternally authorized.

Music flew heavenward triumphantly.

And in the cell he slept, the Bible upon his chest, upon his lips a rapt and rather foolish smile, while beyond the bars of his prison the drab human morning slowly broke.

The Liberated City: III

I REMEMBER (I had left her hotel and we had had another argument) that as I was coming down the Corso (it was incredible how dark the city could be) this infantryman came out of a doorway and he was pretty tight. It was midnight.

Where did a guy, he said, find a girl this time of night?

I said it was pretty late.

He said it was his first day in town and he had a three-day pass and his brother had been killed in a town I don't remember the name of now. It was a town up north.

I said I'd only been up north as far as Siena.

He said he'd been in Siena, too.

He said there were too many Frenchmen in Siena. He said the Frenchmen were telling the girls in Siena all the Americans had a disease and the girls wouldn't date the Americans.

Then he said where could he find a girl this time of night?

I said it was late. I said it was tough finding a girl this

time of night. I said there was still a midnight curfew in this town and most of the girls were off the street by this time but maybe if he went down around the Galleria he could find somebody and I told him to watch out for the MP's because a new outfit from Algiers had come up to do duty in Rome and they were bastards, the Algiers MP's.

He said he had been with the Third when they took Rome. I asked if he remembered how the Third had done MP duty and then when the orders came through to get the girls out of the jeeps because there were too many of them riding around in jeeps, the boys from the Third used to go up to the girls and say (it was the early days): come on, baby, walk. We walked up here from Anzio.

He didn't remember that.

He went down the street toward the Galleria and I remember he said his brother had been killed right next to him in some town I don't remember the name of now. But it was a town up north.

Pollard

SOMEBODY WAS playing the piano. Pollard thought: I know that tune. What is it? I know that tune but I can't remember it now.

He ought to dance. He ought to get out of this chair and dance. Eddie had brought him to the party, and now that he was at the party he ought to dance. Whose party was it? Somebody was always giving a party. Whoever was playing the piano was playing it in the Milan room. Pollard closed his eyes: what was it they had told him about the house in which they were giving the party? Ah, yes, the rooms. Murals, the rooms had beautiful murals, and each room was painted like another Italian city. Somebody had taken him through the rooms when he had come with Eddie, and had said: "Wonderful idea, isn't it, Captain? The whole house, you see, is really Italy. This is Milan: there's the Duomo and that glassed-in thing is the famous Galleria. Have you been in Florence, Captain? A lovely city, The war has spoiled it but it was a lovely city once. Yes, that's the Arno. And Naples, do you recognize it? You've been in Naples, I suppose? So many soldiers now in Naples, aren't there? But isn't the bay magnificent? Do you know Shelley wrote a poem about it? Shelley, yes; no, no—Ode to a Nightingale is Keats, I think. He's buried here in Rome, you know."

Was he? That was nice for Keats. To be buried here in Rome. Well, he was too, he was having a nice military burial right here in Rome.

Then, in one of the rooms, perhaps it was the Sorrento one, the wall showing the summer villas and the sea, there had been surprisingly Dr. Wu, still in the cutaway Pollard had seen him wearing at lunch, the wing collar, and holding a cocktail in his hand.

"Ah, Captain Pollard," the little elegant Chinaman said. "And where is your amusing young lady, Captain?"

My amusing young lady, Pollard thought. I hate my amusing young lady.

"She is so funny," Dr. Wu said. "Did you bring her to the party? Is she here?"

"No," Pollard said. "She's in bed."

"In bed?" said the Chinaman. "But so soon?" Amusing young ladies did not go to bed in China, Pollard guessed, when there were parties. "She is too amusing to go to bed so early. How lonesome for her," Dr Wu said.

"She's got company," Pollard said. "She's got a husband to keep her from getting lonesome."

"Ah?" Dr. Wu's diplomatic eyebrows went up. "Her husband?"

"That's right, doctor. That's what all amusing young ladies have."

"What a pity," Dr. Wu said. "It is such a fine party."

With his eyes closed, in the chair, hearing the piano, Pollard wondered whose house this had been, and who had painted all the cities in it, and what city the bedroom was.

Another party, another requisitioned house. He opened his eyes to see what city he was in. Those white temples, the dust, that partly ruined villa with the portico and the dry marble pool, he knew that place, he had been there once. Of course: Pompeii. He was in Pompeii.

He got up from the chair. He supposed whoever had built the house had liked the idea of journeying from Sorrento to Milan walking from the kitchen to the sitting room. Pompeii, he was in Pompeii again. It had been a hot afternoon in Pompeii and there hadn't been really much to see, a rut in the stone a chariot had made or was supposed to have made, a section of broken wall that had once been, or was supposed to have been, a baker's shop. You couldn't really tell any more. Flies, broken walls, a column, a shallow amphitheater, and a hot and not too interesting afternoon, that had been Pompeii.

He wished he could remember the tune. He was forgetting too many things. He probably couldn't give a fire order correctly any more; that too, the giving of fire orders, seemed so long ago. He straightened his shoulders; ah, yes, Colonel Lakewell explaining how to march. "On the balls of your feet, men, on the balls of your feet." To the left, march, Pollard said, and it pleased him that he could still execute a left flank. Captain Pollard to the right, march, and there had been such congratulations from home when he had come out of Fort Benning, an officer, a success, and Mother was so pleased, it was as though he had just been promoted head salesman, and he knew everything in the manuals then, fire orders, business about the junior officer and the senior officer, the articles of war, close order drill, to the left, march, to the right, march, to the rear, march, and somebody said: "Oh dear—watch out!"

"Excuse me," Pollard said.

"Take it easy, old man," whoever it was said. Pollard tried to see who it was: some second lieutenant. Well, he ranked him, though he probably had qualities of leadership too. That's what they all had, qualities of leadership. It seemed to Pollard he was thinking perfectly clearly so that he wasn't actually tight. It was just a certain difficulty he was having seeing and walking.

"Excuse me," Pollard said, and sat down. He thought he ought to sit down a little. Afterwards he would get up and dance. He would pick one of the rooms to dance in, Milan, Florence, Naples, Rome: there was a nice choice of cities.

"Are you wet?"

"No. But I do hate clumsy people."

They went away. Good-bye, Pollard said, ta-ta; I hate to see you go. He closed his eyes again. It was raining, and in the rain he was on a hill in North Carolina lecturing on flat trajectories. It was idiotic being in the rain but the schedule called for thirteen to fourteen hundred hours flat trajectories on this hill, and he lectured, the rain falling. So many places he had been, and too quickly. There were all sorts of odd things coming back tonight: flat trajectories, a little fifteen-year-old Arab girl in an embroidered vest in a house in Algiers, the night he had been lost in Foggia. By God, he had been around, he had traveled, he'd seen the world, hadn't he, in four years? And survived. Four years out of his life, but he had survived. Men died, as they must be dying now in the mountains below Bologna, but he didn't die. He sat in an office behind a broad flat desk in the Piazza Venezia and every day the chances were better that he would not die at all in this war. He sat there in the chair thinking of his surviving and of Antoinette, and it looked like it was going to be the longest night of his

life; how was he going to beat a night as long as this? He
ought to dance. He ought to get tanked up and dance.
There must be somebody at the party he knew beside Eddie and Dr. Wu. Lois, he remembered how he had tried
in the Albergo to make Lois. He had tried to give Lois the
business because Antoinette was giving him the business.
He was certainly showing leadership tonight, Pollard
thought painfully.

"Do you like dawgs?"

He opened his eyes.

"Dogs?"

Whoever she was, in the uniform, standing near him
talking, her legs were too thick. But she was American.
Now that he thought of it there was a hell of a lot of thick
legs going around in uniforms these days. He ought to try
one of these female soldiers some day. Somebody said once,
he couldn't remember who, that it was like going to bed
with a lady cop.

Exaggerated. He'd seen a pretty Wac once.

"Ah like dawgs. Hound dawgs. Always had a dawg round
the house back home."

"I sort of like cats a little."

"Cats? Well now, a cat never gets to love you the way a
dawg will. Kick hell out of a dawg he'll go right on lovin'
you if he's yours."

That's right, Pollard thought, making an effort to sit up,
dawgs and women. Women weren't dogs, women were cats.
Didn't follow then if women were cats. CO once, where
was it? At Benning, yes; dog barked at him when he was
dressing up the company. CO went after the mutt and
tried kicking his ribs in because dog barked at him
when he was giving the company dress right dress. And the
mutt howling off into the night with maybe a rib broken.

Dress right dress. Hup, hup, come on, Pollard: off your tail. You poor doublecrossed drunken bastard whose girl is with her own true married love. Hup, hup: up you go. If Mother could see you now.

There were, it seemed to him, all sorts of unidentifiable people in and out of uniform standing around in chummy knots, with drinks, or sitting down on chummy sofas and loveseats or in front of chummy pianos. He listened, mostly because she was very good-looking, to a tall blonde Yugoslavian wearing her hair braided in a yellow coronal, describing how and with what difficulties she had fled across the Adriatic with different kinds of peasants belonging to Marshal Tito very close behind her while she fled. The war, it was very terrible, but Pollard thought war or no war, when you were constructed like she was you would just do a lot of running naturally. She was with a major now so that, evidently the running was being postponed. He heard, somewhere, and very briefly, in one of the rooms, an Italian voice saying: "Che bugia!" Then an American accent saying: "What's a bugia?" Then the Italian: "Liar. You very beeg liar. Grandissimo." A thin tall girl was looking at the murals.

"I'm sure it's Pompeii," the thin tall girl said. "It looks just like Pompeii."

"Well, it could be Herculaneum," the officer with her said. "That's a ruin, too."

"No, it's Pompeii, I'm sure."

"Oh, Captain," the officer said. "What is this, Pompeii or Herculaneum?"

"Pompeii," Pollard, the expert, said.

"There," the thin tall girl said.

"Did you go into that house in Pompeii?" the officer said. "The one with the pictures on the walls."

"Of course," the girl said. "Practically everybody goes to Pompeii for the pictures, don't they?"

"I'll bet you blushed," the officer said.

"Darling," the thin tall girl said. "Don't be absurd. I haven't blushed since I went into the little boys' room in public school by mistake."

"What did you do?"

"I compared notes, sweet," the thin tall girl said.

The officer laughed. Pollard could see she was one of the amusing young American ladies, too, the kind Dr. Wu liked so much. Antoinette's kind of an amusing young lady.

"My God," the thin tall girl said. "But they really did have tremendous things in those days, didn't they?"

Then, somewhere, it could have been the Florence room, there was a colonel saying: "We were in there before the infantry. Infantry was still six or seven kilometers from the city when we drove in."

"Were you frightened, Colonel?"

"Frightened? Ma'am, if anybody tells you he wasn't frightened, he's lying. And I'm lying."

A bluff colonel. Played end for West Point. They all played end for West Point. West Point or Notre Dame, and they were always in there before the infantry. That, and it was very fashionable now to say you were frightened. Honest stuff: you were doing it for blueberry pie and you admitted you were frightened. Nobody believed in heroes any more, outside of the citation writers, so now all the modest heroes said they had been frightened. Pollard waited for one of them to say that, ma'am, he wasn't only frightened, he was paralyzed. He ate dirt he was so scared, he wet his drawers and he had tried to dig his way like a rat into the earth with his fingernails he was so scared, then maybe he would believe them. But that wasn't being modestly frightened. None of them would say that because that wasn't fashionable at all. Not at West Point it wasn't, and not at Notre Dame either.

Pollard, walking with great care, went into the Rome room, and at the sandwich table there was a girl eating sandwiches. Somebody had been through a mess sergeant's kitchen and had carried half of it away. The army white bread had been cut down to canape size, the crust removed, and spam, sardines, cheese and ham had been spread on the bread. A big plate of boneless chicken out of a can was on the table beside the sandwiches. The girl eating at the table was not American. She wasn't anywhere near as good-looking as the Yugoslavian who had had such trouble with Tito's peasants. As a matter of fact, Pollard didn't think the girl at the sandwich table was good-looking at all. She was eating the sandwiches very quickly. If Pollard had not come in then and stood beside her at the table she would probably have gone through a considerable number of the sandwiches since the room was almost deserted. She gave Pollard, because he was a captain and an American, a smile which managed to be at the same time timid, inviting and apologetic. She even hesitated in her eating. Pollard smiled at the girl. The murals showed the piazza of Saint Peter's, the gold dome, the enormous horseshoe of the double colonnade, and the twin fountains in the square.

"Hello," Pollard said. "Are they good sandwiches?"

"Bonissimo," the girl said.

"Why don't you have some more?" Pollard said. "Why don't you have a lot of sandwiches?" He picked a handful up from the plate and piled them carelessly into the girl's hands.

"Oh, no, Capitano, grazie," the girl said.

"Go on," Pollard said. "Have a sandwich. Have a couple of sandwiches."

"But they will look at me," the girl said.

"Why will they look at you, Tina?"

"I am not Tina," the girl said.

"Maria," Pollard said.

"No, no. Anna," the girl said.

"Anna?" Pollard said. "Anna what? Anna Maria or Anna Louisa or Anna Banana?"

"Solo Anna."

"How is your father's palazzo, Anna?"

"What?" Anna said. "My father has no palazzo."

"He has a big palazzo," Pollard said. "He's a prince and he has a big palazzo."

"Oh, no," Anna said. "My father is an electrician. I have the guarda di roba in the Teatro Nazionale."

"The what?"

"Where are left the coats."

"Oh," Pollard said. "A check girl."

"Si."

"Do you like people, Anna?"

"Che vuol dire 'people'?"

"La gente."

"Oh. Si. Un po'."

"People," Pollard said. "Do you know the trouble with people?" He leaned forward, toward her, confidentially. "They're alive," he said, and blew into her ear.

"No, no," Anna said. "You must not do that."

"Why don't we go into the garden?" Pollard said. "There must be a giardino in the joint. A beautiful giardino."

"Si. C'è uno."

"Let's go into the garden," Pollard said, "where all the people are dead."

She hesitated. Chicken, and formaggio and pane lay on the table before her. Pollard saw her looking unhappily at the table, and said: "Come on Anna banana. Here, we'll put the sandwiches into a piece of paper." He picked up an enormous number of the canape-sized sandwiches.

Anna giggled. "Oh, no, Capitano. We will be seen."

"Oh, the colonel's fat enough," Pollard said. "He needs a good diet. Come on. We'll go into the beautiful giardino and you can tell me how your father fixes the electricity."

In the garden, there was a stone bench under the trees. Pollard said: "Anna, Anna, Anna. Did you like the party, Anna?"

"Si."

"Did you dance?"

"No."

"How old are you, Anna?"

"Ventitre."

"Are you married, Anna?"

"Si. Sono sposata."

"That's good," Pollard said. "I'm glad to hear you are sposata. Girls named Anna should be sposata. What do you think of the war, Anna?"

"Terriblè."

"And the Americani?"

"Sono carina."

"And Roma?"

"Città bella."

"That's right," Pollard said. "Now we've covered the three important topics in Italy: the war is terrible, the Americans are cute, and Rome is bella. Shall I show you a trick?"

Pollard took a five hundred lire note from his pocket. "You watch now," he said. "I'll make this disappear." He tucked the five hundred lire note down the bodice of her dress, between her not very impressive breasts.

"No, no," Anna said.

"Don't you like the trick?" Pollard said

"No, no."

"All right," Pollard said. "I'll take it out." He put his hand into her dress, and said: "It's lost," and began to search for it.

"No, no," Anna said. "Oh, you are bad," and took his hand away.

She smiled at him in the darkness placatingly, because she did not want him to be offended. After all, he was a captain. She did not know what the influence of this capitano might be in the villa where there was so much food on the table. It had seemed to her such a pity, inside, that so much of the bread with the meat on it had been bitten into and then left, half devoured, on the plate. Now this funny capitano, who was so drunk, had taken her into the garden, and she did not wish to offend him. The sandwiches in the paper they had brought were on the bench beside her. He was an American capitano and later she hoped she would be able to wrap several of the sandwiches in the paper and take them home with her to the children. She thought, too, that if she told him about the difficulties of her life he might be moved to some sympathy with her which would make her stay in the garden with him a simple and profitable conversation interrupted by perhaps simple kisses. She had, these days, because of the difficulties at home, so little appetite for love.

So not to offend him then, she leaned forward and kissed the funny and drunken capitano. But it was a hurried kiss, and she was preoccupied with the thought of the sandwiches so close to her on the bench.

"That's no way to kiss," Pollard said. "What does your husband say when you kiss him like that?"

"My husband," Anna said. "My husband sleeps and plays cards."

"Doesn't he kiss you?"

"Ah, Capitano, you do not know what my house is like," Anna said in a flat, querulous voice. "I do everything, I myself. If I did not work in the guarda di roba the children would go hungry."

"What children?" Pollard said.

"My children," Anna said. Pollard heard both her voice, and the voices in the garden, the grass and the tree voices, and her voice was the complaining and lamenting one. He slept all day, her husband. Why should he get out of bed, he said, when there was no work? Everything, the capitano should understand, was on her shoulders.

"Yes," Pollard said. "Yes."

It was like that since the war, since he, the husband, had come back from the army. Seven years they were married, and she was sixteen when she was married, and the children, did the capitano know what it was when the children, the bambini, the little ones, cried because in the house there was no food? The garden was dark, and Pollard, listening, heard her voice full of complaints and full of dreariness. Antoinette, Lois, and now this one, he was really picking them today. Who cared how many kids she had? They weren't his kids. He didn't come out into the garden to talk about her bambini. A voice full of dismal unhappiness. Shut up, Pollard thought. Why don't you shut up? You and your tough luck stories, shut up, Pollard thought, sitting on the bench beside her in the dark garden.

"Come here," Pollard said. "You're a mile away."

She wasn't even pretty. The cheekbones stood out in her face and she had a sort of timid niceness. But she complained too much. He wished he had the Yugoslavian in the garden. He would wind up in a garden listening to a tough luck story. The ring around a rosie was starting again.

"Come here," Pollard said. "I'll show you how a husband kisses his wife in America."

"Eh, l'amore," Anna said.

"That's right," Pollard said. "L'amore Americano."

Anna smiled at him again with that wavering uncertain mask of friendliness upon her face, and when Pollard took her in his arms she kissed him submissively. He felt her mouth dry and unmoving under his, and when he put his hand upon her breast, the breast was small, unshaped and flabby.

He took his mouth away.

"That's not how you make real love," Pollard said. "In Italy I thought you knew how to make real love."

"All the Americani think of," Anna said, "is love, love, love."

"That's right," Pollard said. "Love, love, love."

Once again Anna did her best to imitate, although she had no desire for it, the actual passion of a kiss, only to feel Pollard force her mouth open.

"No, no," Anna said, trying to take her mouth away.

"Yes," Pollard said.

"No, ti prego, I cannot," Anna said. "Ti prego, Capitano. E impossibile."

If someone were to come into the garden. Well, what if someone were to come into the garden? It was a dago girl and she checked coats and they might look faintly disgusted not only because it was a trifle public and there might possibly be an American girl around.

Pollard bent Anna backward on the stone bench, saying: "Fight, baby. Go on, fight me. I love it when they fight me."

Anna squirmed and fought.

"Capitano," she said. "Per favore. I cannot."

"Yes you can," Pollard said.

"No, ti prego. I cannot. You do not know. I cannot. Ti prego, Capitano. Dio. Oh, Dio."

"That's right," Pollard said. "Beg me, baby. Beg me."

Nobody came into the garden. From the villa whoever it was playing the piano continued to play lightly that tune he knew he had heard somewhere before.

He moved away from her.

"Anna," he said.

She moaned in the darkness, her hair loose, and the skirt showing the thin thighs against the stone.

"Get up," Pollard said. "All the blood will go to your head. Get up, Anna."

Then he saw that he had forced her backwards down upon the sandwiches, and that they had been crushed under her. He put them together for her again in the newspaper.

"Here, Anna," he said. "Don't forget the sandwiches."

She took them.

"You are so bad," she said. "Oh, you are so bad."

"You shouldn't have said no, no," Pollard said.

"Capitano," Anna said. "You like me?"

"Sure," Pollard said.

"Un po'?"

"Un po'," Pollard said. "Now you better go on into the house. I'll stay here. Go on. I want to stay in the garden a while."

She came close to him.

"Oh, you are molto cattivo," she said. "But sometime,

you will come see me? You will take me with you to the hotel?"

"What about your husband?"

"My husband. My husband sleeps and plays cards."

"All right," Pollard said. "I'll take you to the hotel sometime."

"Dancing?" Anna said. "It is so long I have not danced. You will take me to the hotel and we will dance?"

"Sure," Pollard said. "Sometime. Now go on into the house."

"Un bacio prima."

"No."

"Uno!"

Pollard kissed her. "Go on," he said. "Go on into the house now. Don't forget the sandwiches."

She went across the garden, under the dark trees, toward the lit villa, holding the newspaper parcel of sandwiches. Pollard watched her go. If it had to be somebody it should have been the Yugoslavian. He took his handkerchief and wiped his mouth, carefully. He turned and went under the trees along a gravel path in the garden until he came to the big iron gate of the villa. He opened the gate and went out into the street.

The city was incredibly dark.

As he walked it seemed to Pollard that he no longer knew who he was. They had clipped his hair short, squared his shoulders, put him behind a desk in the Piazza Venezia and he was supposed to represent something. But he forgot what it was he was supposed to represent. All he knew right now was that he hated it. He hated this street, with no lights, these buildings, full of alien windows, he hated the darkness of Europe.

I want to go home, he said, as he walked blindly through

the empty and echoing streets, I want to go home.

He was twenty-six years old. Mother had always kept the bedsheets so clean and for breakfast there had been wheatena. He had been blown up in Africa. When the war was over he was going to live an entirely different life. He knew it, he knew exactly the kind of a different life he was going to live after the war was over. He walked through the city, street after street, and now and then as he stumbled he would hold to the wall of some shrouded building waiting until the nausea passed away. His girl, Captain Pollard said, feeling depths of pity for himself opening in him, his girl was with another man who happened to be her husband, and he had gotten a deal. The war was still on but he was not in the war any more. He was finished with the war. He would just rot here in Rome behind a desk. He was twenty-six years old. He would be twenty-seven years old. He would be twenty-eight years old. The only thing that would happen to him would be he would rot and he would grow older. Antoinette. I hate your guts, Antoinette, Pollard said very distinctly to nobody at all in the dark, shrouded and empty streets.

The little hill close by the Colosseum is the Celio. Pollard did not know this nor did he know that it was on this hill Marcus Aurelius had had his villa. Had he known he might not have thought of it with any particular irony. He was to remember the hill not because Marcus Aurelius had had a villa on it at all. He was to say later, when he spoke of it, along with his speaking of the time he had been blown up and of the little Arab girl of fifteen whose breasts were naked under the open embroidered vest, that here one night when he was very drunk and when a girl he knew in Rome he thought he was in love with (it turned out later he wasn't at all, it was just one of those things that happen in a war) had had her husband show up and there had been a hell of a mess because of it, that here, suddenly, by the Colosseum, in the darkness—

They jumped him. Italians, of course. There must have been a couple of them. He couldn't tell. One of them slugged him, hard, possibly with a blackjack, and that was all Captain Pollard remembered except that suddenly he knew what tune it was the piano had been playing. *It's so easy to remember but so hard to forget.* An old Rodgers and Hart tune from way back. Then he went out, and that was all he knew about it, until they found him the next morning lying completely naked on the street near the Colosseum in Rome, Italy.

Giorgio

ONCE MORE, as in the morning when his day had begun and before he had thought of trusting himself to the charity of Mario La Pina, Giorgio sat on a flat stone and heard around him the voices of other men. A fire made of twigs and grass burned on the wet ground. Except for the fire, it was very dark now, and in the dark there were the shapes of many ruins. The fire was burning down behind what had once been the senate house in the Forum, and behind the men around the fire there was the big square mass of an old triumphal arch. The figures of chariots and soldiers and of the emperor Severus Septimius carved on the arch were now obscured. Broken stones and the sections of old columns which had once supported the imperial buildings lay in the dark wet grass. When Giorgio had come toward the men, having seen the small fire, a voice had asked:

"Chi è?"

"Io," he had replied.

"What sort of answer is that?" the voice had said from about the fire. "You ask who it is and he says I. Who is I?"

"Io," Giorgio said, coming into the light of the fire. "Giorgio."

"Ah," the voice said. "The cicerone. Come va, cicerone?" Then Giorgio had seen that it was Emilio, still with the stick he had carved in the morning at the Colosseum, and still with the amused and arrogant look upon his face, squatting down by the fire.

"This is Don Francesco," Emilio said, indicating the man with the partly bald head who also squatted by the light. "And that one," he said, pointing to a broad-shouldered man who was digging in the grass, "is Vito."

It was very late. On the streets there were only drunken soldiers, and the carabinieri, armed, and in patrols of three, guarded the darker alleys. The military vehicles swept the city abruptly with their headlights. The shops were all shuttered. Maddalena would again worry, Giorgio knew, and it was time that he went home, and yet he could not go home again. It was a day that would never end for him. He had gone to Mario La Pina and he had humiliated himself. He had begged for his old job. But they had thrown him out of the Tivoli. He did not belong there with the millionaires of the borsa nera and the conquistadori. His old life had finished and there was no new one to take its place. Let Maddalena worry; at least, here, in the darkness, there were others like himself.

From the Forum there came the sound of someone laughing. Giorgio looked into the darkness. The laughter seemed to come from among the circle of columns of a little temple.

"Who is it?" he asked.

"A woman," Emilio said. "Who else would laugh? She's doing business probably. There, where the vestals had their temple."

"With who?" Giorgio said. "A soldato?".

"Who else comes down for love to the Forum at night?

Everybody else is married or knows the address of a good casino. The soldier takes it where he can."

Emilio poked at the fire with his stick.

There was a movement again in the darkness around them, and a face emerged at the edge of the light, hovering there among the standing stones, and Giorgio, startled, said:

"Chi è?"

"Let him alone," Emilio said. "It's the Maestro." He called: "Buena sera, Maestro."

The eyes flickered in the strange face, and Giorgio saw the thin bearded jaws move. He could see a long black coat that hung from the Maestro's shoulders, a muffler wound about the scrawny throat.

"Eh . . . eh . . ." the face said.

"Tell me, Maestro. What said Santa Caterina?" Emilio called.

"Eh . . . eh . . ."

"What said the good saint?" Emilio called again.

"Eh . . . eh . . ." and the face retreated again into the darkness from which it had emerged.

"Why do you ask him what Santa Caterina said?" Giorgio asked.

"Listen. You'll hear."

Where the broken columns lay and the bushes grew around the floors of the old basilicas they could hear the bearded Maestro moving. Then Giorgio heard a voice, cracked and thin and obsessed: "And Santa Caterina said give him a piece of bread. Can you not see the man is hungry? Eh . . . eh . . ."

Giorgio listened.

"And Santa Caterina said . . ."

It went away.

"Would you believe it?" Emilio said. "The Maestro knew eight languages once. He guided the King of the Belgians through the baths of Caracalla. They say he could pick up a stone and reconstruct the whole history of the Empire from it."

The woman laughed invisibly again in the ruined temple.

"All night he wanders in the Forum," Emilio said. "Nobody knows where he sleeps or what he eats. He must remember still something from Santa Caterina for that is all anyone ever hears him say now."

"Amici," Vito, the broad-shouldered one, called. "Come here. There is something to see."

"What?"

"Come here."

They went to where Vito crouched. "Look," he said, pointing. Emilio, Giorgio and Don Francesco looked, and there, his fur up and his back arched, was a hissing tomcat, and hearing a squealing in the grass, the men looked more closely and saw in the grass three large rats. "Look how big they are," Vito said. "Did you ever see rats that size?"

"Where did they come from?" Don Francesco said.

"The sewers or the Tiber. They're the biggest I've seen."

The hissing tomcat flattened out, the tail moving slowly and menacingly.

"Look at him," Vito said. "The tiger."

"But look at the rats, "Don Francesco said. "They don't run. Look how fat they are. There must be plenty to eat in the Tiber."

"A German or two must be on the bottom still."

"The one you pushed off the Ponte Milvio?" Emilio said.

"Who said I pushed one?" Vito said.

"Everybody says they pushed one," Emilio said. "First

they stabbed him and then they pushed him into the Tiber. In this city even the bambini claim they killed a German."

Giorgio watched the cat. It went forward, slowly, like a miniature tiger, through the grass, flicking its tail, the green illuminated eyes full of a cold fire, and the rats, squealing, moved excitedly about in the grass, their naked tails dragging. But they did not run. They squealed and they moved about, butting each other in their anxiety. They did not seem to look at the cat.

"Some rats," Vito said.

The cat jumped so quickly the men did not see her preparations for the spring. A violent treble squealing flew into the air. It was something to see. To Giorgio, the rats were more terrible than the cat. The cat made incredible leaps. The cat twisted about in the air as he clawed. The rats were awkward. They were fat and heavy and when they jumped they seemed to heave themselves at the cat. There was a furious amount of spitting and the treble squealing. It is against nature, Giorgio thought. It is against nature for rats to be fighting with such passion. What did the Tiber breed now that such rats crawled out of her waters? The cat was screaming. From his shoulder a rat hung. The cat jumped and pivoted to free himself.

It was a thing, Giorgio thought, that no one had ever seen before. Was it because they were hungry they came out of the waters of the Tiber, or because of what they had eaten in the waters of the Tiber since the war?

The fury continued in the dark grass.

Emilio reached out suddenly and brought his walking stick down sharply on the furred shoulders, and the rat, squealing, fell off, and the cat, hissing and in pain, leaped away into the shelter of the stones.

Then the rats, too, although for a moment Giorgio

thought that having finished with the cat they might be equally unafraid of the men, scuttled away.

He felt shaken. He did not know why.

"Emilio," Giorgio said.

"Yes, cicerone?"

"Which are we, Emilio? The rats or the cat?"

"Neither," Emilio said. "Get a stick and you will still be the one who decides. Come on. Let's go back to the fire."

They went back to the fire. Vito broke some twigs and put them on the small flames. Don Francesco warmed his hands.

"Why are you called Don Francesco?" Giorgio asked.

"He studied to be a priest once," Emilio said.

Don Francesco looked at Giorgio. He smiled kindly with the long thin mouth. He did not look like much of a priest.

"What happened, amico?" Giorgio said.

"He fell in love," Emilio said.

"Yes," Don Francesco said. "I fell in love."

"Wait," Emilio said. "He will tell you about the trees in the Garden of Eden. It was something he discovered when he was studying to be a priest. How many trees were there, do you think, Giorgio, in the Garden of Eden from which Adam and Eve were forbidden to eat?"

"One," Giorgio said. "The tree of good and evil."

"Don Francesco says no. He says there were two. He studied to be a priest and then he fell in love with a married woman and now he says he has discovered in the Garden of Eden there were two forbidden trees."

"Two?"

"Yes. Ask him. Tell him, Francesco, about the two forbidden trees."

Don Francesco lifted his bald head.

"There were two," he said. He had a deep voice. The

voice was like a priest's although the face wasn't. "It is in the Bible. They hide it but it is there. It was not because they ate from the tree of knowledge that the Lord drove them out of the garden of happiness. But because of the danger they would eat from the other tree too."

"What tree?" Giorgio asked.

"The tree of immortality," Don Francesco said. "Read it. It is there, in Genesis. He was afraid, the Lord, that man would eat also from the tree of immortality. And then he would possess not only the knowledge of the good and the bad but he would also live forever. Forever," Don Francesco said, his eyes glowing. "He too would become God."

He stopped, rubbing his hands together in the warmth of the fire. Giorgio saw now that the backs of his hands were very hairy.

"You see?" Emilio said. "Two trees."

"What difference does it make how many trees there were?" Vito said. "We're not in the Garden of Eden."

"That's where you're wrong," Emilio said. "We are always in the Garden of Eden. In it and out of it at the same time."

"You're in it," Vito said, "but I'm out of it."

"You're getting old, my friend," Emilio said. "The old are always out of it."

"I'm not so old," Vito said.

"You're old, old," Emilio said. "Can you go down to the Tiber in the wintertime and swim in the ice water as you used to? Now you'd get rheumatism and they'd carry you off to San Giovanni the next day."

"Don't worry about me being old," Vito said. "I've still got a fist."

"Can you take an eighteen-year-old to bed and still make her happy? Once a night and you're finished," Emilio said.

"If I had money," Vito said, "I could still get an eighteen-year-old."

"You see?" Emilio said. "Now you need money before they'd do it with you. You're old. You're out of the Garden of Eden."

Giorgio looked into the fire. The twigs did not burn well. The grass around the edges of the fire had blackened and was curled up. There was nothing to be seen in the flames which had not been seen before. Maddalena would be sitting up, waiting. She would worry. She would think he was hurt and had had an accident. She would think he was drunk or he was playing cards. During the occupation, when it was curfew and he was late, she would sit like that and wait. She was not to blame. The occupation had been in this city, and she had waited. Now there was the liberation, and she waited. Both the occupation and the liberation were already part of the past, and they receded each day more and more. Everything dropped into it, was swallowed up, and disappeared. Stones were left, sections of fallen columns.

"Cicerone," Emilio said. "What is this thing here? What is this kind of platform?"

Giorgio looked. Emilio was leaning against a flat high stone like the edge of a wall which was tufted with wild grass.

"It is a rostra," Giorgio said. "It is a platform from which the orators spoke in the days of the Republic."

"What orators?" Emilio asked.

"Like Cicero," Don Francesco said.

"Once," Giorgio said, "in the early days of the Republic they put the figureheads from ships on here. That made it a rostra. Then the orators spoke. They stood up in the Forum and they made speeches."

"They allowed them?" Vito said.

"Of course," Don Francesco said. "Even under the Caesars."

"Emilio should get up," Vito said. "He could make a speech. Go on, Emilio. Climb up and be a Cicero."

"Some Cicero," Don Francesco said.

"The only difference between him and Cicero," Vito said, "is that Cicero's dead."

"He's dead too," Don Francesco said. "Only he forgot to lie down."

"Shut up," Emilio said.

"Listen. Cicero opened his veins in a bathtub and bled to death. That's the kind of an orator he was."

"No," Giorgio said. "Not Cicero. Petronius did that."

"In a bathtub?" Vito said.

"In Nero's time," Giorgio said. "He sent him a note and Petronius opened his veins in a warm bath."

"Listen to him," Don Francesco said. "A real Tacitus."

"Who is Tacitus?" Vito said.

"A shoemaker on the Via Merulana," Emilio said.

"Who cares?" Vito said. "They're dead. Get up, Emilio. Make a speech."

Emilio clambered up the grass-tufted platform. He turned toward them, smiling sardonically. Behind him was the square darkness of the triumphal arch. The fire flickered. "Fratelli," Emilio said.

"Wait," Don Francesco said. "How can he make a speech? He has to ask permission first. He has to submit a draft."

"To whom?" Vito said.

"Admiral Stone," Don Francesco said.

"Is that true?"

"Of course," Don Francesco said. "This is liberated Italy."

"You hear that, Emilio? You must go to the Alleati before you make a political speech."

"Fratelli," Emilio said again. "Please shut up, fratelli."

"Wait," Vito said. "Why fratelli? I don't see any brothers here."

"What do you know about politics?" Emilio said. "All political speeches have to begin with either signori or fratelli."

"I like signori better."

"Don't show your ignorance," Emilio said. "In politics when your audience has money and relatives in the government you start with signori. You're poor. You're stupid. You're not worth anything. So I start with fratelli."

"Some orator," Vito said admiringly. "I'm already convinced."

"Fratelli," Emilio said. "Brothers of the devaluated lire. As I look down at your repulsive faces, what do I see?"

"Merde," Don Francesco said.

"The only bastard of my poor mother," Vito said.

"Shut up," Emilio said. "Don't interrupt the speaker. This is rhetoric. Roma caput est. That's Latin. Do you know Latin, you uneducated men? Roma caput est."

"Listen," Vito said. "I fart better than he orates."

"Fratelli," Emilio said. "Take the museums. What does a man see in the museums? A leg. A beautiful marble leg. Tremendous. They found it in an imperial house, the archeologists. Dug it up. The leg of maybe a great wrestler. But where is he? Where's the rest of the wrestler that goes with the leg? Where's the bull chest and the giant arms? The archeologists, they only found the leg. He left the leg behind. He was a great wrestler, the best in the world, and all that's left of him is a leg. Il civis romanus. That's Latin again. I'm wasting my education on you."

"A leg," Vito said. "This is some time to talk about a leg. Say something about the grapes. That's more important."

"This year, fratelli, the grapes will taste of gunpowder," Emilio said.

"A vino dei cannoni," Don Francesco said.

"Squeezed from the smaller bombs," Emilio said.

"What about meat?" Giorgio said. "I like politics that talks about meat."

"Ah, meat," Emilio said. "Well, for meat it may be necessary to slice a good steak from the behind of the cicerone's wife. Do you object, cicerone?"

"No," Giorgio said. "She can spare it."

"Good."

"They did it once when Siena was besieged," Don Francesco said.

"Fine," Emilio said. "We have a historical precedent."

He waved the walking stick.

"Fratelli," Emilio said. "Amici and fratelli. Be careful not to steal such military tires as can be identified later by the carabinieri. We are approaching winter. If you are cold and lonely, I recommend a certain Lucia on the Via Marghuta who is pleasant, inexpensive and even permits a man to smoke a cigarette in bed afterwards. The Alleati have promised us a great deal. But the only thing that arrives in any quantity is barbed wire. Eventually I expect to see the peninsula from Taranto to Istria decorated with this symbol of military authority. We are liberated. We have been liberated from cigarettes, shoes, meat, gasoline and our women. As for me, I look forward to a winter full of amusing demonstrations of friendliness on the part of the English. I expect to see the Mediterranean begin soon to fly into the Thames. As for the Americani, the French, and the Russians, all of whom so profoundly admire beautiful Italia, our art, our past, our culture—well, fratelli, all I can say is I would not like to be caught alone in the dark in a men's gabinetto with these great admirers of ours. So, to conclude," Emilio said, and shouted: "Abasso!"

He leaped down from the rostra.

"Abasso what?" Vito said. "What shall we shout down with?"

"Anything," Emilio said. "How can you go wrong?"

"It was quite a speech," Don Francesco said. "Emilio, you should be premier."

"He should open his veins in a bathtub," Vito said. "That's what he should do."

"Come on," Emilio said. "I'm tired of the Forum."

They stood up, Vito, Don Francesco and Giorgio, stretching themselves and cracking their knuckles. The woman in the temple had not laughed for some time. The night was full of stars and it was quite possible the following day would be a nice one. Only the weather was unchanged.

"Put the fire out," Emilie said. "One Nero is enough."

They went through the darkness, walking together across the grassgrown floor of the Forum, following what remained of the paving of what had been the Via Sacra. Emilio walked beside Giorgio, swinging his stick.

"Tell me, cicerone," he said. "What is the difference between the old Romans and us?"

"They're great and they're dead," Giorgio said. "We are neither."

"Correct," Emilio said. "That's an answer I like."

"Emilio," Vito called. "If you were about to die what would you ask for?"

"Me?"

"If they gave you a last request what would you ask for?"

"First a good meal," Emilio said. "Then a girl I saw once in the chorus of a musical show in the Teatro Fontana."

"That's all?"

"The priests wouldn't have their churches long with you for a flock," Giorgio said.

"A man about to die should seek confession and absolution," Don Francesco said. "We have a lot to repent."

"Why?" Emilio said. "What sins do I have to confess? An empty stomach, a flat pocketbook, and a lonely bed. Shall I repent not having had them?"

"That's some theology," Vito said.

"I'm not talking about theology," Emilio said. "I'm talking about true religion. The needs of the human spirit. Well, my spirit needs a good dinner and that girl from the Teatro Fontana."

They walked on, climbing the embankment at the foot of the Palatine, and issuing on the dark Via del Impero. They began to walk toward the Colosseum. At this hour, swept by huge shadows, the monument seemed even mightier than it did when the sunlight lay on its broken tiers. In this section of the city, between the historic hills and the arch of Constantine, the streets had a bad reputation. To Giorgio it seemed another Rome, dangerous, lightless, and slightly criminal.

It was Emilio, who noticed everything, who saw the officer first. The officer was crossing the wide street near the old arch, and it was Emilio who pointed out that an officer at this hour without a vehicle, and alone on the streets, must be a drunken officer.

"But how drunk?" Vito said.

"Such an officer," Emilio said, "would be very drunk."

They watched the officer as he stood a moment under the triumphal arch, holding to the iron chains which were

Night, the stars, and the Via del Tritone.

A whistle.

"Wait a minute, baby. Veni qua."

A cough.

A laugh.

"Quanta costa?"

"You spik, Joe."

"You spik, baby. I listen."

"Tre mille."

"You got a casa?"

"Si."

"She's got a house. She says five bucks for the old lady who rents it and twenty-five for her."

"Ask her if it's for all night."

"Per tutta la sera, signorina?"

"Si."

"She says all night."

"But thirty bucks! What am I, a general?"

"This is Rome, kid."

"It sure ain't Scranton. Listen, for a whole night in Scranton—"

"Come si chiama, honey?" Schulte said.

"Adriana."

There was somebody with them. A girl in a tight skirt and a white blouse. There was somebody named Adriana with them.

"This is my buddy, Harry," Schulte said.

" 'Allo."

"Where are we going?" Harry said.

"A joint. The dame knows a joint."

"I don't want to go to no house with her," Harry said.

"We ain't going to no house yet," Schulte said. "We're going to a joint. A joint with music."

"Senta mala, lui?" Adriana said. "You sick, babbee?"

"He's sick."

"Oh, molto ubriaco," Adriana said. "Make you very sick. No drink so much."

"He's love sick," Schulte said. "He's looking for a girl."

"Oh," Adriana said. "Poveraccio. Una signorina qui or in America?"

"Qui," Schulte said. "In Rome."

"Oh," Adriana said. "We find signorina. Ci sono molti signorina a Roma. No?"

There was an alleyway, with wet cobblestones. Going through the entrance there was a blast of music, light thickened with smoke, and a long bar in a narrow room.

"Hey, Adriana!"

" 'Allo, Johnnee."

"Adriana!"

"Come sta, Gina?"

They knew Adriana all right, but it was a bar and it had dancing.

There were two potted palms next to the orchestra made up of a piano, a violin, a saxophone and an accordion. The accordionist sang as well as played the accordion and there was so little space in that room the violin player had to play among the potted palms. Somebody kept bothering the saxophone player to let him play the saxophone while somebody was breaking glasses and somebody was hollering, "Cognac! Where's the waiter with the goddam cognac?" Sometimes the lights would blow out. The girls who were dancing in this bar kept changing their partners, but not the way they danced, and most of the girls were young and none of them were beautiful and all of them wore the more violent shades of lipstick. Most of them were already registered with the police but some of them had not yet been registered. The waiters knew all the girls and they knew which of the girls had done it before the soldiers came to the city and it was surprising how few.

The waiters said, "What will the girls do when the soldiers go away?" and the girls said, "What will the waiters do when the soldiers go away?" But it was really the whole city which said, "What will we do when the soldiers go away?"

The orchestra played American music. It was American music which had been popular about the time the stock market had crashed. They played the American music very loudly and in a tempo that made even the familiar tunes somewhat unrecognizable to the soldiers. The soldiers did not care and the girls did not know the difference except for some soldier now and then who was a dancer. There were more soldiers than there were girls and not all the girls were willing to go to a room with a soldier for tutta la sera because it was more profitable to go half an hour in the vicinity and then return to the bar. There were many discussions among the girls about the soldiers they had. A blond soldier was looked upon as a genuine Americano and the dark soldiers were all thought to have had Italian parents and to have been born in Naples. The girls smoked as many of the soldiers' cigarettes as were left on the table and took the pack when it was partly emptied and the soldiers weren't looking. The girls would tell the soldiers about a soldier who had been molto generoso and had given them both soap and those chocolates which came in the tin scotoli and did not the soldiers have for their signorinas an equal generosity?

Adriana wore a tight black skirt, a white blouse, and down her throat hung a little silver cross on a thin silver chain. When she smiled she had bad teeth. When she laughed the little silver cross jiggled. When Schulte touched her under the table she slapped his hand.

"Are you still thinking about that Francesca?"

"What if I am?" Harry said.

"Forget about her."

"I don't want to forget about her," Harry said.

"What's so special about her?"

"She was beautiful," Harry said.

"Beautiful," Schulte said. "They're all beautiful. This one's beautiful too, ain't you, baby?"

"Comé?"

"Beautiful. Look at those teeth. There's a hunk of dentistry for you."

"What you say?"

"I said, baby, what a time a dentist would have with you."

"Parole, parole, parole!" Adriana said. "Io capisco niente."

"You'll capish," Schulte said. "Wait. You'll capish. Come on, let's dance."

. The soldier at the table next to the table Harry sat at turned to the soldier at the table with him and said: "Do you know what a soldier is, rebel?"

"No, Frenchy," the other said. "I don't know what a soldier is."

"I'll tell you what a soldier is," Frenchy said. "A soldier is an always."

"I never heard of an always."

"He's always eatin' or he's just finished eatin' or he's thinking of eatin'," Frenchy said. "He's always goin over the hill or he's just come back from goin' over the hill or he's talking about goin' over the hill. He's always losin' his dough playing dice or dealing stud or he's just lost his dough or he's tryin to borrow some more dough to lose.

He's always talkin' about the girls he's laid or is layin' or is going to lay. He's always reading a letter from home or writing a letter home or waitin' for a letter from home. He's always tight or he's goin' to be tight or he's coming out of being tight. Jackass Run, that's what a soldier is."

"What's Jackass Run?"

"Whip the jackass and make him run, that's Jackass Run," Frenchy said.

Somebody passed out. An MP whose name was Healy came in and tried to bring the soldier out of it. He put his thumbs under the soldier's jawsockets and into his throat and lifted him in the chair in which he was sprawled. It was something Healy said he had learned in the medics. But the soldier didn't come out of it and Healy said to let him sleep it off and went to the bar to have a drink.

Adriana and Schulte came back to the table.

"Listen to me," Schulte said. "Are you listening to me?"

"I'm listening," Harry said.

"I fixed us up. Are you listening to me?"

"I don't want to be fixed up."

"Forget about that Francesca. Listen, I fixed us up. Adriana has a friend for you. Are you listening?"

"Fix yourself up. I don't want to be fixed up."

"Listen, there's two rooms in this house. When we get there don't pay the dame right away. Say you'll pay her in the morning. Say we're staying the night and you'll pay her in the morning. Are you listening to me? In the morning we lam and if she hollers give her five bucks and shut her up. Are you listening to me, Harry?"

"Hey, babbee," Adriana said. "Still sick in stomaco?"

"He ain't sick in no stomaco. He's sick in the head."

"Drink drink drink," Adriana said. "All the time drink. What your fidanzata say when you go home?"

"She'll say I love you, baby."

"She say pooh. She say you go back to Italia you drink drink drink all the time."

The orchestra played. Healy was having another drink at the bar when the argument about the Buffalo division started. It started at the table and it went to the bar. It started at the table when the soldier with Frenchy said to Frenchy, "If a nigger come in the bus where I'm riding or come in a show and sit down next to me by God I don't care how good that movie is either me or that nigger is gonna get up and get out of that there movie house."

"Christ," Frenchy said. "A nigger's good as any of you muckers with your GI tail out and I'm going to go on pounding sense into them thick skulls of yours until by God something takes."

"Why you would, Frenchy. I do believe you would. But I heard it's a mighty poor white man likes to nigger-ride."

"Why you dumb Alabama bastard," Frenchy said.

"I ain't for keepin' niggers down but I ain't for holding them up. They can go ahead and advance theirselves far as they want but I don't want and I won't stand for no nigger come rubbin' up against me in a bus or sittin' in my lap in a movie house or longside me in a cafe. I'd shoot a nigger fore I'd allow him to start doin' what he do up North. I do believe that, Frenchy. I do believe I would."

From there it went to the bar. At the bar it got to how when you were in the line with the jigs why the Pinetree boys were always having to go in and take back the ground the boys in the Buffalo lost; and then it went from there to how they should have left all the jigs in Naples or in Leghorn to run the motor pools because all a jig could do anyway was run a truck, in the line they were no good.

"I'm gonna have to pound your thick skull in, you

dumb Alabama bastard," Frenchy said. "I'm just gonna have to."

The colored boy at the bar near Frenchy and near Healy got excited because he said man, bullets don't know no color, man, don't you go saying things like that about my buddies, the colored boy said, and Healy tried to stop it.

"All right, MP," the colored boy said. "All right now, I don't want no trouble with MP's. I had all the trouble I want with MP's."

"Cool off," Healy said. "Can't a man drink without an argument? Go on outside and cool off."

Then Healy took Frenchy and the Alabama boy and the colored boy outside into the street to cool them off a little and the orchestra played and Harry sat at the table with Schulte and Adriana.

"Hey, babbee," Adriana said. "What you think?"

Harry thought: once we all thought we were going to Panama. Everybody was talking how we were going to be shipped to Panama or to some zone of the interior. Panama, or the West Indies, or Alaska. This is some Alaska we got shipped to.

Harry thought: patch on my shoulder, gold stripes on my sleeve, an infantryman's blue badge on my shirt, a pack of butts in my pocket, a drink on the table, here I am, seven thousand miles from nowhere, looking for a girl named Francesca. I won't find her. I'll never find her. She went away with those four hours when we liberated this city. She belongs with those hours. I'll never see her again.

Harry thought: the day we came into Rome we won this war. The day we stayed in it we lost it.

When they went out of the bar into the alleyway, Healy was standing in the alleyway with his forty-five, unholstered, in his hand, flat, and Frenchy and the Alabaman and the colored boy were lying on the wet cobblestones. Healy's face was angry and white and the Alabaman and Frenchy and the colored boy from the Buffalo division were covered with blood. Adriana was terrified at all the blood but Harry and Schulte just looked at it, and Schulte said, wonderingly, "All three of them he conked. All three of them." They went down the alleyway over the wet cobblestones and turned into the dark Via del Plebiscito.

"I wonder what Li'l Abner's doing tonight," Schulte said as they walked with Adriana toward her casa.

Harry thought: what I ought to do is lay down somewhere and go to sleep. Schulte didn't have to go back to Chicago. Schulte and me could go back to Hartford and we could open up a business. A coal and ice business or something after the war. The army don't have to make a bum out of you if you don't let it.

Then he remembered the colonel.

He remembered the colonel when they got to the casa and the signora, who was to be paid for the rooms, a small, bulging woman with a wart, opened the door and cautioned them to be quiet. The signorina who was the friend of Adriana and was to be his signorina had not yet come but she had telephoned the signora of the casa and she would be there subito. Adriana assured him that she would be there subito and he was to go into the room and to lie on the bed if he felt still sick in his stomaco and he was to wait. Adriana and Schulte went into the adjoining room and closed the door and Harry lay on the bed which had a red coverlet and remembered the colonel. It was when he was on the rifle range during maneuvers. It had rained for a week and it was February and there was mud on everything. Even in the tent there was mud. Then this colonel came out to the rifle range driving up in a staff car after a good breakfast and a bed that wasn't in the mud and he came over to where Harry was standing on the firing line. The colonel said, "Well, soldier, how are you doing?"

He came from a hot breakfast and a dry bed, this colonel, and Harry was in his overcoat, muddy. The colonel said, "Well, soldier, how are you doing?" Harry said to the colonel, "Fine, Colonel. I'm doing fine, sir."

Lying on the bed with the red coverlet waiting for the friend of Adriana, Harry said to himself: "I'm yellow. That's why I didn't tell the colonel. The army's made me yellow." Then he fell asleep.

When he opened his eyes he was sick. He saw that the red coverlet had been taken from under him and folded back neatly over the foot of the bed. On the wall opposite him there was a picture he had not noticed before and at first he did not know who the man in the white nightgown in the picture was. The man had a beard and he was sitting in a rock garden and his hands were quietly clasped. The moon in the picture was rising over dark hills and cypress trees and then Harry realized the man in the picture was Jesus. He got up heavily on his elbow, his head turning sickeningly, and the girl in the room said: " 'Allo, Joe."

At first he did not believe it. It did not seem possible, after such a day and the long waiting. The hair was exactly as he remembered it from that afternoon four months ago when he had seen her smiling in the sunlight on the street where he had met the old lady who came from Buffalo and rode on the lake steamers, and the eyes were the eyes he had been searching for. She stood there, smiling, dark-haired and slender, and he said to her, because at first he thought she did not recognize or remember him, "I'm Harry. Don't you remember me? I'm Harry."

" 'Allo, Ar-ree," she said.

"That's it," he said, excited. "That's how you said it. Ar-ree. And I said don't go up, come down. Don't you remember? The fifth of June and I stopped you on the street. I said where's the Piazza Venezia and you said it's too far and you said come to my house and I'll wash you. I was dirty. You gave me a flower. Don't you remember, Francesca?" he said.

"Chi è Francesca?" the girl said.

"You," he said. He got up from the bed. His hair was matted and his dogtags hung out of his opened shirt. "You," he said, "You're Francesca."

"Ma no," the girl said. "Non io."

Then he stopped. He looked at the big bed from which the red coverlet had been neatly folded back so that his boots would not dirty it, and at the room in which he had been waiting, and he said to her, "What are you doing here?"

She did not understand. She looked at him, and smiled again, questioningly and a little afraid. She saw a soldier she did not know, although perhaps it was a soldier who had been with her once and she had forgotten him, and who said she was Francesca. When they talked their language sounded so harsh and so brutal.

"Ma non sono Francesca," the girl said.

"Don't lie to me," Harry said. "I'd know that face anywhere. I waited four months to see it again. Four months up the line I waited."

"Come," the girl said in her own language. "Come to the bed and you will feel better."

"What are you doing in this house?"

"Oh, how drunk you are. Come, darleeng. You will feel better."

"Tell me what you're doing with that Adriana? Why does she go to the phone and call you?"

"Ssh, darleeng. The signora will be angry," she said in her own language.

"Don't tell me to shut up. Answer my question."

"Come," she said in her English then. "Bed, yes? Yes, babbee?"

She tried, with difficulty, and because he was shouting and there would be trouble if he shouted, to draw him toward the bed. He would be quiet there, she thought. All the soldiers were quiet there.

"Yes, babbee? Come."

"Don't call me baby," Harry said. "Don't tell me to go to bed. Don't talk like that."

If only he would be quiet. If only he did not make trouble for the signora with the carabinieri. She drew him toward the bed, and when he sat on the bed she thought if she undressed quickly he would be quiet. She reached down to the hem of her dress and as she drew it up over her head, while her head was still in the folds of the dress, Harry tried to pull the dress down again. Feeling his clumsy, drunken and angry hands on her suddenly, and in the darkness of the dress, she began to scream for Adriana to come to her and to help her.

"What are you calling her for?" Harry said. "Francesca, don't," Harry said. "Francesca."

In her fear now, struggling to escape from the dress, she screamed, "Non sono Francesca! Do not touch me! You are crazy! Do not touch me!"

The adjoining door was pulled open, and Adriana came into the room, saying, "What is it? What is it?" and then Schulte came into the room too.

In the hall the signora had begun knocking on the door.

"Adriana," the girl said, "Adriana, take him away. He is crazy. Why does he call me Francesca? What does he want from me?"

"Madonna," Adriana said. "You'll wake the house."

"She's Francesca," Harry said. "Get out of here. I know her."

"Non sono Francesca! Sono Bianca!"

"On June the fifth I went to her house," Harry said. "She washed me. She gave me a flower and I said I'd be back. I know her."

"She says she ain't Francesca," Schulte said.

The signora knocked and knocked.

"Che cose succede, Adriana?" the signora called. "Adriana, open the door."

"She's Francesca," Harry said.

"I am Bianca!" the girl said. "Madonna, don't I know who I am? I am Bianca!"

"But, of course," Adriana said. "She is Bianca. There is no Francesca here. Be quiet."

Schulte said, "Let's get out of here. Let's get out of here before they call the cops. Come on, Harry. She ain't Francesca."

"She is. She's a damn whore. But she's Francesca."

"Where are you going?" Adriana said. "Where are you going without paying me?"

"Shut up," Schulte said. "Now don't you start."

"Mia soldi!" Adriana said.

"Here," Schulte said. "Now shut up."

"Five hundred lire!" Adriana said. "Five hundred lire he gives me! What shall I do with five hundred lire? The room is five hundred lire. Thief," she said. "Do not let him out of the door. Five hundred lire he gives me!"

"Shut up," Schulte said.

"Give me my money," Adriana said, and she flew at Schulte.

"Get away," Schulte said.

"Thief," Adriana said. "You said you would pay me two thousand lire!"

She clawed at Schulte.

"I'll pay you," Schulte said. "I'll pay you," and back-handed Adriana.

She fell against the bed and from the bed she spat at him.

"Thief!" she screamed. "I spit on you. I spit on your mother. I spit on your America."

"Let's get out of here," Schulte said.

"I'm taking Francesca with me," Harry said.

The girl got the door open. "Signora, signora!" she cried. "Call someone. They are crazy. One is a thief and one is crazy."

"Madonna!" the signora said when she saw what was in the room.

The girl ran out of the room. They heard her crying, "I am Bianca! I am Bianca! I did not give him a flower."

Schulte got him out. Candles were flickering in the hall-way, doors were opening, and in the shaftway dark heads looked out of the windows thinking that once more there would be trouble in the neighborhood and how shameful life had become in respectable houses such as this because of the money one earned from the soldati.

"What is it?" the heads said. "Who is screaming like that?"

"Soldati and the signorini."

"Eh, che disgrazia."

In the morning the carabinieri would be there again and someone would enter a denunciation against the sig-nora of that apartamento from which, in the night, came those terrible screams and curses. The windows finally went down and one tried to sleep as best one could, not knowing where or when the next scandalous but inevitable uproar would begin.

In the street, Harry struggled to escape from Schulte and go back up the dark stairs.

"Let me alone," Harry said. "I'm going to wait here. I'm going to wait until the morning. She'll come out of that house. She'll recognize me. She just thinks she doesn't know me now."

"Listen, Harry," Schulte said. "You can't lay down here like this. Come on. We'll come back in the morning."

"I'll find her," Harry said. "Wherever she is, I'll find her."

"Sure you will," Schulte said. "Come on, Harry."

"Why don't they cheer us any more?" Harry said. "Why is it so goddam cold and dark?"

"The cheering's over, soldier."

"Where are the flags? They put flags out. Every window had a flag. It was like everybody was in love. Where are the flags?"

"Back in the mothballs, soldier."

"She was beautiful. I came into the city and there she was—waiting."

"Come on, Harry," Schulte said. "We all got to find her. Come on, soldier," and then the headlights of the truck flared, the truck pulled up, and the driver leaned out.

"If you guys are going, let's go," the driver said.

Tomorrow, maybe. When it was sunlight again, or maybe not tomorrow, but soon, he would find her. Dusty, cursing and triumphant, under the old gates of the city, in a blaze of glory, that's how he'd come, once more up the road to Rome, and there would be kisses, wine, thrown roses again. That's how he'd find her, that's where she be-longed, there, in the blaze, throwing the roses that did not wither, kissing men who had handcarried their weapons twenty miles up from the sea, and he would find her, that light restored, that quick and undying smile. Then he would say: gee, baby I never forgot you. He would say: honey, I came all this way looking just for you. And say: sugar, without you this war don't mean nothing.

Without her, the rains falling in the empty bomb-craters, dripping from the helmets on the crosses made of sticks on all the little roads from Cassino and Anzio, would mean nothing. Rust filled the mouths of the long guns on the overturned tanks in the mountains and rust ate the treads, and it was all nothing without her.

The Marchese

IT WAS, THE Marchese Aldo Alzani said to himself, rather well done. For an amateur it was a very creditable job. He had had, after all, so little practical experience with this sort of thing. Of course, he had waited a long time, and he had never doubted that, given the opportunity and a fortunate combination of circumstances, he would do it. Nevertheless, now that it was done, one could permit oneself a little justifiable pride. There were the documents now, safely bestowed in the capable hands of Martelli, and here, in the villa. . . .

As he had expected, there was a light burning in the general's study, and his father-in-law was at the desk, writing.

It was amusing to think of the general writing, for he was engaged upon his memoirs, an occupation which, to Aldo, seemed almost a stroke of prophecy. The general had had once a certain success with a very military volume devoted to the first of the African wars in which he had scored quite an imperial triumph. The time obviously had come for the writing of memoirs, and Aldo knew the general thought of himself as a man who had had an im-

pressively distinguished career. The memoirs would have
an olympian sound if the general succeeded in conveying
to the world his own sense of his dramatic importance to
world history, and it would be highlighted by many episodes in which the general would be heard uttering his
most characteristic phrase: "Give me full power and I—"

The failure, or the success, of the specific moment in
history would then hinge upon whether the general had
or had not been granted full power. It was quite depress-
ing. But Aldo consoled himself. There were excellent odds
the memoirs might experience a rather abrupt climax.

The general, glancing up from the scene of his labors,
saw his son-in-law with that detestable little smile upon
his pouting and rather slack mouth, and dressed in a white
tropical suit, standing in the doorway.

"Are you working, Papa?" the Marchese said. "Am I
disturbing you?"

"Come in," the general said. He put the pen down. He
had come, in his memoirs, to that exhilarating moment
when he made his triumphal entry into a certain primitive
capital. It had been a great hour in his career, perhaps the
greatest. Of course now, in the other end of the historical
telescope, the thing had a diminished quality, and what
had been a profoundly stirring episode somehow had taken
on a tarnish. One had to admit, glancing backward, that
what he had conquered that morning, after the hard drive
up from the desert, had had a rather poor luck about it—
the native huts of mud and clay, the unpaved streets in
which dead mules and dead tribesmen lay in equally aban-
doned stenches, and then the colonial mansions them-
villas. The genuine enemies had been distance, heat and
selves, which had turned out to be not very impressive
the flies. It had been more of a military subjugation of

nature than of a difficult enemy. He had been writing this in his memoirs, and endeavoring to blow into the shrunken skin an air of the old splendor, and by recounting the terrible logistical problems he had faced, the military vision he had exhibited, and the determination he had called up among his troops, to impress the neglectful mind of time. The maps, the terrain of the country, old photographs of the primitive capital, and photographs of himself, in full dress, and in battle uniform among his staff officers, lay on the desk before him. Aldo's eyes flickered with a faint irony over the military litter. Precision, of course: Papa would be so very exact with maps, directives, photographs. He carried all his credentials with him into history.

"Well?"

"Is it going all right?" Aldo asked. "You had such difficulty with the first one."

"I'm not a litterateur," Papa said contemptuously. "I write history, not French novels. It is somewhat more difficult."

"Of course. Nevertheless, they are both sold in the railroad stations."

"Spare me the wit," the general said.

"Where is Maria?"

"She was in earlier with Cespa."

"Ah," Aldo said. "Our eloquent Guido."

"At least he isn't cynical," the general said, looking at his son-in-law.

"And I am, Papa?"

"You are corrupt, like all your generation," the general said. "It is only too bad that Italy has you to depend on."

"Not at all. I depend on Italy."

The general growled to himself. The memoirs had stirred the ghost of a national passion in him. He, Italy, the Party, destiny and history, had all conspired to make a tremendous moment in a sunbaked overgrown village which had been the capital of a primitive and defeated kingdom. But time had rubbed the brightness off the dream. A shadow, petulant and irritable, crossed his face. "Corrupt," he said. "You will drag us down into your cynicism with you."

"Papa," Aldo sighed. "I'm afraid you do not understand me, after all. You persist in regarding me as a platoon of infantry. Really, I'm not. And besides, you know, our natures are so different." He lit a cigarette. "For example," he said to his father-in-law, "how corrupt would you say I am capable of being?"

The general looked hard at his son-in-law. The casual and detested face, with its small blond mustache, looked smilingly back at him.

"As corrupt as you thought amusing."

"Ah, no. Much more. As corrupt as I thought necessary. The necessity makes it amusing."

"Very interesting," the general said. "You are unique. Do you mind now if I preferred the room empty?"

"In a moment," Aldo said. "Do you know, I have been thinking, that it might be wiser, seeing how difficult things are now, for you to retire?"

The general was not sure he had heard. He turned slowly to face his son-in-law.

"Retire?" he said.

"From public life," Aldo said. "You know: one sits under a lime tree, writing in the long afternoons one's memoirs, and occasionally a journalist comes to interview one. A private, quiet, and very restful retirement."

"Are you suggesting," the general said slowly, looking

at him, "that I resign from the army?"

"Oh, much more. I am suggesting a complete resignation. Commander, Viceroy, Duke—all of them. After all," and Aldo smiled whimsically at his father-in-law, "there was a time when you were none of these, and I suppose you were not too unhappy. You could be happy again, Papa. It would be a quiet life—but then, a safe one."

"Safe?"

"Yes, safe. I hardy think they would try to assassinate you while you were engaged on your memoirs. They might, of course. But I hardly think so."

The general looked unbelievingly at his son-in-law. Aldo might have been discussing the weather. "But why should they try to assassinate me?"

"They are so patriotic, Papa. Like Guido."

"I conquered an empire for them," the general said with difficulty. "They wouldn't dare."

"What empire? A waterless desert and a country full of flies."

"No," the general said. "Who else had such a victory? Who else had the King's personal thanks?"

"Ah, Papa," Aldo said. "But who else was foolish enough to have written directives to a battalion of artillery and to have neglected to destroy the directives?"

"What?" the general said. "What directives? What battalion of artillery?"

"My dear general, have you forgotten? On the eighth of September you issued a series of directives to the battalions stationed about the city commanding them not to fire at the Germans. Do you recall? It was very unwise. You see, if the Epuration Committee were to have possession of these directives, signed quite clearly in your distinguished handwriting, and if it were perfectly obvious from these military epistles that in a large measure you were responsible for the betrayal of the city on the eighth, while certain unhappy patriots on the Via Ostia were dying in rather sanguinary bunches, under the German machine guns, and thinking you, my dear Papa, the hero of Africa, were also at that moment giving your life in the defense of the city—" Aldo paused. He glanced with exaggerated sympathy at his father-in-law. It was such an obvious predicament. They would hardly, the patriots on the Via Ostia, have understood such a complicated military maneuver in which one defended a city by silencing its defenses. "My dear Papa," he said. "If they knew, the reaction would be tremendous."

The general knew exactly how tremendous the reaction would be. He got up abruptly, and with almost an indecent haste yanked open the lower drawer of the desk at which he was writing the history of his impressive life. But it was useless, as he knew it would be useless. Papers, documents, letters—but not the packet, buried, as he had thought, safely. He straightened, and turned again to his son-in-law, his blond, indifferent, casually smiling, incomprehensible and suddenly dangerous son-in-law.

"Where are they?"

"My dear Papa, where would they be? In the hands of the chief of detectives of the Ministry of Internal Security."

The general would not believe it. "They were here," he said hoarsely. "In this drawer, locked. How did they get to the Ministry?"

"But, Papa," Aldo said. "I brought them."

Because it was still incredible, and because he would not give up certain simple family assumptions, the general said, with difficulty, but as calmly as he could, "But why? Why would you, the husband of my own daughter, take

them to the police?" For whatever else he might be, Aldo
was still his son-in-law. "Why? Am I stupid? What profit
will you have from it?"

"But why not?" Aldo said, reasonably. "Why do you assume that I, with my talents, would not? You see how little
you understand me."

"Do you know what you have done? Do you have any
idea of what will happen now?"

"Papa, I am not stupid. Of course I know."

"Do you know what they will say? Do you know what
slanders the journals will invent?"

"Awful things," Aldo said.

"They will crucify me."

"Oh, no, Papa. Why do all you military men and politi-
cians talk of crucifixions? They are religious ceremonies.
Shoot you, yes. Imprison you. But not crucify."

"You're joking," the general said. "Of course." He stood
up. "You must be." Aldo joked; they all joked; it was that
kind of a generation. Discipline was what they needed, all
of them; the rigors of a camp, the exactions of a long
march. They were cynical and they joked.

"It is something that amuses you," the general said. "I
should not have allowed myself to believe it." Nevertheless, the packet was gone.

"I do wish you would treat me seriously," Aldo said.
"After all, I have just delivered what might well be your
death sentence into the hands of the Ministry. My own
father-in-law's," he said, a little indignantly. "And yet you
insist on pretending I'm joking. Not at all; even though
you would like to believe it. I am serious." Aldo smiled.
"Come, Papa. I am not a battalion. You cannot issue a
directive. Sit down, and we will discuss the virtues of your
retirement from public life."

"Retire?" the general said. "Do you think with this they will let me retire quietly? They'll want my head."

"Really?" Aldo said. "That so much photographed head?"

"Don't mock me," the general said thickly.

"Am I mocking you, Papa?"

"Don't mock me, you son of a bitch," the general said. "Old as I am, I'll strangle you with my own hands if you mock me."

He sat down, shaking, in the chair next to the desk on which were scattered the neat pages describing the episodes of the taking of the capital.

He looked at Aldo, as though he were trying to identify him, as though he were aware suddenly that Aldo was a stranger. "Who are you?" he said heavily. "I took you for a spoiled Tuscan aristocrat, without a penny, who married my daughter. I was mistaken. She wanted a title. I bought her a title." He paused. "But now it seems I bought more than a bankrupt aristocrat. Now it seems I purchased a snake."

Aldo smiled.

"There, Papa," he said. "We approach the truth."

"What I don't understand," the old man said, "what is difficult for me to understand, is why you did it. You are not a socialist. So it can't be that you care for my political disgrace. You're not a patriot. You are nothing. Yet you did it."

"As I said: I am unique."

"Then why?" the general said.

It was the second time today he had been asked that question. Martelli had asked it, for other reasons, and now the old man asked it, for still other reasons.

"But it's perfectly obvious."

"Is it? Why should you want to drag me down? Why should you want the disgrace of your father-in-law? It's not obvious."

"You bought me," Aldo said. "My dear general, you said yourself you bought me."

"Others have bought you."

"Ah, but I was never purchased by a family of flax manufacturers from Milan before. By a petit bourgeois. A petit bourgeois with immense ambitions. Do you know, Papa? I detest ambitious people."

"Yes?" the general said tightly.

"Such ambitions. Of such scope. The father's and the daughter's. A man of steel, the father was known as. Were you not, Papa? Unyielding, inflexible. Quite: and with a daughter of approximately the same metal. I detest people of steel."

"You seem to detest a great deal."

"Yes? I do, don't I? I detested it when my father-in-law, the magnified petit bourgeois, sat and rang a little bell, and I, most punctually, most obediently, came trotting up. And the daughter, too, rang her little bell. Oh, not audibly. But I heard it, the little tinkling bell, and I trotted up to the bedroom. Your little spoiled aristocrat came trotting up day in and day out to the daughter of the son of the flax manufacturer from Milan. You have no idea how boring it was. How could you? You were so busy with your triumphs, and your daughter with hers, and only I, the poor Marchese, had no triumphs. You see, Papa? It was an intolerable situation."

"I bought you!" the general said violently.

"How true," Aldo said thinly, and smiled again. "Therefore, I sold you."

The old man glared at him. "Get out. Get out of here."

Aldo stood up, adjusting the sleeves of his white tropical jacket. "Withered is the laurel," he said, "and aged the brow. We are all, Papa, servants of the State." He smiled piously. "Addio; and sleep well."

He went out of the study, through the dark apartment, experiencing a cold and malicious elation. He had waited an incredibly long time for this, and it had been pleasant. He had not actually ever believed it would take place, but a kind history had provided him with the unlooked-for opportunity.

He felt wonderful; his soul had been out in the sun of revenge, in the sea of retaliation, and it was amazing how refreshing, how invigorating that sort of thing could be. He felt wonderful.

Not finding Maria in the apartment he descended the stairs and went out of the villa into the little private park which surrounded it. He lit a cigarette, cupping the small flame, looked at the dark sky thick with stars, and began to walk under the trees. It was extraordinary, he thought: had not the war come, had not the regime stupidly committed itself to the war, and therefore, to oblivion, all its grandiloquence wiped out, he might have gone on being the bored, slightly contemptible figure at the bars on the Via Veneto who was always, despite the fact that it was his name she assumed, referred to as "the husband of the general's elder daughter." But time had put out a great paw and stroked all their little pretensions, their miniature splendors, and their world fell apart: regime, daughter, general, the evening crowds at the bars. But among the ruins he was at home; chaos was the time for talent, and it was quite clear to him now what talents he had.

Some distance in among the trees he heard voices: Maria's, and then, the dramatic bass of Cespa. The Marchese discreetly chose the nearest shadows: Cespa, and Maria, in a summer dress, he could see, in among the trees. It was not quite what he had expected; but then, why not? He remembered Maria's "but he seems so strong," meaning Cespa, after lunch; (and she, of course, he thought sardonically, was so, so weak); and recalled that face of a third-rate evangelist. Yes, why not here under the trees in the darkness? He was very curious to hear what the conversation might be.

"Do you think so, Marchesa?" he heard Guido say.

"It would be insane not to," Maria said. "If I were a man certainly that is what I would wish."

"Perhaps I have thought of it."

"Have you?"

"A great deal. Someone must; eventually, it is a choice someone must make. If only to restore order and decency in our moral and social life. "

(Ah, Guido was still restoring order and decency. Aldo grimaced, faintly.)

"You are capable. I know you are capable, Guido."

(So it was Guido. Between lunch and midnight it had become Guido.)

"Am I?"

(Tell him he is, Aldo thought. The gentleman wishes you ever so gently to massage his vanity.)

"To be a man," Maria said. "There are so many opportunities when one is a man."

"And if you were a man, Marchesa?"

"Climb. Dio, I'd climb!"

"One gets dizzy."

"Not if one is not alone."

"Would I have a mountaineering companion? An Alpinist, Marchesa?"

"If you wished."

"You, signora?"

"Mountains are lovely. Particularly the high ones."

(Yes, but ah, the fall, my dear, Aldo thought. Papa is failing now. A vertigo is seizing him. And it is such a long way down.)

"Petrarch climbed," Guido said. "But when he was on top of Mount Ventoux and had seen the four countries, there was nothing left for him except to descend."

"But he climbed," Maria said. "He did not find excuses or invent scruples. He climbed. All my life I have been dragged down by unambitious men. All my life."

"Isn't the Marchese ambitious?"

"Aldo?" she laughed.

(How well she knows me. Or thinks she does. Papa, too, thought he did. Papa was in his study now, digesting that knowledge. And you, too, my dear: in a little time, in a little time.)

"But it is so cold in the mountains," Guido said.

(How he clung to that image. Poor Cespa: he probably thought that in society this was how one talked—in second hand literary images. At that, he was not altogether wrong.)

"But there would be snowdrifts. And the winds. He would be in danger, signora. Such a man, climbing, would encounter a great deal of danger."

"What is danger?" Maria said. "It would be exciting."

(How reckless we are! But the greatest fall one takes ever is out of bed, and into another one. That's your heights, my love.)

"Ah, signora. Where would one find such a woman?" Cespa said.

(She would be smiling now, a bony cat, her ears back and purring. But, of course. Where?)

And Maria: "Yes. Where would one?".

(The climax, now. Come, come, signor Cespa: the lady is asking where would one.)

"Here, perhaps? In the darkness. Under these trees, signora?"

"Perhaps," Maria said.

"And having found her," Guido said, "he begins to climb Mount Blanc, until he reaches—"

"The top."

"Or her lips."

(Splendid! He had not heard anything as sickening in years. But now, of course, he would lean forward, gallantly, in the dark.) And he leaned forward. (With ardent eyes. And there would be banal music. And he would . . .)

But instead there was the shot; high up, from the one lighted window in the villa.

Maria, startled, pushed Cespa away, hearing it. "Guido," she said. "What is it?" staring into the darkness toward the house.

Guido listened. There was no repetition of the sound.

"Nothing, my dear."

"But it was like a gun. It sounded like a gun. Who would be shooting here?"

"One of the servants?"

"They have no guns."

"Then it was nothing. You thought it was a gun." he said.

Aldo turned and went noiselessly and carefully out of the grove. He thought of the study, and the pages of the manuscript of the memoirs lying on his father-in-law's desk, the large handwriting, the episodes numbered, the history abruptly ended. He wondered if the manuscript had been damaged at all, and whether the old man, who would not

now get any older, had done it sitting at the desk in front
of his memoirs, and whether he had read, before he did it,
once more carefully the pages of description he had written
of the afternoon when, hot and triumphant, the great caval-
cade he had commanded had rolled into that primitive and
death-filled capital, thinking: "But I did not expect him to
do that. Or did I? Yes, perhaps I did. Perhaps that is what
I wanted, after all."

Now, in the park, there was Maria and Cespa. He
thought perhaps it might not be wise to force an immedi-
ate break with Maria. Cespa would climb; yes, the man
would climb that political Mount Ventoux, and perhaps
that evangelical head might prove useful. One never knew;
the country was chaotic, and it was impossible to see what
was about to happen, and who, among the noisy claimants
for power, would seize and hold it? It might be profitable
now, since Maria would know nothing, for him to pretend
ignorance also, and to be at hand when Cespa began to
climb. He lit another cigarette, thinking that, yes, it was
wiser to wait; and besides, having Guido now, her little
bell wouldn't tinkle so often, if at all. Perhaps he could
even arrange to have Pepi come down from Switzerland.
It would be amusing: she and Guido, Pepi and himself,
and the conquest of Mount Ventoux.

Poor Papa. He had been quite right. It was too bad that
Italy had him to depend on.

Still, all that was tomorrow.

Carla

THREE TIMES Mama had changed the bedsheets. It was with great difficulty that the dottore had obtained ice and made an icepack and now Carla lay in bed, very white, still bleeding, but the danger was almost past.

"Do not tell her," Carla had said to the doctor. "Please, dottore. Do not tell her."

"But I must," the doctor said. "She is your mother, cara."

"Please, dottore. It is dead. She does not have to know now."

"No, cara," the doctor said. "I really must. If you were my daughter I would want to know."

So the doctor had told Mama.

Mama's face looked as though someone had struck her. "Ohimè!" she had wailed. It was the shame, of course, although Carla felt no shame. The shame and the respectability. She felt nothing except a terrible exhaustion. For there had been pain; almost as much pain as if she had actually given birth.

"Please, signora," the doctor said. "Control yourself."

"Can I be a watchdog?" Mama said. "Can I have eyes everywhere?"

"Stay calm, signora," the doctor said. "It is over. She has

hurt herself badly and she must rest. What will your shouting help now?"

When the doctor had gone, leaving the pills she was to take and cautioning her she must be very quiet or else there was danger of another hemorrhage, Mama took a damp cloth and wiped the sweat from her forehead. Then she took the red ribbon and bound up her loose dark hair.

"Un disastro," Mama said. "Un disastro."

It would have been better if Mama had not known. She was not capable of bearing, in addition to her other troubles, this new calamity. Carla lay in the bed thinking how stupid the dottore had been to tell her. It was too difficult a thing for Mama to understand and, besides, the child was dead now.

Mama lamented. Had the father been home she would not have dared to have done this. But they do not fear the mother, Mama said, overwhelmed with pity for herself. The mother is nothing. With the mother they do what they want. A voice, Mama's voice, over and over, burdened with its own misery, but Carla could not feel any sympathy for her. She did not even wish to be here in her own house. It would have been better to have been taken anonymously to some hospital.

"Who was the man?" Mama said. "How can you lie there like that and not answer me? Who was it?"

"E non importa," Carla said.

"Whose bed did you crawl into? Tell me. While my eyes were elsewhere, whose bed did you open?"

Carla did not answer.

"Grigorio," Mama said. "It was the American."

"E non importa!"

"My heart told me," Mama said. "Yes: when he came into the house my heart warned me. A soldato. Are you happy now you have had your soldato, figlia mia?"

"Mama," Carla said, turning her head on the pillow.

"Are you content now? He listened to you play the piano. He took you for a walk to the gelateria. And I was blind. Blind and stupid to think the end would be different."

She cried.

The tears issued disfiguringly from her eyes. For this too had happened: the war, the taking of her husband as a prisoner, and now this too, the family disgrace.

"Nothing," Mama said. "You feel nothing for my pain."

It was true; she felt nothing. A deadness separated her from the world. The blood, secretly flowing, had emptied the world of what importance tears or hysterics or domestic shame might have. It was not as though her mother but a curiously unhappy marionette wept. Nevertheless she said:

"Don't cry, Mama."

"I'll weep," her mother said. "As the Virgin wept, I'll weep." And then:

"And he, Grigorio? Does he know?"

"Yes."

"Will he marry you?"

"No."

"Why? He enjoyed himself. Why shouldn't he marry you and take you afterwards to America as so many of them do?"

"He is married," Carla said.

"Che bel amore!" Mama said. "What pleasure you had!"

"Please, Mama."

"I'll tell Antonio. If Antonio knows he'll break all his bones."

"It has nothing to do with Antonio."

"Nothing? The sister's shame is the brother's."

"There is no shame," Carla said.

"He's finished with you. He ate from the best dish in the house and now he gets up from the table and walks off. Che gioia! He walks off! And you, my daughter? Inside, the professore is waiting. What shall I tell him? My daughter, excuse me, went into a bed with a foreign soldato. But he's finished, he's wiped his mouth, it was an excellent meal, and now he's finished. Now my daughter, excuse me, is ready for a countryman of her own."

"Mama, Mama," Carla said tiredly. "You don't understand."

"I understand the professore wants to marry you, loves you, and the other made a fool of you."

"You'll never understand."

"I understand. Too well I understand. You could not wait. The blood boiled in you. You were in a hurry. Oh, how well I understand!"

"No. You don't."

"Dio mio, one thing I pray: send them away! Send them back where they came from! Let the ocean take them and their food and their money! Let them ruin and disgrace their own country! Dio, ti prego," Mama said passionately, "send them away!"

She got up heavily from the chair.

"Another secret," she said, "to lock away in silence." She looked at her daughter. "What shall I tell the professore?"

"I don't want to see him."

"But the man has waited."

"Please, Mama."

"No," Mama said. There was an obstinate look now on her thin face. "From now on you do what I say. From now on I'll keep a chain on you." She went to the door. "Professore," she called.

"Mama, please."

"From now on I'll be a watchdog," Mama said. "Do you hear me, my daughter? A watchdog."

The professore came into the room, his face full of concern for her, and his cold pipe, as always, fixed in his mouth. "Come si sente?" he said, and Carla, not wishing to hurt him, answered, "Bene, grazie, Professore."

"Bravo," he said.

Then, as one slaps an object a child has hurt itself on, he said indignantly, "The camionettas. They should be prohibited. One can be killed on those terrible ladders."

"It was my fault," Carla said.

"Sit, Professore," Mama said, indicating the chair beside the bed.

"How was the concert?" Carla asked.

"Terribile."

"Who sang?"

"Ceccarelli. With the university choral society. The Don Giovanni." He grimaced. "It was terrible. Twice I myself heard the soprano crack in the duet." She saw him then, for a moment, with his violin, uncomfortable in the iron folding chair in the small radio station orchestra, a diminutive and earnest figure, still capable of feeling something about the music. He would suffer when the soprano was bad in the Don Giovanni. He would look from under his eyebrows at the musician beside him, and make that almost imperceptible gesture with his shoulder that said: what could one expect? This was the kind of soprano they had now.

"Perhaps I should go, eh, signora?" the professore said. "She should rest."

"No, no," Mama said. "Sit. Carla wants to talk."

"It is late."

"The clock can wait."

He looked at his cold pipe. "I must ask Grigorio to sell me another tin of tobacco," he said. "There's no tobacco to be found anywhere. Will you ask him if he comes to the house, Carla? I will pay him."

"He's going away," Mama said.

"Who, Grigorio?"

"Si. Another city. His company goes tomorrow."

"So suddenly?"

"Si. It is the army."

"E vero, Carla?" the professore said.

"He is going away, yes," Carla said.

"Che peccato! I needed tobacco."

"It's better they all go," Mama said. "All the Americani."

"But why?"

"They are here too long already."

The professore tapped his pipe. "Soldiers are soldiers," he said. "Many people dislike the Americani now who cheered them four months ago. But not I."

"No?"

"People look and see them, the soldati, with food, with cigarettes, with benzina. And having nothing, naturally, they're jealous. But do you know what I say?"

"What do you say, Professore?" Carla said.

He put the pipe carefully back into his mouth.

"They fight," he said, "so they eat. We do not fight, so we do not eat."

He looked at Mama.

"E justo, no, signora?"

Mama did not answer. Even if it were just, she would not have answered.

When Mama had gone from the room, leaving them alone, the professore began to speak of the news in the paper. "They say in a month or two," he said, "the powerhouses will be repaired. Twenty kilowatts of electricity, that's what they promise us. It will be good to have light again, no, Carla?"

"Yes, it will be very good."

"Light!" he said. "I can hear how they will shout when the light goes on again. Luce! Luce! You'll hear it all over the city."

"Yes."

"Things go slow. In two months the electricity, then perhaps the trolleys will run again, and people won't have to fall off camionettas when they travel. And if they clear the mines out of the sea, fish will come in. Piece by piece we'll put ourselves together again."

"Yes," Carla said. "But it will not be the same."

"Well," the professore said, "I will be content if it is nearly the same."

There was silence, and he sucked on his pipe, looking at the candles burning in the room.

"Do I look very ugly, Professore?" Carla asked.

"Ugly? But no."

"I must look so ugly now."

"No," the professore said. "If there is anybody ugly in this room, it's me."

"You are not ugly," Carla said.

"Of course. I know my face."

He touched his chin and stroked his blunt short nose. "With such a face," he said, "I'm no good for the king, and the queen couldn't use me either."

"You must not talk like that," Carla said. "I like your face."

"Bé . . ."

"It is a good face," Carla said.

"Music is my only virtue," the professore said. It must

be difficult for him, Carla thought, with the pleasure of tobacco. Yet he would insist on paying. He would be precise in his obligations, his very small, indomitable pride. Except that now Grigorio would not be here to bring the tobacco.

"Yes," the professore said. "No bono per il re, neanche per la regina."

"Oh, no," Carla said.

He looked at her, "I am too serious, no?"

"No."

"Yes, I am a little too serious. It has a comic effect." Why should he insist so on his defects? She saw him, exerting that small pride of his, that diminutive honesty, so that the world might not think he was deluding himself. He was contemplating the pipe again. "Well, we must live with ourselves, however God made us." He looked at Carla from under his eyebrows as he must have looked at the musician beside him when the soprano went bad in the Don Giovanni. "But I am faithful. If I had to recommend myself, I would say, the professore, there's a faithful one." He smiled at her. "You see, cara? I have the dull virtues."

He reached out to touch her hand, timidly. It was very cold, and the veins were visible, thin and blue. She, lying there, still knew the secret going-away of her blood, and still felt, even now when he touched her, that lifelessness that seemed to separate her from the world. "Remember, cara," the professore said. "We Italiani, we are fools; we may even be dull, some of us; but we have suffered together. Those who have not suffered with us cannot understand us. Never," he said. "One thing I know: the poor should never marry the rich, a cripple should not marry one who walks straight, and the Italian should never marry the foreigner. They will always be strangers."

He paused.

"Ricordi questa," he said.

She did not answer.

He stood up, short, unhappily earnest, with the pipe from which he had only a frustrating pleasure still in his mouth. "Cosi," he said. "It is time I went. Tomorrow I will come to see you before I go to the station."

"Yes, "Carla said. "Domani."

"Shall I blow out the candles? Would you like to sleep now?"

"Si."

"Buonanotte, Carla."

"Buonanotte, Professore."

He blew out the candles and went quietly out of the room and then at last she was alone and the room was dark. The pain was gone now, and there was only the exhaustion, and that separation from the world. Grigorio would have felt badly and he would have pitied her. But she did not want him to feel pity. What had happened had happened because she had thought she would not see him again. In the camionetta, driving through the streets of the city, in the darkness, touching a stranger's shoulder, touching an alien knee, she had said again and again: non ti vedro piu. The child would have grown up with bad teeth and crooked bones. Grigorio would go away, time, an ocean, the love of another woman she had never seen, separating them, and in the camionetta she had seen it all.

She heard the bells of the Church of the Blessed Sacrament. It was past midnight. Everywhere there was darkness. Each lay down to sleep in a bed soiled either by tears or blood. Now the professore was walking home. He would be afraid, because of the robberies, of the unlit streets. His shadow, taller than he was, went earnestly before him. The stars lit small areas of the sky; between the lit areas it was cold and dark, and in front of a man went his tall shadow.

The heart beat, hardly audible. The bones were so thin and breakable. Blood came so easily. She was warm, suddenly warm; and thirsty, too; and her head was so heavy. It was very dark; she was in the darkness, thin and so easily breakable, the darkness was cold, then it was swept by heat, in waves, the edges lit by starlike areas; and she wanted Grigorio, she was thirsty and she wanted Grigorio now, feeling the great separation, the wall between her and the world, and he would be going away, he was going away, time, an ocean, another world taking him, and she was grown up, now she was grown up because in the camionetta she had learned to look at the reality, bells were ringing in the Church of the Blessed Sacrament and she was grown up, she was no longer a child, and it was so warm, the cold swept by the heat, in waves, Grigorio, Grigorio, who was going away, and there was sunlight, bells, sunlight and bells and she was running down the street in the sunlight, hearing the bells. It was three o'clock.

She was late, running, and the children ran with her as she ran, singing, "Caramelli, bambi; cioccolata, segnori," in the street, holding out their unwashed hands, singing, "Cioccolata, segnori . . ." In the hallway (the elevator did not run, it would never run again) the wife of the portiere sat, knitting, her needles flickering rapidly through an inexhaustible ball of yarn. "Buon giorno, signorina," the wife of the portiere said. She was ugly; Carla had not realized how ugly she was; she was ugly now, and she wore a look of malicious triumph. "He's gone away," she said. "Your soldato's gone away." The needles clicked and flew; "He won't close the shutters at three o'clock in the afternoon any more, my dear." The wife of the portiere laughed. "He's taken all his real American coffee with him."

She ran upstairs. "Grigorio, Grigorio," she said. But the room was empty. Her head turned; she was so tired, and so frightened, and her head was so heavy. The shutters were not closed, and the Egyptian strip was on the wall again. She had made the signora take it down because of the vermin and it was on the wall again. In the courtyard, from the apartments, where all the radios were playing the music of the operas, heads leaned from the windows.

"Yes, he's gone," they shouted.

"He slept with her and now he's gone. Now she's ready for a countryman of her own. . . ."

"She'll take a cripple if he'll have her now. . . ."

"Eh, our women! He made love to her and the little fool let him and now he's gone away. . . ."

Then, as she watched, from the brocaded figures, the profiled angular gods of the Egyptian strip, a swarm of vermin began to crawl.

She ran.

"Caramelli, bambi; cioccolata, segnori . . ." the children sang.

In the piazza trolleys were stalled, a long line of them, the motormen sitting immovably on their stools in the cars, waiting. "Any minute," the people said, "any minute they'll start. They're waiting for the lightning."

They glanced up at the sky. It was cloudless.

"Any minute," the people said. "When the lightning comes they'll start."

"Carla, Carla!" the professore called. He was standing in the middle of the street, looking unhappily after her. He was carrying his violin case and the music pages of a sonata. "Why is she running away from me?" he said.

"Let her run," Mama said, wiping her red hands. "She'll get tired. I've got a chain on her now."

The music pages of the sonata fluttered.

"We'll play duets," the professore said. He sang the Don Giovanni, cracking. "Every Sunday we can sit and play duets, Carla at the piano, I with my violin. Why is she running?"

"Run," Antonio shouted. "Run to the North Pole! I know what those girls do who play in the restaurants and the hotels. No sister of mine . . ."

"Grigorio, Grigorio," she cried, running.

Uncle Luigi was waiting on the bridge. He was old; he wore a straw hat; he was leading a horse. "Where is the child?" he said. "I have everything ready. Where is the child?"

The horse whinnied.

"Where is the child?" Uncle Luigi said. "I fixed the farm up—the hay, the fields, the house. We'll go on the horse. Everything is all ready for him. Where is the child?"

A camionetta chugged across the bridge. "There's room for one more," the driver said. "I always take exactly twenty-two. There's room for one more." There was an explosion; the wheel sank, air hissing from a tire. "If you wait," said the driver, "I know a garage where they buy tires from the soldiers. At night they change the marks of the treads. . . ."

On a broken bicycle Antonio rode up. He was bitter. "I can't get in," he said. "They say there's work but I can't get past the barbed wire."

He kicked the bicycle.

"I asked if there was work," Antonio said. "Galeazzo has gone to work for them. Cesare is driving a truck for them. Pietro works in the kitchen and steals sugar. Danilo is an interpreter. But I can't get in. There's too much barbed wire."

At the gelateria she thought she would find him. He was always here, in the early evening, drinking a vermouth, listening to the people.

"What?" said the waiter. "Grigorio? No, I haven't seen a soldier. Besides, my feet hurt." The sun shone remorselessly; flies buzzed over the little cakes on the counter; the padrone polished the caffe espresso urn. "My feet hurt," the waiter said, "and there are too many soldiers."

The square was hot and deserted. The bead curtain rattled in the doorway of the gelateria. A jeep, brilliantly green, raced down the hot street. "Signorini, aspet'," they called from the jeep. "Shall we bring those little watery sausages to the house? Would you like us to steal sugar or bring you soap or recommend your brother for a job with the Alleati?"

The wheels said: aspet', aspet', signorina.

It was three o'clock. Bells from the churches were still ringing. It did not get later. It stayed three o'clock. All the shutters of the houses were closed against the heat of the day. In her green kimono, wearing slippers, Mama ran out of the doorway of the palazzetta. She carried a big steaming bowl of fettucini. "We'll make a festa," she cried. "When your papa comes home, we'll make a festa." She sat down and wept.

"Nobody know how lonely I've been," Mama said, sitting and weeping disfiguring tears.

There was a garden in front of the palazzetta. It was the garden in which the trees were always green and were always the same trees. There, on the bench in front of the bust of Verdi, was Grigorio. He was talking to an old man. "It will be a bad winter," the old man was saying. "Everywhere it will be a bad winter."

"Grigorio," she said happily.

He looked up. "Carlaccio," he said. He smiled pityingly. "Was it bad, carissima?" he said.

"No," she said. "The pain's gone now."

"It's all my fault," he said.

"No," she said. "The fault is no one's."

He stroked her hair. It was bound with a red ribbon. In the bright air the swallows twittered, and she knew that behind the shutters the eyes of the neighborhood watched them.

"I was so frightened," she said. "I thought you had gone."

"Cara," he said.

"But you will go soon," she said. "I only wanted to delay it. But if the war is over you will go home, no?"

"If the war is over," he said.

"You will be happy to go home, isn't it true?" It was difficult for her to say it.

"I've been away a long time, cara," he said gently.

"But you will be happy to go home. It is bad," she said, forcing herself to say it, "to be away a long time from the person one loves."

"I have another life, cara," he said, "like all soldiers. A life before I came here."

The children ran out of the palazzetta; they searched the ground for the stubs of cigarettes; "caramelli, bambi; cioccolata, segnori . . ." she heard them sing. From the chimneypots the swallows flew like arrowheads. On the Tiber they would be sculling now and lying on the decks of the bath-houses.

"You'll fall in love again," he said. "You're not eighteen yet. People fall in love many times in their lives."

The shutters opened; heads leaned out. "Look," they

said. "She believes him. But last week on the Via Angelica a South Africano took a young girl and . . ."

"It's the negri; the negri I'm afraid of . . ."

"She went to the Albergo Splendide and a Frenchman there, an officer from Morocco, said yes there was work if she would . . ."

"The Polacchi, they are the beasts of Europe. . . ."

"Are not the yellow ones Chinese? In Bice's apartment, when I went to ask for some salt, there was a yellow one, in the bed, fast asleep. . . ."

"Soldati. The soldati have ruined us. We have on our backs the soldati of all the armies of the world. . . ."

"Grigorio," she cried.

He was going away.

"Arriverderci, cara mia," he said, going away.

She ran down the path; it was turning dark; she was so tired, and it was turning dark. "Will you come back?" she cried. There was a wind and the sound of water, the sound of distance, time and water. "Will you come back?" she cried.

In all the windows the heads turned. They shouted:

"Will you come back?"

"Caramelli, bambi," the children sang; "cioccolata, segnori. . . ."

"Carla!" the professore shouted.

"Let her run," Mama said. "I have a chain on her now."

"Barbed wire," Antonio said. "There's too much barbed wire."

He went away, as the darkness gathered, and there was a sound of water, time and distance, an enormously hollow sound, but always, as he went, he looked back to her with love. And with pity, for he had pitied her, although she did not want the pity, there in the courtyard of the palazz-

etta, standing, among the children singing: caramelli,
bambi; cioccolata, segnori. . . .

She was alone, in the darkness, the bells of the Church
of the Blessed Sacrament throbbing into silence.

The Sentence

THE SUN SHONE.

One would not have thought the sun would be shining; that the afternoon would be as flawless, and that after what had happened, after the blood on the Ponte Umberto and the blood on the Lungotevere, after the hysteria, the tumult, and his death, after the passing of the sentence, the sun would go down, as it was going down now, quietly, perfectly, flooding the sky of late summer with such magnificent colors.

They stood, the men, at the little chiosco, drinking a lemonade made by the wife of the padrone, in which the lemon pips swam, and watched the sun, and they thought of what had happened during the day when the sentence had been passed.

"Tell us," the men said to the man who had been there and had seen all of it, the eyewitness, "tell us," they said, "what happened?"

You should know (the man who had been there, the eyewitness, said) that I was not one of those whom he had personally injured. There's no son dead in the house be-

cause of him, nor a husband of one's married daughter—
and yet, can I say he has not injured me? Who can say, in
the city, he has not had some injury, or has not had to endure some suffering, because of him? And yet . . .

. . . Well, it was a cool morning. September, you know
how pleasant our mornings can be, and already, when I
came to the Palazzo, there were an enormous number of
people along the Lungotevere and in the squares as far
south as the Piazza Cavour and in the park around the
castle of Sant' Angelo where, they say, the popes once kept
lions. Why did I go? Well, curiosity: and I was somehow
involved. Yes, the curiosity, of course; because of the newspapers and because it was the day sentence was to be passed on him; but, then, I felt involved, too. Besides, there's
no work, now: where else is one to go? And I have enough
of my wife eight hours a night. . . .

. . . But such a crowd! From all the quarters of the city.
One saw many who wore the little black strip in the lapel
and the little star—the sign of the relations of the dead.
But, in the street, outside the Palazzo, it was impossible
to know anything actual. Talk—

. . . That he would be acquitted—

. . . That the court was corrupt and not to be trusted—

. . . That attempts would be made by sympathizers of the
regime to free him—

. . . And then, about ten o'clock, it was said that the
Court was assembling, and there was a great roar from the
people. There were so many of them, standing along the
Lungotevere, and crowding into the courtyard of the Palazzo, and they had been waiting for the Court to assemble,
and now when the news came there was this great cry. One
heard this cry, this shout, and one felt, at the same time,
the almost automatic surge of the people toward the Pa-

lazzo, toward the long marble hall in which the chamber was where the Court was now assembling to judge him. The sun was now climbing higher, and the heat was increasing, and I, who do not often think of these things, thought for a moment of what these people were who had come from all the quarters of the city to the Palace of Justice to hear the judgment of the Court. There was so much humiliation here, so many bad memories. This one does not forget how, one evening, he was arrested, casually, after curfew, although he was only late a few minutes and he had been forced to walk so far. And that one had stood for so many intolerable days in the long queues for bread; and another still awakes at night in a sweat like a child because of the fear during the bombings; in another some old military insult still rankles; another endures shame because he was compelled to sing some detested song or participate in some infamous act or share in some petty tyranny; and another has had sons killed in Libya or in the north; and one has wept, and one has cursed, and all, all have been in some measure, in some fashion, wronged. Yes: the Lungotevere was crowded with all our unhappiness, and I, who normally feel so little, felt it, and when they roared, there, hearing the Court was assembled, it was as though, in a wilderness, a volcano began to erupt, and out of that dead smoking mouth poured many of our petty rages as well as the more important agonies—

. . . And then one could feel that slow enormous movement, the many bodies moving together, toward the long marble corridor and toward the oak doors of the chamber in which he was awaiting sentence, moving and moving.

. . . Myself, I could see little: a straw hat, a bald head, an amber comb holding a woman's hair; and there were children, too, among them.

. . . Even if I had wanted to escape I could not have escaped. I moved, reluctantly, not shouting, although all about me they were shouting, but somehow something prevented me from shouting with them, and I could not have escaped even if I had wanted, and I did not, I think, want to.

. . . In the courtyard there are the statues. You know them? The lawgivers, down the ages. All marble, the ancient ones, and in togas, and the new ones, from our time, in marble frock coats, with marble lace shirtfronts. All admonitory fingers and contemplative brows. Well: someone was on the old Greek's shoulders—what's his name? The one sitting down, with his knees wide, the father of legality? He had a client on his antique shoulders, I saw, who kept screaming: abasso la giustizia! And I remember thinking: why does he shout down with justice? But it was something to shout, and, at least, he was more comfortable than I was, on the old Greek's back.

. . . And the roar increased. It was deafening—women (the one with the amber comb, I remember particularly) screaming, and the men—well, there was one, a fat one with a broken nose, and whose eyes bulged, near me, and he shouted: bestie! bestie! But it was hard to know which beasts he meant.

. . . It must have been then, although I was not near enough actually to witness it myself, that they forced the oak doors of the chamber in which the Court was sitting, for there was a tremendous shout. I heard: they have opened the doors! There must have been nothing the carabinieri could do; and, after all, they did not dare to use their guns. It would have been unthinkable to use their guns. We surged up the steps of the Palazzo, between the statues of the lawgivers, and I, of course, was carried along, trying with difficulty to see what was actually happening. And it was then, I suppose, having forced the doors, they must have seen him: for he was in the court, awaiting sentence—in his slept-in suit, the opened collar, his arm in the white sling, standing beside his attorney, and even I can imagine what fear he must have experienced.

. . . Then the shouting and the inhuman howling was greater than ever.

. . . It is him! It is him!

. . . The spy!

. . . The torturer!

. . . The hangman of Rome!

. . . (And he was all these things. Whatever we may think, he was all these things.)

. . . And they they shouted: Give him to us! Faciamo giustizia con le nostre mani! Yes: with our hands.

. . . And through the enormous and boiling crowd you could hear those, who did not know what was happening, asking of those who thought they knew:

Chi è?

Lui! Lui!

E lui! E la bestia!

And then:

Paghi lui per tutto!

. . . Yes: they would pay him for everyone and for everything. They would pay him for all and they would pay him for each. The carabinieri were helpless, of course, and the Court itself must have been in panic. For it was not what the magistrates had expected. This was to be a trial, carefully prepared for, carefully announced, of great political import and dignity: a calm dispensation of the law, a ceremony of witnesses and speeches, in which careers would be made and reputations enhanced, climaxed at last by a sol-

emn sentence handed down by His Excellency, the Presi-
dent, and photographed by the newsreels. They had, all
the distinguished gentlemen of the Court, so carefully
groomed themselves for this moment, and justice, in their
hands, was to come forth, neatly packaged, tied with their
little sanctioned bows. They would avenge the people, of
course, for, after all, they were the instruments of the
people, but the people did not wait. And now, facing that
huge and undignified flood of hate, they saw their effective
scenery, so carefully erected, and before which they were
to perform, torn apart, and the drama, so carefully re-
hearsed, come to another, and unforeseen, last act.

. . . As for myself, well, outside the doors, on the balus-
trade which surrounds the porch of the Court, I saw an
Englishman, a colonel, with a little riding crop such as
their officers use, shouting at the people; shouting and, one
must confess, with rather futile anger, beating at the air
with his riding crop. Unfortunately, he shouted in English;
and his interpreter, who was with him, was compelled to
translate his anger so that the people might understand.

He would shout, in his own language, waving his little
whip, and then the interpreter would shout too. He shouted for us to go home, to wait, to be calm, to be patient, for
they would try him, they would administer justice, they
were here in our interests to do justice. . . .

And so on; about what one would expect, for one has
heard it all before, although it was possible to feel sorry for
the English colonel with his little whip, so angrily and so
futilely lecturing that flood in a language not even his own.
And Bernardini, too, tried: and he has a reputation—for
he spent many years in exile, and was perhaps one of the
few politicos who did not sell himself to the regime, and
the people knew it. I could see him, above their heads: you

know his face, how sharp it is, those extraordinary eyes and that narrow bitter ironic mouth: and yet, even for Bernardini, it was useless.

Go home! I could hear him shouting.

Citizens, friends, people of the city! And it was all useless. Had he been the old Greek himself, outside there on his pedestal, the father of justice, it would not have helped. Perhaps shooting would have helped: but who would have dared to order the shooting? It would have been the end of all their careers, and in Rome, if they had fired then on the people, on the widows and the sisters of the dead, there would have been such blood as the city has never known.

. . . So the Englishman was swept away; and Bernardini, too—all of them; the whole Court, and all the pleading, the reasoning, the threatening, it was all swept away: and they dragged him out of the chamber. . . .

. . . By then, he was already pounded and bloody—for someone had, in the seizing, half gouged an eye from his head . . . and the arm, which was broken when they captured him, must have been terribly wrenched . . . and so, begging them, blinded, he came down the stairs of the Palazzo, knowing then he would not live through the morning. . . .

. . . And the shouting: ah, it was no longer shouting. I, myself, who had not shouted until then, was not conscious of my own voice, how harsh and how unlike my own it was, coming from my own throat. I fought, too, now, to get closer to the center of that violence: to see him, to see the blood, and to, perhaps, add my blow—for, I think, I would have struck him, too. I think I could not have stopped myself from adding my blow to the uncountable number of blows which fell on him. For all the city beat him: every alley, every palazzetta, every square and marketplace beat him: those he had injured and those he himself had not personally injured, beat him. And on the Lungotevere, there was blood—but it was not ours. . . .

. . . For once, in twenty years, the blood was not ours. . . .

. . . You know how, on the Ponte Umberto, there are the trolley tracks: well, he was unconscious then, and they had thrown him so that he lay across the tracks, and there was a trolley, on the bridge, and they went into the trolley, and the motorman . . .

. . . Well, I was shouting, and there was the body, lying on the tracks, and the motorman . . .

. . . They wanted, I think, some unimaginable death for him, some terrible form of it. Yes: one feels, now, after it is over, a little sick; kill him, one thinks, but not so, not with such bestiality. Well, and have you and I had to lift the lids on those coffins, to go there into the caves and to look at what bones are left, and to identify, by a ring or a gold tooth, what one had once loved? Have we had their tears, you and I?

. . . But then, the motorman would not let them use the trolley. . . .

. . . And when I looked again, there he was, unconscious and bloody, lifted, limply, on the parapet of the bridge— and someone, it was difficult to tell who, for they were screaming so, the women in black worse than the others, threw him down; down, yes: the fifty feet of air into the yellow Tiber.

. . . I was there, and that I saw.

. . . How, sinking into the water, one thought forever, the head suddenly reappeared, the mouth spluttering, and water running from the dark hair—for the Tiber was icy and he was not yet dead.

. . . And he began to swim, with the broken arm, thinking that beyond the Ponte Sant'Angelo there was safety, and thinking some miracle would intervene, thinking that they would not even in the water pursue him now to his death.

. . . God knows how he swam: bloody, an eye almost gone, his broken arm, dragged down by his clothes—but he swam: and then, from a boathouse, near the steps which go down to the river from the Lungotevere, I saw—

. . . Yes: a rowboat. Those in the boat were young men, and they were naked, except for bathing trunks, and their bodies were very brown because of the sun. They rowed the boat out and when they came to where he was swimming in the water they hit him with the oar. One thought: but he must sink. He must go under. But he did not sink. There was the sun, the young men in the rowboat, naked, and the oar hitting him.

. . . It could not go on. It was not possible. The howling from the Ponte Umberto and the Ponte Sant'Angelo and from the waterstairs and from the Tiber was undiminished. Then they hit him again: and he sank.

. . . And afterwards, I was so terribly thirsty.

The sun was going down. The man, the eyewitness, who had been there and who had seen it all, drank the lemonade the wife of the padrone of the little chiosco had made, but from which she had not strained the lemon pips.

"How long is he dead now?" the padrone of the little chiosco said.

"Almost three hours," the man who had seen it all replied.

"Well," the wife said. "He's better off. He's better off where he is than we are now."

"I am not so sure of that," the man who had been there said.

"Why?" said the wife.

"I agree with him," the padrone said. "If I were sure that in the other place there was spaghetti and vino dei castelli I might perhaps say yes. But none of us are sure."

"No," the wife said. "They are better off in the other place."

"And why?" said her husband.

"Nobody comes back here," the wife of the padrone said. "It must be better if they stay."

The city, for the chiosco was on the Janiculum hill, near the monument to Garibaldi, lay spread beneath them. It was a fine day, and this sunset now would be one of the splendid Roman sunsets. They looked down into the city and drank their lemonade.

"Well," said the man who had been there, "it would have been same if they had shot him. After all, there is only one thing better than being shot."

"What?" said the padrone.

"Not to be shot," the eyewitness said. Having finished his lemonade, he said good-bye to the padrone and to his wife, and began to walk down the hill, toward the city where his life was.